Robert Banks Stewart, a writer/producer, has been responsible for a string of successful British television drama series. He co-created and produced the Bafta-nominated *Shoestring*, created and produced *Bergerac*, adapted several of H.E. Bates' novels, as well as producing the opening series of *The Darling Buds of May*, and produced the initial series of *Lovejoy* and John Buchan's *Hannay*. He has written a number of television plays, including an acclaimed NBC co-production of A.J.Cronin's *Shannon's Way*, and *Between the Covers*, winner of a Gold Drama Award at the New York Film and TV Festival. Over the years he has contributed to many famous tv series, including *The Avengers*, *Callan*, *Public Eye*, *Doctor Who*, *Danger Man*, *The Saint*, the BBC's Emmy-nominated *Legend of Robin Hood*, *Adam Adamant*, *The Human Jungle*, *Van der Valk*, *The Sweeney*, *My Uncle Silas*, and the Writers Guild award-winning *Arthur of the Britons*.

THE HURRICANE'S TAIL

Robert Banks Stewart

First published by Kaleidoscope Publishing, 2012.

Copyright © Robert Banks Stewart, 2012.

This novel is a work of fiction. Apart from public figures and known locations mentioned, the names, places, characters and events portrayed are the work of the author's imagination. Any resemblance to actual places or persons, living or dead, is entirely coincidental.

No image or text may be reproduced by any means without the express written permission of Kaleidoscope Publishing.

Kaleidoscope Publishing
42 Victoriana Way
Handsworth Wood
B20 2SZ
United Kingdom
www.kaleidoscopepublishing.co.uk

ISBN 978-1-900203-34-0

Layout and design by Rob Moss.

To my three sons, Alex, Andy and Angus, always my best friends.

Prologue

Harper was only a minute late, but because he always liked to be thought of as a complete professional, he took the stairs to the first floor three at a time, no sweat for a six footer in his mid-forties, lean-limbed and gym-fit.

The surprise rendezvous was a shabby 1930s office block with mean little metal window frames and a cracked stucco facade, stained with rust from the guttering under its lawnmower-green tiled roof. Even so, Harper thought it odd that there wasn't some kind of entry-phone, considering the two men he was to meet had sounded so secretive, dangerous even, when they'd phoned.

It was a conference call, both of them on the line at their end, but from separate offices, which he found disconcerting, even though one of them hardly spoke. He felt uneasy about the cold-chisel tones of the one who did most of the talking.

However, it was clear a job had come up, and equally clear that he'd better heed their summons.

On a swelteringly hot day, he wore sandals, cotton trousers, and a coral-coloured T-shirt, nothing flash, except maybe for the fake Rolex on his wrist and the Cutler and Gross sun-glasses. He wondered if they'd have expected him in a neatly-pressed suit?

Walking cautiously along the first-floor landing, he noted that the inside of the place had the sour, musty smell you get in minor civil service buildings and schools. He pressed a buzzer on a grimy light oak door with a spyglass in it.

After a moment, a gangly, curly blonde-haired secretary, almost as tall as him, in baggy shorts and inviting long legs, opened the door.

'I'm Harper Buchanan.'

'Yes, I know. Come in.'

He followed her through her drab outer office, admiring the backs of her knees and her highly-sprung rear as they went. Pity about the rest of her, he thought.

They entered a larger office whose wooden-slat Venetian blinds over the Crittal windows were almost completely closed despite the heat, and it took Harper a few seconds to focus on the two men and their surroundings, as the secretary left, not even announcing him either by presence or by name.

The pair of them sat behind an unrestored partner's desk with a fraying red leather top, on which a tiny battery fan was vainly whirring in the muggy atmosphere.

Both had their backs to him, didn't even bother to turn around, which rendered them to Harper as couple of mere silhouettes against the glow from the flat-screen television mounted on a wall-arm above. One of them had pressed freeze-frame on the remote, and there, on the screen, was the image of a man getting out of a car.

Harper did a double-take. The subject of the picture, who'd had no clue he was being filmed, was himself…

As he stared ruefully at his own image, he thought: what if I'd been picking my nose, or worse, feeling my crotch? The thought amused him and he gave a chuckle, which he saw didn't amuse either of them as they turned to face him.

The taller of the two men, fanning himself with a Panama hat and smoking a cigar in an old-fashioned ivory holder, spoke first.

'Take a seat, Buchanan.'

Harper instantly recognised the voice: the one with the frosty lip on the conference phone call. The upper-class drawl resonated in the stifling room, as if it came from a radio play with hammy actors, and the usual hollow sound.

Sitting down in a cheap, hard, uncomfortable folding plastic chair to one side of the desk, Harper could make this man out more clearly now. In his thirties, he wore a crumpled sand-coloured linen designer suit, white cotton shirt, and what looked like the salmon-and-cucumber Garrick Club tie. Harper couldn't be certain because of the light. As the man removed his banded Panama, he displayed a floppy blond hairstyle with centre parting, a complete giveaway, an almost certain public school badge, the style presumably unchanged since his sixth-form days at Eton or Harrow.

'Your snoop was a smart operator,' Harper said. 'Never got wind of him.'

'Mobile phones with their in-built video cameras make it so easy nowadays. We were just carrying out a bit of routine homework,' said the second man, a short, balding fatso of fifty, with gold-rimmed glasses, squeaking in the flutey, ball-less counter-tenor voice that so often goes with excessive flab.

He was munching a hamburger, and in profile, in the dim light, Harper could see salad stuff smeared all around his letterbox mouth. In a Donegal tweed jacket he was sweating calories. Harper decided: this man has a private Hampstead school written all over him, with just a tell-tale touch of a Middle-European accent.

'Listen, Buchanan, we drew up a list of candidates who could do this job for us. The camera helped us narrow it to you,' Fatso said, spitting food into the silvery light.

His colleague set down his Panama, opened a folder. 'We've decided that you're the right chap for the job.'

'The very man we were looking for,' added Fatso, stabbing at the TV remote with a greasy finger, achieving a full-screen close-up of Harper.

'Not a lot of choice, of course,' drawled the other one, as a half inch of cigar ash dropped onto the desk and he blew it away in a cloud with a deft wave of his hat brim. The coloured band fell off, and he kept trying to fix it back on for the rest of the interview.

Harper was beginning to be irritated by the double act. It was as if, in keeping with the hot weather, they felt some homage to a Graham Greene thriller was appropriate, and they weren't going to leave off, not yet.

'Suppose you start by telling me what this is about?' Harper challenged them. Christ, that little fan on the desk was useless.

He hated this interview, this office, the dangerous smell of these two jokers behind the desk. Almost as strong as the smell of that hamburger.

'We'll come to explanations in a moment' said Fatso. 'A few extra details first. We note that you don't smoke, don't drink much, or take drugs. Is there anything else?'

Harper felt a little humour would do no harm. 'You mean do my privates hang left or right?' he chortled, squeezing his crotch to underline the joke.

The tall one didn't smile. His tone was even chillier. 'Don't try being funny with us. This is important. How much sleep do you need at night, for example?'

Oh, thought Harper. We're into psychology, at the shallow end, are we? These guys might be straight from Guantanamo, or London's Belmarsh at least.

'In my profession,' Harper said scornfully, 'when I sleep, I sleep normal hours. You want to know if I'm alert?'

'Are you? Always?'

'Well, on that screen you've practically zoomed in on my eyeballs. No yellowing there, no tell-tale coke rings, right?' he said sardonically.

'We said we know you aren't on drugs, Buchanan,' said the burger king. 'To do this, you'd have to go to ground for a bit. Who'd notice?'

Harper shrugged. 'You mean in my private life? Nobody, I think, not for a few weeks at any rate. I'm single, divorced, that is – living alone at the moment. But I expect you've already sussed that out.'

The fat man inspected the serrated remains of his sesame bun, discovered he had no meat left, and dropped it in a wastebin. The thin one took a packet of mints from his pocket, popped one in his mouth and didn't offer them around.

'One final query,' he asked, sucking on his mint. 'When was the last time you used your gun?'

'Why don't you just ask me how good I am?' Harper said.

'We've heard you're good. Indeed, very deadly,'

'Well, that's it, then,' said Harper. Playfully, he picked up the Panama hat and stuck it on his head. 'Now, suppose you tell me what this job is?'

When he left, they pulled up the blinds, watching Harper get into his car, a blue Saab soft-top, in the courtyard below. He started the car, setting the roof to automatically fold back, his dark frame and brown arms standing out against the white leather upholstery as he selected gear. The Rolex, fake or not, glinted in the sunlight.

The tall man mused: 'Cool black guy, driving a smart car like that? I shouldn't be surprised if he doesn't have a hard time, being stopped by the police.'

His companion shrugged, taking off his jacket, and filling the room with what seemed like the pungent aroma of a second hamburger. 'Oh, very likely. Then I expect he gives them a hard time, because of who he actually is! He has a sharp mind has our friend, and plenty of lip.'

'And a bloody good aim, too, let's hope, does Detective Sergeant Buchanan,' said the other.

They watched Harper drive off to join the choking traffic and pollution along the Great West Road, in what was one of London's fluke heat waves, when they might not even need the new retractable

roof at Wimbledon's Centre Court.

Part one

Just enough space for a bullet

One

The clapboard Pentacostal chapel was painted in pink, eu-de-nil, pale blue, yellow, and flake white, going on grey. With its fretted gables and elegant verandah, it looked like an ice-cream sundae against its rainforest backdrop.

Over a hundred years old, it had been built as a personal pulpit by a discredited Scottish minister called the Rev. Nairn Crimond, who was drummed out of the St. Andrew's church on the island at the age of fifty-eight, when he left his wife to live with a beautiful, twenty-three-year-old Creole, Marie-Therese, from Martinique, and sired lusty twins.

He said that despite his sermons telling people how to live, he himself hadn't really been alive for at least fifteen years, and finally tearing off his dog collar was somehow symbolic as he rediscovered his libido.

For all its sickly colouring, the chapel was a favourite of the Prime Minister, Sir Walter Julien, whose official limousine with its national flag was among the cars parked in the street outside. Two menacing-looking motorcycle cops sat stiffly on their Harley-Davidsons, and a couple of dark suited presidential-style bodyguards with regulation Rayban aviators and bulging armpits, lounged against the Prime Minister's Daimler.

It was a blustery morning, the kind seldom mentioned by freebee travel writers or the hard sell holiday brochures, where the West Indies was always perceived as a desert island paradise of blue-green seas, gently caressing palm-fringed, golden beaches.

Clouds like wirewool straggled across the sky. The wind, fondly known in the Caribbean as the Gentle Trades, but regularly much more squally and dangerous, especially at the tail-end of a hurricane like now, chopped up the water, sprayed the sand, convulsed the palms, rocked the boats and rattled most of the tin roofs.

Nevertheless, it did nothing to drown out the sound or dispel the joy of the gospel singing that came from within the chapel, situated just below *Les Deux Enclumes* – the Two Anvils – in the volcanic mountain range that dominated the North-West tip of the island.

The inside of the wooden building was almost as colourful as the exterior, decked out with flowers and filled with a congregation in its Sunday best. The women, wearing striking floral dresses of every hue, had white lace gloves, carried folded parasols, and topped it off with a collection of hats to rival an Easter Parade.

In fact it was a parade day, for it was Abolition Day, the annual celebration of the date when slavery was abolished in this once British-owned Caribbean island. Traditionally it was marked by a fancy dress show, when they wore the uniforms of English redcoats, French fusiliers, and the rags of slaves and their children.

A good number of the congregation were theatrically got up for the parade, giving this morning's service a festive air.

Such lightness of spirit, however, evaded Sir Walter Julien, who was in the front pew with his wife Emilie and their five children ranging from Hamish, their eldest son of twenty-three, down to the baby, Hattie, whom he held under one arm, his song-book raised awkwardly in his free hand.

A tall, debonair man, Sir Walter was going grey at his temples. He was often considered to be the double of the American actor Morgan Freeman. But he'd met Freeman once when he was filming on a neighbouring island, and personally didn't see much resemblance. Emilie, who also met the star, loyally reckoned that her husband was far better looking.

As he glanced around at the happy faces of the regular choir of gospel singers and the people in the pews, Sir Walter remembered his first visit to this chapel as a three-year-old, when his parents, like all black people, prayed that their world would change, if not in their own lifetime, at least in their children's. Caribbean poverty and economic dependence on European countries far away, seemed in those days destined to last for ever.

The only alternative was to pull up your roots, pack your flimsy suitcase and sail across the Atlantic to try your luck, starting with one of the menial jobs they reserved exclusively for West Indians. Unless, of course you were a successful cricketer or a calypso singer, then you were headed straight up the track.

Walter Julien had had his own dreams in his youth, that he would come to Britain and make something of himself, not as a lavatory cleaner or a bus conductor, but as a scholar. And ultimately, because of his diligent schoolwork, he did, winning a place on a Commonwealth grant to London University.

Living in a cheap bedsit in Brixton, one of the areas of London where the black immigrants had somehow established a residential bridgehead, otherwise known as a ghetto, he worked most nights in coffee bars and hamburger joints, usually until well after midnight, then studied hard in the small hours.

He finally gained a first-class Law degree.

Several top London legal firms offered him a job and he could have started a whole new life. But after three years he was homesick for his island, its lush tropical forests and beaches, and more importantly because he was proud of his heritage, he promptly went back to the West Indies.

As a solicitor he specialised in the criminal courts, took an interest in politics and was eventually elected to the island Parliament, rising over the years to become a government Minister and then subsequently by popular vote, Prime Minister.

Along the way, he married Emilie, a physiotherapist, whom he first met on an Underground platform at Earls Court in London, went out with several times, lost contact, then found her again, to his – and her – delight, in Basseterre on the island of St Kitt's, and this time it was serious love and marriage.

He wondered if this was the last Sunday he would ever spend with his family.

The hymn was nearly at an end, and Eugene Gwilt, the huge, jovial preacher, with a fierce black beard and a completely bald, blue-black scalp, was giving the last verse all of his 'holy roller' enthusiasm. His tiny wife, Rusty, in a lime green hat she'd made herself, big enough to grace the top of a standard lamp, played the wheezy old chapel organ; she was transported like a concert pianist at the pearly gates.

Sir Walter had promised Eugene he'd deliver a short address to his flock, and now, as the song finished with a loud vocal flourish and a chorus of fervent hallelujahs, the preacher beamed even more broadly. Sir Walter prayed that his friend wouldn't lay his introduction on too thick. He usually did.

'Folks,' said the Reverend Gwilt, 'it cannot have escaped your attention that we are honoured this Sabbath mornin' by the esteemed presence in our midst of our Prime Minister, brother Sir Walter Julien.'

A big round of applause.

Then, turning towards Sir Walter with a bow fit for royalty: 'Sir, it would be a fitting end to our service, especially on this commemorative day, to offer you our humble chapel as a platform for a few words.'

Sir Walter handed Hattie over to Emilie and left the pew to make his address. He looked around with affection at faces in the congregation. Some of them were his oldest friends since schooldays, and he felt guilty that he couldn't tell them what was about to happen.

Only Emilie and a few close government aides were in on it.

It had to be that secret because of the death threats.

Downtown, the capital's main shopping street, Shaftesbury Boulevard, was virtually deserted, except for the jeep parked outside Aitkens & Jeffrey, the smart men's tailors. Although the sign on the door of the shop, with its Savile Row-style windows and gilt and maroon-painted facade, said *Closed*, there were two figures visible inside, by the long, brassbound counter.

With his accustomed slow precision, Henry Aitkens, who wore his black jacket and striped trousers as though Sunday was any other day of the week, finished packing the large, flat cardboard box that lay before him, smoothing tissue paper neatly across the top and reaching for the sellotape to seal the lid. There were quite a few garments within.

"Do you want to check your list?"

'Never mind that,' said the T-shirted Rastafarian who waited impatiently. 'I'm late. We need these things pretty damn quick.'

Grabbing the box, he made for the door, forgetting that Aitkens had locked it as they arrived. Aitkens unhurriedly brought the key from his pocket, picking up a piece of paper from the counter as he came over to let the Rasta out.

'You forgot the list.'

'Don't matter, so long as it's all there.'

As he watched the Rastafarian climb into the jeep and drive away, Aitkens realised he'd become part of a conspiracy, albeit a small part. But they'd made it very plain he'd better keep his mouth shut, or else.

Actually, they needn't have worried. Henry Aitkens was a profoundly discreet man. In fact, he'd worked in Savile Row in London, albeit as a lowly ironer of clothes, but he knew about discretion. However, he couldn't help being curious about why they wanted those items, under cover of a Sunday morning.

Especially since he thought he knew a customer to whom his shop had sold identical clothes.

Two

Beyond the august, well-guarded portals of the British Foreign and Commonwealth Office in Whitehall, there exists a little-known but breathtaking example of eccentric Victorian architecture, the Durbar Courtyard, a pure piece of Indian Raj-style grandeur. Like some inner part of the Taj Mahal, with soaring pillars and high, pointed Moslem arches, it was said to have hugely pleased the Great Queen and Empress, then ruler of a third of the world.

She was also, of course, ruler of a large part of the Caribbean, the hemisphere under discussion by the three men who were strolling around the marbled, mosaic courtyard, still feeling the unaccustomed heatwave in London, which the weather forecasters had, as usual, failed to detect.

Detective Sergeant Harper Buchanan had changed into his best suit and tie. The tall man with the Panama hat, whom he'd met earlier, turned out to be a senior Commonwealth Office diplomat, the Hon. Jonathan Walmsley. The third man now with them, a jowly character around fifty, with greying hair cropped close to his skull, and boiled blue eyes, was Chief Superintendent Vince Norris from Special Branch.

They explained that the fat man at the original interview had been a Home Office psychologist, brought in to "assess" Buchanan. God help all police officers who are cracking up, thought Harper. Probably prescribed to stay in their official rest centres (i.e. nice country clubs), with their feet up, watching endless TV cop-operas, drinking and eating junk food like Fatso.

Harper, who counted himself as always fit-for-purpose – a term invented by one Home Secretary – often thought it entirely dubious that the police force all over the country clocked up more sick days off than any other public service.

'Your station will be told you've been sent on detachment.' said Norris. 'To fill a last-minute vacancy on a criminal psychology course at Hendon Police College. Fits in nicely with the pressure to widen black cops' horizons at the top end of the Met,' he added.

Harper was squinting up at the damascene surrounds to the arches, highlighted in the late afternoon sun. It looked as if he was admiring the decorative painting. But secretly he was thinking what a poncy place these Foreign Office posers worked in. Hardly like his no-nonsense red-brick cop shop across the river. And as for Norris and his so-called 'horizons.'.. bound to be one of those racist bastards at heart.

'Look, people in my outfit aren't stupid,' said Harper. 'Detective Sergeants, especially black ones, don't get whipped off their duties that quick, to attend fancy lectures.'

'Yeah, you're probably right, but sod your mates, anyway,' Norris shrugged. 'Otherwise, our apologies for any unexpected personal inconvenience.'

Harper was resentful. 'Thanks very much. But I'm a working detective, not some bloody nanny for a politician.'

Walmlsey, puffing a cigar, an up-to-the-minute, do-it-all mobile phone poking out of the top pocket of his jacket – almost as if he hoped it would soon shrill impressively for his attention, maybe even play the Eton boating song – cut in: 'Sir Walter Julien's not just any politician, Sergeant Buchanan,' he said. 'The Commonwealth Office considers him a Prime Minister we want to stay on good terms with.'

'Besides, chummy, he's West Indian, just as you're a West Indian,' Norris added.

Harper stopped walking, looking at them angrily.

'Listen… first off, don't call me chummy, okay? I resent false intimacy. I'm as fucking English as either of you. I was born here. I went to an English grammar school, then to an English university.

I was married to an English girl, I don't live in an all-black district, and what's more, I've never even set foot in the Caribbean!'

Walmsley and Norris exchanged an uneasy look at Harper's forthrightness.

'Still, it's the thought that counts, isn't it,' said Walmlsey. 'On our side. And I believe your parents came from the same island as the man we want you to guard?'

Norris, who always felt intimidated by diplomats, especially walking around anywhere in Whitehall like the Durbar Courtyard, even on a Sunday afternoon, said: 'You'd better fill Sergeant Buchanan in a bit more.'

'All right,' said Walmsley. 'Here's the situation: Sir Walter Julien's coming to London, unknown to everybody but his nearest and dearest. He has to undergo a complicated heart operation, because of an abnormally-structured valve. Otherwise he's dead. It's vital his opponents don't know about this, especially that he's quit the island. If they find out, there's a strong risk of a coup, and they've threatened his life as it is. His absence would provoke an almost certain take-over.'

'Politics definitely sound a bit rough over there,' said Harper.

A navy-blue uniformed Foreign Office messenger came out from an archway into the courtyard, handing Walmsley a note. He took it with a curt nod and scanned its contents.

'It's what's behind some of the politics,' said Walmsley, stuffing the note into his pocket. 'Organised crime, especially the big drug cartels that stretch all the way from Colombia to Miami, using the Caribbean as a bridge, or a feeder to Europe.'

'Some of the islands feel they've been dragged accidentally into a rather nasty whirlpool,' he added, pointing out – somewhat proudly – the involvement of the Royal Navy, including Sub-Lieutenant Prince William, for their efforts at surveillance and arrest of maritime drug-runners.

My God, Harper thought, I bet this mop-haired smoothie reckons he's headed for promotion, maybe even a diplomatic post that will lead inevitably to a Knighthood.

'Sir Walter's island Parliament's in recess at the moment,' he drawled. 'He's put it about that he's busy writing a book, and he intends to stay at home for a few weeks.'

There was a sudden blast of music – and, Christ, it *was* the Eton Boating Song! Walmsley's mobile quivered to life like an unseen hand in his pocket. With a sigh, concealing his gratitude at the call, thus underlining his importance, he walked a few paces away so as to talk out of earshot.

'You should be flattered, Sergeant,' said Norris. 'You're just the sort of bloke Sir Walter will get along with.'

'Oh, really? Because of my colour?,' Harper said, belligerently.

'Not necessarily. They say he's bit of an intellectual. Went to a British university like you did, and he's fond of music and cricket, as we gather you are.'

Harper said drily: 'Oh, right, I'll make a point of wearing my egg-and-bacon tie.'

'Is that a joke or what?'

'No it isn't, is it, Sergeant Buchanan?' said Walmsley, overhearing and nodding deferentially, if a touch reluctantly.

Briskly snapping his phone shut he rejoined them reciting Wisden-style: 'Opening batsman for Sussex University, played on four occasions for the county side. Highest innings, 84 not out, including eight fours, two sixes, against Kent at Canterbury. Recently became a member of the MCC, hence the egg-and-bacon tie.'

Harper shook his head admiringly.

'Hey, man, you sure did check the score on me!' he said, regretting, even as he spoke, that he'd lapsed into a parody of the lilting, cliched West Indian sound of a bloke wearing a tea-cosy hat.

Walmsley patted the phone, now back in his top pocket, as if it was a career diplomat's essential pacemaker.

'That was a message from my office. In a few hours, if all goes according to plan, Sir Walter Julien will be aboard a Virgin Atlantic flight to Gatwick.'

'You'd better take good care of our man, Sergeant,' said Norris.

Walmsley nodded sombrely. 'If anything happens to him, it could have a destablising effect on the whole Caribbean scene.'

'That should make it feel more like police business,' added Norris.

Three

Sir Walter had announced he'd be brief, but Emilie permitted herself a slight smile.

Fifteen minutes on, the Prime Minister was still on his feet, like all politicians warming to his theme. His soft passionate style reminded her of Nelson Mandela, whom all the world admired. Especially her husband. And now there was the American President, Barack Obama. God, how the world was changing!

The subject of what might be his last speech for some time – if only his listeners in the chapel had known it – was the increasing amount of drug based graft and corruption, violence and murder, that looped over the West Indies nowadays.

'The Mafia to the North in Miami, the cocaine growers and suppliers in South America… the Caribbean squeezed in between.'

'So a hundred and fifty years ago, folks, we got rid of slavery,' he was saying, 'but how about the slavery of people caught in the clutches of evil, often invisible men, who are either the drug barons, or those who aid and abet the filthy drug trade? Those dark forces that combine business and organised crime, and seek to destroy you and me and our peaceful islands?'

Emilie Julien, in their pew, silently prayed: 'Please Lord, please watch over my husband, he has such a lot of important work to do.'

At the back of the chapel, Chief Inspector Eddie Carmona, seated between two female companions, was thinking about his own crime workload.

A Creole in his forties, from Trinidad, Carmona had that odd physical combination, red hair from his Spanish genes and a coffee-coloured skin. Not exactly a handsome face, but the eyes were sharp, and there was a quiet authority and vitality about him, a humorous turn to his mouth, and a soft spoken, self-deprecating wit that women found profoundly attractive.

The honey-haired woman on his left, Margot Sheridan, was late thirties, tall, flat-chested, a prim Canadian spinster and member of the Bahai World Faith until she discovered the greater pull of sex and love with Eddie, whom she knew was twice divorced.

Six months after he met her, he brought the other girl, Inez Salassu, home to dinner, with some story that he'd rescued her from an unsatisfactory relationship with a violent criminal on bail. Inez, in her twenties, was a Puerto Rican with dark, flashing eyes and a good body. They had to put her up for a night or two. Eventually, in a convivial game of sexual noughts and crosses, he became the X in the middle, and a menage was established.

Margot was a schoolteacher and Inez a bank clerk. They kept their domestic set-up well away from their professional careers, except that a few of Eddie Carmona's colleagues, being cops, knew about it, and around the office his private lifestyle earned him a mixture of good natured envy, not say to admiration.

But with Carmona, a tough, experienced detective, his special assignment came first. His office wasn't located in the main CID building. It was hidden away in a crummy ex-sugar warehouse behind the fruit and flower market.

Seconded from the Trinidadian police HQ in Port of Spain, he was boss of JIBOC, the Joint Investigation Bureau of the Caribbean, staffed by a select band of cops drawn from a number of island nations in the federation, financed by them to act as an undercover task force.

To combat, in fact, some of the very crime and corruption that Prime Minister Julien was talking about.

Carmona liked and respected Sir Walter. Admittedly the island's economy was in a poor state, but which country's wasn't these days? There had been blips in Sir Walter's government, notably a scandal over the construction of a new hospital, but the Minister responsible had gone to prison.

His opponents claimed Sir Walter was too much of a one man-band, and it was probably true that he ran things with almost presidential control. Yet, although there was periodic unrest and demonstrations, his rule was paternalistic rather than despotic.

By and large, he was the kind of honest, robust politician they needed in this corner of the world to keep things stable. Unfortunately there were those 'dark forces' he had mentioned, greedy men who plotted to overthrow leaders like Julien, to gain their own ends.

As Carmona glanced across the aisle, he wondered if he might be looking at one of them. In the pew opposite was Maitland Harbinson, leader of the UPP, the radical United People's Party that formed the Opposition to the present government.

Harbinson was here today representing his party at the Abolition Day parade. He sat alongside several island dignitaries, including David Imrie, the British Consul, Monseigneur Claude Jarret – half the population was Catholic due to the French influence – and the burly, uniformed figure of Colonel Theodore Marcel, commander of the armed forces, who doubled as Minister of Defence.

Around forty, Harbinson looked more like a college professor than a politician, an image he had deliberately cultivated since his student days at the University of the West Indies, Kingston, Jamaica. But Carmona knew of his ruthless streak and wasn't fooled by the tousled, curly hair, the saucer-sized 'intellectual' glasses, the neat, trendy, casual clothes that he was reputed to buy on trips to New York. Today he was wearing a faded grey, light-weight corduroy suit, tieless, with a silk shirt the colour of lemon-curd.

Carmona had a number of reasons for disliking Harbinson. Some of them were confidential, in the police files, about his closet homosexuality, which had been noted, but not, in today's climate, held against him. Others were simply personal, but to Carmona, who had developed his own sixth sense about people in the course of his police career, they set up question marks about the man's character.

Harbinson, he was sure, had a cocaine habit, maybe to add zest to his gay adventures. Like so many coke-heads he had a short fuse, and Carmona recalled an occasion when, turning up ticketless at the last minute for a fully booked inter-island flight, Harbinson flew into a rage and insisted on another passenger being ordered off the plane to make room for him. There was something slightly sinister, too, about the way the airline duty manager gave in. Carmona believed there was some coercion involved, a few heavy threats in the air.

Another time, dining with friends at the fashionable Hotel Bakoua on the neighbouring island of Martinique, Carmona witnessed a row between Harbinson and a French journalist known for his investigative skills. It had something to do with a story the writer had done for his his paper in Fort-de-France about Harbinson's suspected involvement in a student riot six months ago that was believed to have been deliberately triggered off by the UPP. Two students were killed and a lot of people hurt.

Some time later that evening, in the hotel's underground car park, Carmona found the journalist semi-conscious, covered in blood. The Frenchman couldn't prove it, but he was sure the thugs who beat him up were Harbinson's UPP cronies.

Sir Walter was winding up. 'I thank you, Reverend, both for your fine service and for asking me to speak to you folks. At Government House it's open day for the kids and their fancy dress parade. I hope it will be fun for everyone, as well as reminding you of the brave struggles of our brothers in the past to ensure a better future for all of us today.'

Incongruously, in church, he got a round of rapturous, election-style applause.

Happily the sun had come out and the wind had dropped by the time the service ended.

Eddie Carmona and the Reverend Gwilt stood outside the chapel watching Sir Walter and Emilie leave with their children in their Daimler.

'All that security! Who'd have his job?' said Gwilt. 'But it's good for him to have the chance to worship with his wife and kids.'

'Yeah, even if he has to bring the household cavalry with him on a Sunday,' said Carmona cynically, nodding at the motorcycle outriders and the two bodyguards squeezed in front beside the driver.

'He that fears God fears no evil, for he carries His holy shield,' said the preacher.

Inspector Carmona said: 'Tell that to the bastard extremists who send him death threats,' and then, realising where he was, added, 'Sorry, Reverend, no other words for them.'

As Sir Walter and his family travelled back to Government house, a man was getting dressed in the clothes that the Rastafarian had brought from the tailor's. The clothes were exactly like those being worn by the Prime Minister this very morning.

George Cotter, who stared at his reflection in the cheval mirror, was also identical to Sir Walter Julien, almost his double, in fact, except that he was a shade fatter, hence the need for clothes that would fit.

'Wrist watch worn on the right wrist, jacket never buttoned, is that right? You sure the tie and the shoes are okay?'

He turned from the mirror to look for reassurance from the tall, well-dressed man who was present along with the Rastafarian who delivered the tailor's box. Louis Machin studied the double for a moment.

'Perfect,' he said. 'I could hardly detect the deception myself.'

Four

Harper, an authorised firearms officer, had no difficulty in drawing his revolver from the armoury at the police station in South London where he worked.

Presenting his AFO permit to the Chief Inspector in charge of the arms store, Harper made the excuse that he might have some free time to put in a bit of target practice at the Hendon College indoor range.

After that, he had a cup of tea in the ground-floor canteen with his boss, Detective Chief Inspector Carol Smart, and a couple of plain-clothes colleagues. Smart had been discreetly advised that Harper was needed for a specific assignment, but not told about its exact nature.

Harper, who liked and respected Smart, a first-class officer, found it awkward to withhold the real reason for his sudden absence. Fortunately, even though she knew her one and only black detective was being hauled out by a higher authority, DCI Smart decided not to seek more information.

The other two, both detective constables, displayed cool indifference to the news that he'd been co-opted onto a criminal psychology seminar. Harper was reminded of the general lack of real comradeship he'd encountered in the Metropolitan Police force.

They called it institutional racism. They were always banging on about how it was being challenged and would in time be changed. Commissioners came and went, there were employment tribunal cases involving officers – black and Asian – suing for non-promotion because of apparent bias.

But Harper reckoned it might not take too many years before black and Asian officers were generally thought to be equal to white ones, maybe even sometimes cleverer.

One of the problems was that often on their patch in London and in the North of the country, the incidence of gun crimes and stabbings involving black and Asian people, was dispiritingly high. It didn't help matters.

For her own part, DCI Smart reflected that maybe Harper's problems, of which she was well aware, were compounded by his very Englishness, verging on an apparent sense of superiority because of his university and sporting background. Class divisions didn't bother her that much, being a Scot, particularly from a city like Aberdeen that seemed to have only one accent, no matter who you were.

Harper had been fast tracked for promotion. It certainly gave him an air of easy social confidence, whether real or not. But she suspected that a few of her men, conscious that they were less well educated or as cultivated as Harper, were resentful. Consequently there was a touch of what might even be called reverse snobbery.

To the Afro-Caribbean in the street, of course, Harper wasn't just fuzz, he was worse. The worst insult you could throw at someone like him: a Bounty Bar coconut cop, brown on the outside, a whitey within.

Collecting a few items from his locker in the basement, Harper went out to his car, placing his holstered Smith & Wesson carefully under a newspaper on the seat beside him. In the four years since he'd gained his firearms licence, he'd never actually had to use a gun in any shoot-out, and he sincerely hoped he wouldn't have to on this job.

He remembered the first time he'd brought a weapon back home. Coming off duty from a stake-out that had lasted through the night, he'd left it nonchalantly on a coffee table and gone to take a shower.

Tessa, his wife, had got up to make them breakfast, and he found her standing there in her nightdress, staring at it with fear and fascination. She couldn't take her eyes off it, as if it was a deadly snake that had crawled into their house.

That was when they were still in love, and she was always touchingly concerned for his safety. But there was also, he knew then from the look in her eyes, an underlying repugnance that her husband would sometimes have to carry this weapon as an occasional tool of his job.

Maybe that was the moment when it all started to go wrong. They'd met and married while they were both students at Sussex. They found themselves living in bed-sits in a crumbling, Regency house on Marine Parade in Brighton which, despite its spectacular view of the beach and the pier, was as seedy as you could get. The paint was flaking, the landlords were flaky, many people were sexually flaky; but students revelled in being bohemian. And there was no place like Brighton to lighten up, to enjoy to the full their lives outside of their serious studies.

As well as reading French and History like Harper, Tessa was a talented musician, a cellist, and ultimately she went on to the Royal College of Music, and from there to a place in the strings of the London Symphony Orchestra. Harper was intensely proud of her, as she was of him, and his advancement as a cop in the Met.

Having totally different careers was usually a recipe for a success-ful relationship, or so they thought at first. Plenty to talk about, acceptable advice proffered from either side, and of course, healthiest of all, your work more or less left behind once over the doorstep. But they didn't detect that the differences in their routines would, in the long run, caused their marriage to fail.

The pressure of his shift work, her absences at rehearsals and on the orchestra's tours, aroused unhappy tensions, and gradually there was no shared home life at all. It seemed to happen without either of them being able to do anything about it, and finally, when he discovered she was having an affair with another player, a flautist, they called a halt and split, and after that they got a quickie divorce.

Before driving off, Harper sat back for a moment listening on his radio to the soothing sound of the Albinoni Concerto Grosso, one of his favourites.

Somewhere in there was Tessa's cello. Oh, shit.

Special Branch had fully briefed him about his bodyguard duties. Prime Minister Walter Julien was booked into a highly-expensive private hospital in St. John's Wood, much frequented by unhealthy Russian oligarths and Hong Kong millionaires, whisky-drinking Arab Sheikhs from Dubai and around the Middle East, with acute liver problems, and rich VIP's and celebrities of all kinds, usually show business, referred from – where else? – Harley Street.

There was, as Harper knew, a multi-million pound 'industry' in private medicine, especially for mega-rich foreigners, while ordinary British hospital patients might wait for weeks or even months, until they were, well, dead.

Though he'd never had occasion to visit the hospital, Harper knew it quite well, situated as it was alongside Lord's, the home of English cricket and the MCC, of which Harper, as Walmsley had confirmed, really was a member, entitled to wear the egg-and-bacon striped necktie, along with many of the current luminaries of London.

He would have to go home now and pack a suitcase, since he would be staying with Sir Walter at the hospital, possibly for some weeks.

As he switched on the ignition, Harper wondered if this assignment might not turn out to be more interesting than it seemed.

Five

On the island, Government House was a huge, white stuccoed colonial pile with a colonnaded facade, an imposing canopied entrance, and a first floor balcony that ran right around the building. Originally built by one of the Earls of Pembroke, from Wiltshire, who owned several sugar plantations, it was set in a hundred acres of manicured lawns, tropical plants and flower-beds, with various outbuildings and stables, plus swimming pool and tennis court.

Subsequently becoming the official residence of the British Governor-General, before independence, it stood in a prime position above *Le Ruban Jaune* – the Yellow Ribbon – an idyllic beach lined with palms. At the top of a path leading down to the beach was a revolving wooden summerhouse, which the Prime Minister, Sir Walter Julien, used as his personal study-retreat, where he worked on his papers and wrote his speeches.

Now there was great excitement and activity on the lawns immediately in front of the house, as the children, with the help of relatives, prepared for the Abolition Day fancy dress parade.

The national flag was draped over the balustrade of the balcony, above the entrance. A ten-man steel band was playing with great gusto. There were two large marquee tents with their sides rolled up to reveal tables laden with food and drink.

The loud metallic rhythms of the steel band wafted cheerfully through the open french windows of the bedroom on the first floor.

Sitting on the edge of the bed, his shirt undone, Sir Walter Julien was having a check-up by his doctor, an elderly Belgian physician, Charles Chaumet.

A dapper widower in a striped blazer and a bright red bow-tie, Chaumet had practised in the Caribbean since quitting his job on a cruise liner.

He'd been the Juliens' family doctor now for over twenty years and had delivered every single child.

Doctor Chaumet was, inevitably, one of the few who knew that Sir Walter needed an urgent heart operation.

'Well, your clockwork seems to be ticking evenly for the moment,' he said, packing away his stethescope. A pretty young nurse was preparing a syringe to inject the Prime Minister with one of his heart drugs.

'The irony is, Charlie, I've never felt better.'

'Good. Just how you need to be right now,' said Chaumet, cheerfully putting the needle into him with the brisk nonchalance of someone pinning on a charity flag. He also applied a trinitrate glycerine patch.

As he rebuttoned his shirt, Julien observed: 'Of course the real damn irony is that those people who want me dead don't know about this!'

'I e-mailed your heart consultant in London a few hours ago,' said Chaumet. 'He now has your complete data.'

Sir Walter moved over to the window, gazing down at the people milling about on the lawn. Even though he was only sixty-two, why not just retire? Take it easy, take his chances? The heat would be off. Maybe his health would improve without an operation?

'You're sure I have to go all the way to London for this?'

'Carl Hardwicke is the best man in the world for this sort of job, Walter. And if you don't have it done quick...' He gave a warning shrug.

At that moment there was a knock at the door. The nurse looked at Sir Walter, who nodded. As she opened the door, Louis Machin, his private secretary, stood there with the double, George Cotter, by his side.

'Prime Minister,' said Machin, 'meet… the Prime Minister.'

Sir Walter scrutinised his impersonator closely, as both Chaumet and the nurse reacted at his appearance.

'Although I should be the last to judge,' he told Machin, 'you seem to have done a first-class job.'

Cotter, who'd been an unemployed french polisher in Barbados until a week ago, when he got this completely out-of-the-blue approach, and the offer of untold money from heaven, grinned.

'Hey, how long have I got to practise?' he queried.

Machin looked at his watch. 'Five minutes at the most.' He shook his head at Sir Walter apologetically. 'Sorry, sir, but we finally chose him only last night. We had to be certain he was the nearest likeness we could get.'

'Just have to make the best of it, then,' said Sir Walter. 'I'll give him a quick briefing.' He turned to the doctor. 'Well, what do you think of my stand-in, Charlie?'

Chaumet nodded approval. 'Most convincing, I'd say.'

'You judge the Prime Minister fit enough to make the journey, Doctor?' Machin enquired.

'Yes, just as long as he has the nurse flying with him and they carry the proper equipment on the plane,' said Chaumet. 'And, may I add, full personal protection in London – just in case.'

'The Commonwealth Office is taking care of all that,' Machin assured him.

Doctor Chaumet collected his bag. 'Well, I'll be off. Pity you can't take your own bodyguards.'

'That would give the game away,' said Sir Walter. 'I can't even take my wife!'

Chaumet nodded sympathetically. 'Brave woman, Emilie,' he said, shaking hands with his old friend. 'Wish you all the luck, Walter,' he said, and just for once he didn't manage to seem nonchalant.

Ten minutes later, a military band in white jackets and pith helmets, was playing on the Government House lawn as the children proudly paraded past the flag-draped balcony where the Prime Minister and his wife stood waving encouragement.

In the background, his secretary, Machin, carefully searched the faces of the crowd below. Among those watching was Maitland Harbinson, talking to the British Consul. No one, it seemed, suspected they were looking at Sir Walter Julien's double. Not even the preacher, Eugene Gwilt or his wife, Rusty.

It would be all right so long as Emilie and the stand-in stayed up on the balcony.

A few miles away, a Virgin Atlantic crew bus stopped on a street corner to pick up a waiting Stewardess with her overnight bag. Climbing into the bus, the girl noticed the two additional crew, about whom she'd been forewarned.

Sir Walter Julien gave her a broad smile. In his Captain's outfit and cap, he looked handsomely convincing. Smiling back at him, she sat down next to the other new crew member, Julien's travelling nurse, now having exchanged her uniform for a Stewardess's outfit.

Later, Sir Walter, seated beside the two pilots in the cockpit of the Boeing 747, glanced wistfully down at the island coastline as the aircraft climbed swiftly after take-off.

He could see Government House quite clearly above Yellow Ribbon Beach, the tents and the crowd on the lawn. He thought of his children, whom he knew would keep the secret, especially the unsuspecting baby, Hattie, who simply gurgled with pleasure when he gave her a farewell kiss, and that last tearful hug from his wife, Emilie.

Not just a brave woman, as Charlie Chaumet had said. A woman in a million.

Six

Harper let himself into his apartment in one of the Edwardian mansion blocks that overlooked Battersea Park. He'd acquired it a year ago, after his divorce from Tessa.

A friend of theirs, who graduated at university with them, and who was nowadays a successful interior designer, had taken over the place and produced an ultra-modern, high-tech living space with white walls and minimalist furniture, but good paintings and prints and soft Italian lighting, not to say flat-screen TVs in every room, including the bathroom. During the transformation, they slept together a few times, but the liaison was purely physical, and he knew anyhow that she was in love with a dentist in Sydney, where indeed she now worked.

To begin with, Harper found the décor of the upmarket property a shade soulless. He was used to a certain almost comforting amount of clutter when living with his parents, his sister and brother, crammed together in a tiny terraced house in a then run-down area of Acton. Then a series of modest flats with his wife.

But after a few months be started to appreciate the grace and functional simplicity of the bachelor apartment. It had no history for him, and his natural depression at the collapse of his marriage lifted as he got on with his job.

The only sentiment on show was a shelf of framed pictures: Tessa giving a recital, his parents, Arthur and Lucy Buchanan, sister Rosemary, married to a boat-builder in Scarborough, and younger brother Lennie.

His father, now dead, was proud but unsure of Harper's chosen career as a cop. But he would have been proudest of Lennie, who was a Tottenham Hotspur soccer player, and one of England's top black players, having become their chief striker, earning a dozen international caps already. Not to say a fortune in wages every week.

As Harper checked his answerphone and heard his mother's voice making her weekly call to enquire how he was (she still lived in the same Acton house, alone and fiercely independent), he thought of his parents' hard fight to survive after their arrival in the late Sixties from the Caribbean.

Arthur Buchanan had worked as a railway track-layer, and was also an amateur boxer. Eventually he'd turned professional, won a few fights, and used the purse money to buy a shoe-repair shop, employing a skill he'd learned from his own father back home. The business never made much money, but he and Lucy were able to help with their childrens' education, with extra coaching and refinements like music lessons for him, ballet for Rosemary. Lennie, at fifteen, needed nothing more than soccer gear.

Harper made a few calls, cancelling the newspapers and his Filipino cleaner until further notice. He left a note for the milkman, went through his mail, and paid a few urgent bills. As he packed, he wondered whether he should call his mother and explain that he'd be away for a while, but decided he'd get in touch later from the hospital and not let her in on his new role. She'd just sit and worry for days.

Finally he rang Virgin Atlantic to find out the progress of Sir Walter's flight.

Seven

The Virgin jet was more than half way across the Atlantic and passengers were watching their seat-back in-flight movies. The one showing in so-called Upper Class at the moment was an English Tourist Board film, extolling the sights of London, highly selective, over-colourful, with clichéd views of the capital and an even more cliché-filled commentary by a well known actor with a plummy voice, guaranteed to induce sleep.

Sir Walter, who'd come through from the cockpit, sat next to his Nurse. Both in their airline uniforms, they would be assumed to be having a break. The nurse, although she had her seat headphones on, was dozing.

Sir Walter watched the travelogue with bored indifference. He took out his wallet and removed a slightly crushed photograph of Emilie and their five offspring.

The film narrator was droning on. '…and across the River Thames from the famous Tower of London, with its blood soaked history thanks to Henry the Eighth, with its Crown Jewels and Beefeaters – that's the colourfully attired guards, not a reference to their food tastes! – we find at Greenwich the O2 Millenium Dome, contrasting with the magnificent Royal Naval College buildings, and beyond, the Greenwich Observatory, giving its name, not to say its great astronomical history, to world timekeeping.'

It was at that moment that Sir Walter experienced a now familiar stab of pain around his heart. He winced, began to sweat as the next pain hit him.

Fighting down his panic, he took a deep breath, gripping the arm of his seat tightly, accidentally disconnecting the Nurse's headset. Waking immediately, she saw the Prime Minister's distress.

'Quick!' she whispered urgently, 'Let me get you back to the oxygen in the crew quarters.'

Sir Walter was still trying to keep his breathing under control, despite what now felt like a tight steel band around his chest. 'Don't know if I can make it! Can't you bring the oxygen out here?' he gasped.

'No, it'll attract too much attention,' she said. 'Keep taking deep breaths and lean on me.'

They got up and made for the door to the forward section, Sir Walter donning his dark glasses and carrying his pilot's cap under his arm, trying to look relaxed. He still had the family snapshot in his hand. As they reached the door he stumbled a bit. The Nurse managed to grab him, and for a moment they stood there while he regained his breath.

In the nearby seating area, an elderly American woman, reading her book through a magnifying glass, glanced up and saw what was happening.

'That's odd, damned odd,' she said to herself audibly. The passenger beside her, a West Indian businessman who was engrossed in his laptop computer, turned to her.

'I beg your pardon?'

The woman nodded towards the door. 'Over there. Surely that's one of our pilots? Whaddya make of that? Is he drunk?' She had a rasping voice, pure bronchial Bronx.

The businessman frowned as he saw Sir Walter stumbling again as he went through the doorway and out of sight. His sunglasses fell off and and the snapshot dropped from his grasp. They were both left behind on the floor as the pair disappeared from view.

'It's a goddam frightening thought, dontcha think? A pilot, for heaven sakes!' said the woman.

But her neighbour was already on his feet, walking over and picking up the glasses and the snapshot. He looked closely at the photograph with a slightly astonished expression, then moved to a magazine rack and fished around for a particular publication, a glossy Caribbean news magazine.

'Well, whaddya think?' asked the American woman, as he resumed his seat. 'You figure he was stinko?'

The businessman, not really listening to her, was flipping over pages in the magazine. Finally he found what he was looking for – a picture of Prime Minister Sir Walter Julien, taken in the Government House garden with three of his children. The same man! Something stinks for sure, thought Winston Wicklow, a smart up-and-coming data systems analyst with a chemical company.

And what's more, secretly a keen supporter of the UPP.

The Virgin flight from the Caribbean arrived at Gatwick in the early morning and there was little delay at Immigration or the baggage carousel; passengers were soon wheeling their trolleys through Customs and into the main concourse from the baggage hall, where the usual excited crowd of relatives and friends thronged the other side of the barrier alongside chauffeurs with their hands-free mobile mikes curled around one ear, as they held aloft scrawled and printed signs to signal to their clients.

Winston Wicklow, who was one of the first passengers to emerge, paused discreetly by the bookstand. He watched the tough old New York dame go stumping by, in an all-tartan mac, already wearing a plastic rain hat over her hennaed hair. She'd obviously heard about the British weather.

After about half an hour the outflow of passengers thinned to a trickle, as the last victims of Customs body searches, including sniffer dogs, emerged, with expressions ranging from rueful, to anger and exasperation at having their reunion with loved ones delayed.

Wicklow waited patiently. He'd bought a newspaper, scanning it to make himself seem more like a casual bystander. He decided his vigil was finally rewarded when a group of aircrew emerged from Customs, two pilots and a flight engineer, then a bunch of male stewards and stewardesses. He looked closely at their faces, but if it was Sir Walter Julien he'd seen earlier, he wasn't among them.

Then, checking his watch, he was about to turn away when he saw a yellow light flashing behind a frosted glass door to one side of the Customs area exit. As the door slid open automatically, an electric courtesy buggy for carrying infirm passengers, was driven out, it's light flashing and a warning bleep-bleep sounding.

Seated in the back with the Stewardess who was beside him on the plane, was the man he was almost positive was Sir Walter, still wearing his uniform. In front, beside the driver, was a well-groomed, good-looking West-Indian, in a grey flannel suit and a tie with red and gold stripes.

As he watched Sir Walter and the girl, and Detective Sergeant Harper, being transported from the terminal, Wicklow took out his mobile phone.

Outside the terminal building a car waited on a double yellow line, the hated vultures, over-zealous duty police and traffic wardens, having been told officially to ignore it.

Sir Walter and Harper got in as the Nurse and a plain-clothes police driver, detailed from Special Branch, loaded the bags from the buggy into the car boot.

'Were you expecting someone like me as a bodyguard?' asked Harper.

'Someone like you?'

'I mean a guy same as you? Black?'

'I didn't suggest it,' said Sir Walter, a little surprised, by the question and the tone of voice. 'In fact, I never gave the matter any thought, but maybe it makes sense.'

'I suppose that once I get rid of this Walter Mitty outfit, we could pass for a couple of dudes from under the mango tree,' he continued with amusement.

'My orders are to take you straight to the hospital,' said Harper. 'I expect you could use some sleep ?'

'I certainly could, Harper. That is your name, isn't it?'

'Christian name, sir,' he corrected. 'I'm Detective Sergeant Harper Buchanan.'

'We'll stick with Harper, okay?' He smiled. 'After all, for the time being I'm not meant to be me, and I dare say you're not supposed to be you.'

At the third try, Wicklow got through. He estimated it would be past midnight at the other end, but it couldn't be helped. The man he was calling might be asleep, but he'd soon be wide awake when he heard the reason for his call.

A subdued voice answered. 'Harbinson?'

'This is Winston Wicklow. Remember me? We've met a couple of times at your rallies. Sorry if I woke you.'

'What can I do for you at this hour?' asked Harbinson, woozy and distinctly cross. He'd been to dinner, had lots of wine, and before turning in, a tumbler of rum and one of his regular 5mg Zolpidem tablets.

'I'm in England, at Gatwick Airport', said Wicklow. 'Listen, something very curious seems to be going on… if the man I've just seen is our Prime Minister.'

Harbinson sat up sharply in bed.

'What did you say?' His voice croaky.

'How can Sir Walter Julien be in England? He was here till last evening at the Abolition ceremonies.'

Wicklow cut in. 'Well, it must have been his double.'

And he told Harbinson about the incident of the unsteady airline pilot and the family snapshot.

'I'd check who Sir Walter's doctor is, if I was you. The guy looked ill, like he was having some sort of a turn.'

Eight

Mr Carl Hardwicke arrived at the hospital as usual after lunch, parking his Aston Martin in one of the spaces reserved for consultants. A heart surgeon with a Harley Street consulting room as well as his NHS hospital work, he was surprisingly young, in his early forties. Impeccably attired, a yellow rose in his buttonhole, spectacles on a gold chain, he didn't even bother to lock the car as he strolled into the hospital with the debonair manner of a physician picking up several thousand pounds a day.

He'd spent the morning seeing a string of people at Harley Street, now he would do his private hospital examinations and after-care, followed by three operations scheduled for later in the afternoon.

The well-appointed reception area, more like the foyer of a five-star luxury hotel than a hospital, was filled with wealthy-looking people waiting for consultations. Hardwicke saw his private medical secretary, Sally Ivenhaugh, sorting out some files behind the desk, and went over to check his patient list.

'Your new patient, Mr Ballantyne, is here' she told him. 'He arrived this morning.' They both knew who the patient really was. But Sally, who had the bright charm and polish of an ambitious businesswoman, but was actually a mother-of-three and breadwinner with an invalid husband, spoke the cover name firmly for the benefit of the receptionist, Elena Saplimides.

'Jolly good. When's Mr Ballantyne's appointment?'

'Two-thirty,' said Sally. 'It's that now.'

Hardwicke turned his famous charm on the pretty Greek Cypriot receptionist. 'Perhaps you'd ring Mr Ballantyne's suite, give him my compliments, and let him know I'll see him now.'

As Hardwicke, in shirt-sleeves, conducted a series of tests on Sir Walter's naked torso, Harper sat in a corner of the specialist's consulting room, feeling rather uncomfortable.

He knew that his presence, however official, was an intrusion into normal hospital privacy. Added to which, Harper saw disapproving looks from Sally, the attractive assistant, who'd spotted his shoulder holster earlier, and seemed nervy, as if she feared some kind of gun battle might be about to ensue.

The surgeon was indulging in typical specialist's small talk. 'Do a spot of scuba diving myself, twice a year, in Bequia, off St Vincent, in the Grenadines. Got my Divemaster's Certificate last time. You know the island?'

Sir Walter nodded: 'Of course.'

'Used to be a lovely hideaway, unspoiled, cheap, the perfect beachcomber place. Now you run into half of Hampstead or Notting Hill there. Ruined, I'm afraid.'

Harper wondered if he'd ever have the opportunity to visit his roots in the West Indies before the islands were trampled to death by tourists like Carl Hardwicke.

Hardwicke pulled on his jacket, fluffing up the flower in his buttonhole, indicating the pre-operative exploration was over.

'Well,' he said, 'apart from the little bit of bother we know we have to deal with, you seem admirably fit. As soon as we do an up-to-date MRI scan, we'll set a day to do the repair work.'

Sir Walter asked: 'How do you rate my chances?'

Hardwicke sat down at his desk, scribbling some clinical notes with a gold pen. 'Oh, I should say you'll be as good as new. You'll be able to go on doing your job for as many years as you want to.'

'If I last that long,' said Sir Walter cynically. 'And I don't mean my health.'

'Just take it easy for a day or two. As you can see, we're like a posh hotel here,' said Hardwicke.

'Posh prison for me,' Sir Walter replied, as he went behind the screen to change. Harper got up and stretched his legs. The surgeon grabbed some files and X-rays from Sally, and giving Harper a brisk nod, went off to do his rounds of those bountiful patients in their £1000 a night rooms.

As she tidied her boss's desk, Sally looked over at Harper.

'I expect you're surprised by our weather?'

'Should I be?

'We've been having an unusually warm spell in London. I always think overseas visitors are in for a shock when they come from a hot country,' she said, with a friendlier smile.

'Actually, I'm a native Londoner, I live in Battersea,' said Harper smiling back at her, enjoying her slightly flustered reaction.

Nine

Although Government House was the most securely guarded establishment on the island, with laser-beam alarm systems and live-wire fences, the cove with the Prime Minister's private beach and his summer-house above it, could be overlooked from the sea.

It was just after breakfast, the sun already quite strong.

Rounding a nearby headland was a powerful luxury cruiser, *Pygmalion*, frequently loaned to Maitland Harbinson by one of the rich patrons of his party. Her sleek white hull ploughed lazily through the water half a mile offshore.

On the flying bridge, Harbinson was at the wheel. Beside him, looking through binoculars, was Frank Van Molder, an albino Dutchman, a paid organiser for the UPP. A former solicitor's clerk, he'd done time for embezzlement, and had to leave his home island of Saba to find alternative employment. For a while he worked as a car salesman, but was again caught with his hand in the till. In prison he shared a cell with Harbinson who'd been gaoled for assault at a political rally, and as a result gained his present job.

Van Molder trained his unblinking pale pink eyes through the glasses on a swimmer just off the beach. He pursed his thin, bloodless lips, with what seemed a permanent rim of spittle around them, watching the man swim back to the shore in a strong, fluent crawl, eventually reaching the shallows and wading up onto the beach.

'Wicklow could just have been suffering from jet-lag – imagining things,' said Harbinson, easing the twin throttles back, letting the cruiser drift. He didn't want to draw attention to their presence.

'If he's right, this man is a damn good likeness,' said Van Molder. 'I could swear I'm looking at Walter Julien.'

Harbinson took the binoculars from him, studying the figure on the beach, who'd picked up a towel to dry himself and was climbing up the path to the summerhouse. The Prime Minister's two familiar bodyguards were seated at a table playing cards. Nearby, on a sunbed, Emilie Julien, in a vivid orange one-piece swimsuit, lay reading a book. Harbinson noted that she didn't even raise her eyes from her book as the man passed her and sat down at the table.

There was a heap of banknotes in the middle and they appeared to be playing poker. The man picked up a hand, joined the game, and placed a bet.

Suddenly, Harbinson exclaimed: 'It isn't him!'

Van Molder was startled: 'What? How can you be sure?'

'Think! Remember what he repeatedly proclaims: that he's Prime-Minister-Pure okay? He's always harping on about it, preaching against the so-called evils of addiction? So what have we here?'

'Take a look,' said Harbinson, handing back the glasses, then answering his own question: 'Strict personal rules, huh?

Walter Julien boasts he doesn't smoke, doesn't drink, and doesn't gamble.'

Yet Van Molder could see that the man who joined the table was lighting a cigar, pushing stake money into the pot, and lifting what looked like a large glass of rum.

In the Caribbean dusk, before it would become dark with a bump, Van Molder parked his car in an alleyway down near the harbour.

He didn't much like the company of the man seated next to him, but he needed him. It was over a year since he'd seen Reuben Spence, and since then the bloody fool had dyed his hair corn yellow, and wore fake diamond earrings in both ears. He said it was his girlfriend's idea. A blond black guy, added to his own albino appearance. Christ!

So much for their dual low profile! Still, they weren't reckoning on seeing anybody; or, more accurately, anyone spotting them.

Reuben was another alumnus of the island's Point Pleasant prison, and a housebreaker with a special skill in cracking safes, which might be necessary. He had his canvas toolbag on his knees.

'Right, let's go and take a look,' said Van Molder getting out, softly closing his car door, and wincing when Reuben slammed his.

Fortunately, loud music from the sleazy waterfront bars and brothels drifted on the already dampening night air.

Moving cautiously to the mouth of the alleyway, they gazed across the poorly-lit street at the old-fashioned wooden-framed house where Dr. Charles Chaumet and his two partners ran their practice. It had once been a Seaman's Mission, and Van Molder knew that none of the doctors lived there. A sign in the window gave an emergency service phone number.

There was a light in the upstairs window of Chaumet's surgery facing the street. They could see the spry little Belgian still working at his desk.

Van Molder glanced at his watch. 'He should be gone soon. What do you make of it?' he asked.

'Dead easy,' said Reuben. 'Just so long as we can black out that doc's window, and they keep playin' the music good and loud round here.'

At that moment a police car came around a corner, and they quickly backed into the shadows until it passed by.

Chaumet's light went off in his surgery and a few minutes later he emerged, locking up. He got into his Mini and drove off.

As Reuben had forecast, it looked like a pushover. He forced the lock on a rear door, and they were inside without any fuss. Upstairs they even discovered what they hadn't been able to discern from street level, that the doctor's surgery had thick velour curtains, which were quickly drawn.

A search through Chaumet's desk and cupboards revealed nothing. Van Molder checked the main computer, linked to the three practice doctors, in the general office next door. But the information he was after about Sir Walter Julien proved elusive. It had to be in the safe.

Reuben, despite being too slow for Van Molder's liking, and irritably singing and talking to himself all the while, nevertheless blew the small Chubb safe efficiently. Though it produced a horribly loud bang indoors, it was virtually undetectable to the rest of the world, thanks to muffling with mattresses from examination couches and a pile of nurse's uniforms and sheets, and the loud street music.

In the safe, Van Molder found a box of confidential patient files on disk.

It took him very little time to find Sir Walter Julien's medical data CD that had been relayed to Mr Carl Hardwicke at the hospital in London. As Van Molder digested the information on the computer, he ordered Reuben to start turning over the surgery, to make it look like a conventional drug robbery.

'Steal as many drugs as you can,' he said.

'You mean that, boss? asked Reuben.

'Yes, make it look like a drug robbery – as a cover.'

When he heard this, Reuben gave a comical, wheezing sound in his throat, and suddenly Van Molder realised his safebreaker was high as a kite on some substance or other. Thank God the job was nearly done, though.

'Whaddya mean, 'cover?' I use fucking drugs,' Reuben giggled. 'I hope there's plenty of my kinda stuff,' he said, with relish, getting down to the task of trashing the place.

Dr Chaumet was annoyed with himself as he parked his Mini outside the surgery, to which he'd returned. He kept forgetting things these days. Sometimes he blamed the climate, sometimes the blood pressure pills he prescribed for himself.

But he was thinking as he fumbled for his keys: maybe I'm just getting too old to practise? If that were true, then he had professional misgivings, though he still considered himself to be a competent physician. Although he was worried, he had completely forgotten to take his bag with him for the homecall he'd promised to make first thing next morning.

Now, as he unlocked the front door, he wondered if his ears were playing tricks as well. For he thought he could hear the smashing of glass and someone shrieking. Or was it one of those high-pitched singers they called Rap merchants, who never seemed to draw breath, in the coarsely named Black Pussy Club nearby?

At the top of the stairs, as he opened the door of his surgery and saw Reuben overturning a big glass medicine cabinet, he knew his hearing was fine.

Reuben stared at the man in the doorway. Van Molder, still in another office, was unaware of Chaumet's reappearance. But then the doctor spoke.

'What in heaven's name do you think you're doing!' he challenged, reacting as Van Molder also stepped into view.

Reuben didn't bother to answer. He simply pulled out the gun he carried nowadays, and before the Dutchman could intervene, shot the old man through the chest.

All in a split second, Chaumet remembered the German officer who fired his Luger at him at close range, in the hand-to-hand fighting in 1944 for Antwerp, his birthplace, a battle he was proud to have fought in. The bullet had gone through his right shoulder.

This time he was not so lucky, as he staggered back onto the landing and crashed through the balustrade onto the marble floor of the entrance hall below, quite dead.

Ten

Along the Quai de la Tournelle, beside the River Seine and Notre Dame in Paris, is the row of bookstalls, known throughout the world, where you can buy rare second-hand books and prints. There is a wide choice of stuff, most of it eccentric ephemera, the real antiquarian book trade being located up the road, around the Sorbonne.

In fact, the bookstalls are mostly metal boxes that fold out, permanently fixed to the riverside parapet. Over these, the *bouquinistes* spread their canopies or umbrellas to protect their wares from both sun and rain. Today, as in the rest of Europe, the sun was blazing in Paris and the boulevards were suffocating with heat and traffic pollution.

Vincent Joussier had already drunk half a litre of the white wine he kept chilled in a thermal picnic bag under his stall, where he specialised in Caribbean art. Since he came from Guadelope himself, there were lots of prints and drawings of that island and the other French islands in the Lesser Antilles chain, including Martinique and St Barthelemy.

Joussier, in his fifties, with a beret and a white Van Dyke beard, was of mixed race – but strenuously Parisian, having lived in the city for more than twenty years.

A customer, a tall woman from Alsace, was bargaining with him over a colourful print of a 16th century map, supposedly made by pirates. Settling on 15 euros, twice its real value, Joussier rolled it up and neatly slipped it into a cardboard cylinder. As the woman walked off with her change, pleased with her purchase, he withdrew from his pocket a silver snuffbox. Then, using the 20 euro note she'd just given him, he deftly made a funnel and gave himself a quick snort of cocaine.

In a street across the other side of the Quai, with its endless flow of traffic, Inspector Guy Blasson sat in his car watching Joussier. A digital camera with a powerful zoom lens lay on his lap. He'd had his man under observation for at least an hour and a half, taken a few shots of him.

But it wasn't the bookseller's personal habits that interested Blasson, a senior drug squad officer who, at fifty-five, with a penchant for good food and booze, was neither the right shape nor age to be dressed in the traditional flic's garb, jeans and the black leather jacket. For this sort of job he felt bound to look casual.

Joussier was a known dealer, on the outer fringes of a much bigger organization they were hoping to bust. They could pull him in any time they liked. But they'd had a tip from an informer in a Paris suburb notorious for its drug culture, that he was due to meet with someone higher up the ladder. It could be nothing. Or it could be quite interesting.

As he peered across the road at the dapper Joussier, Blasson looked at his watch and scowled. He should have been accompanied by another, lower ranking officer, Sergeant Plennard, who hadn't managed to turn up so far. When they did, whatever the excuse, they'd be in trouble.

On another reach of the Seine, just outside Paris, to the North West, where the river meanders around the edge of the Bois de Boulogne, two sleek skiffs were racing each other, each rower sculling powerfully.

One of them, a bull-necked, red-faced man with a moustache, his midriff bulging against his white singlet, panted with the exertion, keeping his craft at least length ahead of the competition, a taller, slimmer figure in a loose shirt, baseball cap and dark glasses.

'Why don't you just give up, Plennard?' shouted the stout man. 'You'll never take me over the last stretch!'

The other rower merely gave a contemptuous grunt and kept up an even rhythm. Somehow there seemed to be potentially more power there, as if it was all being held in reserve.

'Okay, you asked for it!' barked the rower in the lead, beginning to increase his stroke rate.

But just as he sculled faster, so the second rower stepped up their rate, too, and the oars were biting deeper into the water, until after a minute or two the skiffs were slicing along abreast of each other.

Gradually the one who'd caught up started to forge ahead, and continued to increase the lead – by at least half a length – as they flashed past some prearranged finishing point. The tubby man, even redder in the face now, sagged over his oars, trying to get his wind back. He even used a puffer from a pocket in his shorts.

'You bitch,' he said ruefully as his opponent took off her glasses and cap, hunching up with exhaustion, her long dark hair lank with sweat.

'It's all in the wrists, Claude,' she grinned. 'Five euros you owe me.'

Sergeant Charlotte Plennard was obviously quite beautiful.

A tough beauty at that.

Eleven

Inspector Eddie Carmona was back in his office behind the market-place, sitting at his desk, trying to put together the shaver he kept in a drawer, which had somehow disintegrated when he'd tried to unclog it after a couple of months of non-use.

He'd been called out just after five o'clock from his bungalow on Lacey Plantation, where they used to breed silkworms, hence the name, to the surgery. An early morning cleaner, an unmarried mother who was always early – she rose at four-thirty, did her work, then got home in time to see her kids off to school – had discovered the body of Doctor Chaumet.

Carmona was sleepless, grumpy at having to get out of bed at such an hour, and missing his usual breakfast on the verandah with his two cheerful concubines. But most of all he hated to wear a creased, second-day shirt and an overnight growth of stubble. With his light brown skin it always looked like rusty metal filings. He was waiting for a life-saving cup of coffee which Joe Guarnac, a darkly handsome detective of Arawak Indian descent, who'd come in early to finish typing an overdue report, was obligingly filtering.

As boss of the Caribbean's undercover Joint Investigation Bureau, which was always alerted immediately to drug related crimes, Carmona appreciated the local police summons, though it did seem like just another sordid murder for stealing substances.

But Carmona was saddened by news of the victim. Ever since he came to the island to work with JIBOC he'd known Charlie Chaumet, and liked him a lot.

The old doctor was good company, and good medicine. Carmona had reason to be grateful to him when Inez became pregnant. Margaret had been very sporting, insisting that Inez should have the baby, since she felt her own chance had past. But Inez began to have severe complications, due to two previous abortions whilst living with that bastard from whom Eddie had rescued her.

Chaumet was a sympathetic, ever-attentive doctor, and finally when Inez had a miscarriage, he'd come to the bungalow and supervised her transfer to the Palm Grove Hospital, and made sure she was well cared for. And didn't overlook the subsequent counselling that she needed after losing a baby.

This morning there he was, lying in the surgery hallway, half his chest blown away, his skull caved in from the fall. Not strictly a senseless crime if it involved the theft of drugs, but tragically unlucky when Carmona heard that he'd left his daughter's house before dinner, to drive back and collect his bag. He'd said he would return for his meal, but didn't. She didn't worry because he'd become a bit dithery.

Nevertheless, as Carmona at last got the shaving head reassembled, and razored his chin, he was thinking about that professional piece of safe blowing. Why go to the trouble of breaking a safe? Or could there have been more valuable drugs kept in there? He'd know the answer when he talked later in the morning to the other doctors in the practice.

But somehow – he couldn't explain it, even to himself – it didn't feel like a normal robbery by desperate druggies. Nor did it have the hallmark of the big boys of the trade. They didn't go in for raiding small surgeries.

No, there was something odd about this one, but he couldn't quite work out what it was that bothered him. Nevertheless, he assumed it would turn out to have something to do with drugs.

As Joe brought him a steaming mug of decaff in a Coronation mug, he reflected on how drugs seem to be related to much of the Bureau's work.

Which made him think about one of his best detectives, Sergeant Charlotte Plennard, who was on the other side of the Atlantic for just that reason.

But Eddie Carmona, smart cop though he was, didn't connect any of it up at this time of day, and why should he?

Twelve

In Paris it had suddenly rained. It was a heavy summer shower that lashed down, becoming a huge downpour, jumping off the pavements and streets, which had all the booksellers on the banks of the Seine frantically adjusting their makeshift canopies to protect their stock.

Joussier was fastening a corner of his candy striped plastic covers when a teenage youth scurried up and dodged underneath, out of the deluge. He might have been simply a passer-by seeking shelter, but he certainly didn't look like the type to buy any books, except maybe porno ones, and not the vintage classics like, de Sade, Frank Harris, William S. Burroughs, etc. which some of Joussier's neighbours specialised in.

Over the road, Blasson, who'd set his windscreen wipers going, was munching on a salami-filled baguette as he observed a quick conversation taking place, then the furtive handover of money.

The Inspector's interest waned. Just another customer, on the path to self-destruction? For a dedicated cop, Blasson, married, but with no children, hadn't any particular moral stance about the exploitation of youth. If the kids got hooked on drugs, it was their own damn fault. Blasson's only stake in the sordid business was catching the top-level scum who were bringing the stuff into France.

Joussier put the 50 euros he'd been paid into a cigar box. Then he reached into a stack of books, flipped open a big hollowed-out tome, titled ironically, *Herbal Cures from the Rain Forests*, and extracted a small white sachet.

The young man stuck it in his pocket and walked swiftly away, though the downpour was, if anything, even heavier. Joussier lit a Gitane, innocently rearranging some hanging prints.

As Blasson felt his car lurch slightly, his eyes flickered up to his rear mirror. Another vehicle had pulled in tight behind him, nudging his rear bumper. He saw Sergeant Charlotte Plennard jump out. She opened the passenger door and settled in beside him.

Still chewing on his sandwich, he mustered an admonishing expression. 'Thanks for coming. You're an hour late.'

'Sorry, boss man' said Charlotte. 'I got caught up in some strong-arm stuff, helping out on another case,' she fibbed. As always, of course, by her use of 'boss man' in deference to his rank, she managed to slip in a bit of seduction.

She'd changed into a worn pair of jeans, her Spanish leather boots, and a large-sized man's Chevignon jacket with stuffed, shapeless pockets. Her hair was pinned up severely. She unhitched a satchel from her shoulder. It had a portrait of the mad scientist, Doctor Mabbutt, from the kid's tv series, on the flap. Big joke!

Though he had to admit he liked her conversation and her mind, and found her very attractive, Blasson was nonetheless often uncomfortable working with this thirty-year-old officer who'd been seconded to Paris a month ago from her outfit in the West Indies.

She'd been sent over as part of the current exercise, code named Operation Hurricane, since the trouble blew from one hemisphere to another.

Charlotte, he knew, was born in Martinique of parents who belonged to that French island's aristocracy. Her insouciance, which sometimes amounted to insurbordination, and frequently exasperated him, stemmed from the confidence her sort of upbringing had given her. She hadn't ever explained, though, how with that background she turned out to be a cop. Blasson would have been surprised if he'd known why.

She slipped off her boots, curling her toes within rather masculine woollen socks. 'So, what's happening?'

Blasson nodded towards the booksellers. 'There's a guy over there from your part of the world. He's from Guadeloupe. See him?'

'What's with all that bourgeois beard-and-beret shit?'

'He's lived in Paris for years. Name's Vincent Joussier. Street drug-dealer with a soul as black as his ass. Rich enough to own a farm in Marne-la-Vallee, yet he still likes to stand around selling books.'

'What's our interest in him?'

We know he deals in cut-down Colombian stuff,' said Blasson. 'A few hours ago we had a tip-off that he'd boasted in a cafe that he'd been 'promoted,' whatever that means, and he had a meeting today with someone important, for whom he'd found a special recruit.'

'And what does that bit mean?' asked Charlotte.

Blasson shrugged. 'Who knows? That's why we're watching.'

Charlotte lit a thin cigar with a Zippo from her satchel, having found it by removing her mobile phone, a personal organiser, a bunch of keys, a packet of Kiss Cool mint sweets, and two lipsticks.

She blew out a cloud of smoke. 'Would Joussier really arrange to see a top contact out here in the open?'

'Can you think of a better cover?' said Blasson. 'Also, it might depend on their reason for meeting.'

Blasson reached under his seat and pulled out a bottle of Pelforth beer.

'You don't happen to have an opener among your hardware, do you?'

Charlotte, smiling, dug in one of her pockets and brought out a red Swiss Army knife. Selecting the bottle opener, she handed it to him.

'If you come from the Caribbean, you're ready for anything,' she said sweetly.

Thirteen

Harper concluded his phone conversation with Chief Superintendent Norris of Special Branch, assuring him that everything was fine so far. He put the receiver down in the comfortable sitting room and walked out onto the balcony of the hospital's penthouse suite.

Sir Walter and Jonathan Walmsley from the Commonwealth Office were having coffee. Sir Walter was shaking his head as they looked towards the neighbouring Lord's cricket ground, where he'd so often been an honoured guest when the West Indies Test team were playing. There was almost always one or two players from his own island in the side.

'Funny place to find myself as a hospital patient. Many a time it's been a matter of life or death cricket-wise down there, too,' he remarked drily.

'Oh, yes, indeed, Sir Walter,' Walmsley chuckled, then wondered immediately if that had been the correct thing to do in the circumstances. Fortunately Harper appeared.

'I ought to be out here on the balcony with you,' he apologised. 'For your safety.'

'Sergeant Buchanan has a keen interest in cricket, too.' said Walmsley.

Sir Walter smiled: 'I thought I recognised the tie – MCC, that right, Harper?'

'Honorary member,' said Harper. 'I've played a bit of County stuff,' he replied modestly. 'If you don't mind me saying so, it's better not to stand out here for any length of time.'

Sir Walter frowned. 'Surely you're exaggerating?'

'Two reasons,' Harper said. 'You might be recognised by somebody on another balcony, and you're presenting yourself as a target from any number of angles,' he explained, pointing to the surrounding buildings.

'I'm afraid the Sergeant's right,' said Walmsley diplomatically, ushering him back indoors. 'Can't be too careful.'

As they re-entered the sitting room the phone rang. Sir Walter was moving to answer when Harper beat him to it.

'Let me take that,' he warned, lifting the receiver.

Sir Walter, irked, sighed quietly. 'Jesus, I really am a prisoner here! I can't even answer my calls!'

'For your own good, Prime Minister,' Walmsley assured him. 'Anyway, it won't be long before you're operated on,' he confided, once again feeling he'd said quite the wrong thing.

'Mrs Ballantyne?' Sir Walter heard Harper say into the phone. Then he saw him signalling for him to go and take it in private, in the bedroom.

When the door was finally shut, Walmsley collected his shiny crocodile-skin briefcase and Panama hat, preparing to take his leave.

'Glad you're getting on well with him. Rather a superior sort of chap, don't you think?'

And Harper could have sworn he was mentally adding: 'For a black politician,' or something to that effect.

Walmsley announced: 'Time for me to get back to Whitehall,' as if the statement carried implicit urgency.

In fact, he was going home to his Georgian house at Strand-on-the-Green, in Chiswick, for a swim, having the good fortune to have married the daughter of a stockbroker who'd escaped the global financial crunch fiasco, and had a elegant, blue hulled motor-cruiser moored by their front door. But naturally he couldn't tell Harper that, especially since the Sergeant had resented being assigned to this job.

Emilie Julien sat talking to her husband on a scrambled phone line.

She was on the back terrace of Government House, that looked towards the Two Anvils and the flanking mountains. She tried to keep her voice light and sound optimistic, but she was missing Walter desperately. She wondered how she ever went along with this crazy scheme to protect his life and leadership, agreeing not to be in London by his bedside.

First they compared the different times of day, and then the weather, as people do, and chatted on about their children, especially baby Hattie's teething problems, and finally: 'Walter, honey, I just don't know what the hell I'm doing sitting here, and what you are doing there!'

'You know why, sweetheart,' said Sir Walter, gazing dismally at the repro paintings on his bedroom walls of Olde English coaching inns, bucolic squires and huntsmen with coats as red as a fox's blood.

'Main thing is, are they looking after you okay?' asked Emilie.

'Sure they are,' Sir Walter told her. 'I have a round-the-clock police bodyguard. How's my double making out?'

'So far so good,' she said. 'Shit scared, but he's being well paid, isn't he?'

Sir Walter laughed. 'Believe me, I don't know anybody who could cope with this the way you're doing, Emilie,' he said.

'Never mind me, honey-pie. Come home soon, safe and sound. Me and the kids are missing you something sore,' she said.

And not wishing to lower his spirits at this moment, she purposely never told him that his dear friend, Doctor Charlie Chaumet, had been murdered.

Like JIBOC's Inspector Eddie Carmona, she didn't understand its significance.

Fourteen

Charlotte and Blasson had a long wait, the latter's tummy rumbling from a combination of undeserved hunger and at least two more Pelforths. But just as some of the booksellers were beginning to repack their boxes and they reckoned their stake-out had been in vain, they got lucky.

Blasson was yawning over the sports pages of *Le Soir* – he liked to back horses, and was often mysteriously unwell, absent from duty, when there was a race meeting at Longchamps or Chantilly. Charlotte was lighting her umpteenth cheroot when she saw the tall, handsome man get out of a taxi on their side of the Quai.

He was well dressed, tanned, carrying a briefcase, and looked like a top business executive. Charlotte stared at him with the shock of recognition, as he turned away from them, stooping to pay the cab driver.

'My God, surely it can't be…?' she murmured to herself

'Quoi?' said Blasson, not even looking up from the racing page.

'The man over there, leaving the taxi,' she said, sitting forward, a note of complete astonishment in her voice. 'When he turns I'll be able… Shit!' she exclaimed. 'It really is him!'

Now Blasson was fully alert, the newspaper down. 'Who?'

'He's from Martinique! Raphael Tabard's his name. He owns an export company in Fort-de-France, specialising in tropical perfume essences.'

'You know him personally?' asked the Inspector, as they watched Tabard wait for a break in the traffic, then hurry across the road to the riverside pavement.

'Yes, of course, I've met him back home, socially, several times.'

She was remembering one occasion. It was at a party hosted by her brother Leon, who now ran the Plennard family banana plantation. Raphael Tabard had been one of the guests. She was also remembering that he made a pass at her, when his wife was standing just a few yards away.

'Perfume essences innocently exported to Europe?' mused Blasson. 'And what else, I wonder? We're growing fucking warm, Sergeant. With luck, we'll bust 'em all quite soon,' he enthused.

'I was beginning to wonder whether my trip here was going to be worthwhile,' said Charlotte.

Blasson swore again. 'I came here early this morning to try and get a bug fixed on the wall so that we could overhear any conversations. But most of these bookworms were here before me, keen for business. You can tell there's a recession,' he said, frustratedly watching Tabard reach Joussier's stall.

The two men were talking, the former making a show of leafing through some prints, as if he was interested in buying.

'Well, we're certainly one step ahead,' said Charlotte. 'We know Tabard's identity, and it shouldn't be difficult to keep track of his movements in Paris.'

'Is he another spin-off Frenchman?'

'You mean a *Beke*?'

'Yeah, you know, one of the Caribbean French, so-called white upper crust, like you.'

Charlotte was about to take umbrage at his slightly derogatory tone when her eye was drawn to a figure arriving at the top of a flight of steps from the cobbled river embankment below, only a dozen yards or so from Joussier's pitch.

He was gaunt, probably late thirties, but could be less, and might have abused himself with drink and drugs, or both. Or perhaps he was older, looking younger? His face was thin and had deeply-etched, hard lines, with a long sharp nose, strangely mesmerising. His blond hair was in a ponytail, with a velvet ring, the tail teazled out like a real horse's tail, and despite the humid air, he had an ankle-length, grey green overcoat draped cloak-style around his shoulders. It gave him an almost medieval look.

He also looked decidedly menacing. Pausing for a moment, he strolled in the direction of Joussier and Tabard.

'Now we have a third party,' said Charlotte.

'I don't suppose he's another social acquaintance of yours?' enquired Blasson wryly.

'No, but he's damned attractive,' she said.

Blasson looked sharply at her, almost as if she'd insulted him. 'What, that creepy ponce?'

'I like ponytails, I like horses,' Charlotte replied.

No chance for him there, thought Blasson.

He became a cop again. 'Okay, this guy gives you some kind of frisson, Sergeant. But looking at him I'd say he's a nasty sort. So who the hell is he?'

Whoever he was, the real business was obviously between him and Raphael Tabard. Could that be the explanation of the 'recruit' Joussier had mentioned? Blasson's camera shutter whirred as he photographed them.

The newcomer and Tabard soon left the Quai, talking earnestly, choosing a safe moment to cross one of Parisian motorists' favourite racetracks, walking towards the peaceful haven of the Jardin des Plantes, further along the banks of the Seine.

As the Quai was one-way, Blasson had to drive fast, back up the Boulevard St Michel and do a quick left on the Rue des Ecoles, to catch up with the pair as they sauntered into the famed botanic gardens.

He parked his car and stuck the special exemption sign on the windscreen. It was a fatuous police invention for official unmarked vehicles, 'Driver Delivering Urgent Surgical Spare Parts', it said, without any regard to the proximity of a hospital. But it always seemed to work.

Tabard and the Ponytail were walking along the stately avenue, flanked by flowerbeds, that led from the entrance to the tropical glass-houses.

Charlotte and the Inspector, camera around his neck like a tourist, hurried after them. His paunch certainly helped to create that appearance. They were forced into a stride rather too hasty to fool any real horticulturist, even though they paused to show a spurious passing interest in the myriad of colourful plants and shrubs in full bloom at this time of year. The two men in front entered the main conservatory, dutifully closing the heavy, condensation-misted door behind them, as instructed.

Inside, they paid for two tickets from the bored attendant, who professed not to have any change and quickly made herself a few euros profit, as she'd craftily been doing all day.

Blasson and Charlotte reached the door. 'Let's go in,' he said. 'Nice, steamy heat. You can pretend you're back in Martinique.'

'No, thanks, Paris suits me fine for the moment.'

They paid the exact amount for their tickets, disappointing the attendant, and entered the dense green jungle of exotic plants and trees surrounding rock pools stiff with lotus lillies. They could see their quarry at one end, through a handy palm screen of Copernicia Cerifera. But they were unable to move closer, since Tabard would have recognised Charlotte. In any case the two men kept glancing around, obviously taking care not to be overheard.

To Tabard, Maurice Caubec was a bit of a surprise. Joussier had found him within a few hours, and swore he was the best man for the job. But Tabard had expected to meet someone with the hard stamp of an ex-Legionnaire, not this weirdo, who looked like a drug addict, and you never trusted them. And ponytails weren't exactly inconspicuous.

The more they talked, however, the more convinced he became that Caubec didn't use drugs. But he did become aware of an icy inner layer to the man. It was in the way he moved his hands, it was in his body language It was also in his unemotional, monotone voice.

He'd heard from Joussier about how Caubec, wanted for armed robbery in Carcassone, in the south near the Pyrenees, had joined the Legion, and how he had come to be regarded, even by his comrades, as ruthless. Sent to fight in Chad, he earned a reputation for the pleasure he enjoyed in taking human lives.

After he'd been involved in a village massacre, for which he was facing a military trial, he'd deserted, succeeding in smuggling himself back to Marseilles and the French mainland, and going underground.

Where he became a contract killer, a deadly name passed around, with so far three well-paid, well-planned murders to his credit. And only one miss.

In other words he came with excellent references for the task that Tabard had been outlining to him.

'Joussier has told you my fee?' Caubec asked.

'Thirty thousand euros? Pricey.'

'A little higher than my usual, since it's last-minute,' Caubec explained.

Tabard nodded agreement, though he knew from Joussier that Caubec was broke, having led a high life since his last wage earner. Apparently he was living in some dump on the outskirts of Paris.

'Plus expenses,' Caubec added.

Tabard brought out a fat buff envelope. 'There's half the amount as a down payment, plus all the expenses you'll need.'

Caubec stuffed it in one of his coat pockets. 'How about the rest? Where do I collect?'

Tabard said: 'We'll talk about that later.' He opened his briefcase and handed him a photograph.

'This is the man who is your target.'

'So where do I find him?' asked Caubec, studying his intended victim.

'It's all in the envelope.'

'You people don't waste any time, do you ?' said Caubec, putting the photograph away.

The two men sauntered out of the hothouse, unaware that they were being watched.

If Charlotte had been near enough to catch a glimpse of the man in the picture, she would certainly have been alarmed. The photograph was of Sir Walter Julien.

Fifteen

Hardwicke had said the hospital was like a posh hotel, and Harper felt it certainly lived up to the description.

He had slept comfortably on the sitting room couch-bed provided for patients' relatives, and now he and Sir Walter were eating breakfast delivered by room service on a trolley with silver salvers and hot toast, tightly wrapped in napkins. He'd started with a plate of green figs, and was now enjoying two perfectly grilled Arbroath kippers.

Sir Walter was tucking in, too. Before him was the kind of fry-up that transport cafes liked to call "Full English" or "everything on a plate." Harper thought that maybe, facing an operation, he felt like the condemned man, entitled to a hearty last meal.

'I hope you don't find this boring, Harper?' said Sir Walter.

'Not a bit. Beats a police canteen hollow,' Harper quipped.

'No, I mean being a bodyguard, cooped up with me. I'm here, I'm going nowhere, so what's all the fuss?'

'Presumably for the same reason your journey was so secret.' said Harper. 'Somebody wants you dead.'

'Okay, but since I'm now completely incognito, why can't I just be like an ordinary bloke? Just an another indistinguishable black guy?'

Harper gave him a wry look. 'Because we black guys are not quite like a row of Chinese guys, Prime Minister.'

Sir Walter smiled back, enjoying the joke. 'No, maybe not. So, do I get the sense you dislike this job they've given you.'

'Not at all,' Harper lied.

'When it's all over – and I hope to God it soon will be – maybe you'd like to come and stay with us at Government House?' said Sir Walter. 'You've probably already visited my island?'

When Harper explained that he'd never even set foot in the West Indies, Sir Walter, astonished, stopped eating his breakfast.

'Well, now, that's something for you to look forward to. You and perhaps your wife?' he added.

'Very kind of you,' replied Harper. 'But I'm not married – not any more.'

'Didn't work out, huh? You have any kids?'

'Fortunately, if that's the right word, no.' said Harper. 'How about you?'

'I've got five, but most of all I've got a real peach of a wife, Emilie.'

'Yeah, she sounds quite a lady. It must be tough for her, staying at home, pretending you're still there.'

Sir Walter shrugged. 'She wants me to live. A long time. We love each other.'

He poured Harper and himself some more coffee. 'Was your missus… black?'

'No.' said Harper. He paused. 'But there wasn't a problem there. It's just that our careers cut across each other's. She's an orchestra player. Our hours were never compatible, eventually our lives became so. We were divorced last year.'

'Sorry to hear that. And your folks?'

Harper told him all about his parents and their early struggles after emigrating to the U.K. How they'd given their children the best they could.

Sir Walter, remembering his own life in London in the Sixties, listened intently.

'Looks like you haven't fared too badly, Harper,' he said. 'You got to go to a university, and who knows, one day you might end up as the first black Metropolitan Commissioner!' he grinned.

Harper dearly wanted to tell him about Scotland Yard and the Metroplitan Police culture and the so-called Independent Police Complaints Commission and all that, but he decided to give it a miss.

'The real star is my young brother, Lennox. Or Lennie to us, his family, and his fans,' said Harper.

Sir Walter stared at him. 'You don't mean Lennie Buchanan, the Spurs and England footballer?'

Harper nodded. 'That's him.'

Sir Walter: 'Listen you're talking to one of his greatest admirers! We watch your Premier League games on our satellite tv!'

Harper shook his head at this unexpected connection with the man he'd been detailed to guard. 'Lennie would be thrilled if he knew he had a Prime Minister among his fans.'

When I'm recovered – any chance of meeting him?' asked Sir Walter, and Harper could tell he meant it.

'I'm sure it could be arranged,' he smiled.

Several floors below, at hospital reception, Elena Saplimides smiled over the desk at the man who said he was a radio journalist.

He was very different to the sort of brash young reporters from television and local London radio stations who plagued the hospital whenever there was some story involving a celebrity patient. But, then, of course, he was French. And he had lots of Gallic charm.

'Who did you say you work for?' she asked, not quite having made out the name first time.

'Radio Caraibes Francaise,' he smiled. He patted the tape-machine he had slung over his shoulder. 'You see, here ....' indicating a sticker with a logo and the initials 'RCF'.

'I'm sorry, what does it stand for?'

He took it slower this time, translating. 'Caribbean Radio.' I am trying to set up an interview.'

'I see,' said Elena warily. 'And who would that be with?' she enquired.

'One of your patients, Sir Walter Julien. Might it be possible to contact him, you think?'

'If you'll wait a moment, I'll just check the register.'

Crossing to a computer, she went through a screen display. Returning to the desk, she shook her head: 'I'm sorry, sir, we've no one here under that name.'

Ah, but perhaps he uses another name, to be discreet, you understand? Let me describe him. Sir Walter is tall, a West Indian VIP in his sixties. You know him, yes?'

The Cypriot girl was now even more cautious. She was thinking of 'Mr Ballantyne' but hoped her face didn't show it. 'We do have people of all nationalities here, sir.'

'But surely a West Indian with a title?'

'I'm very sorry, sir, but I'm afraid in any case I'm not permitted to divulge information about patients,' she said. 'However, if you'd like a word with our Medical Director?'

'Thank you, that won't be necessary,' said the man. I'll try another source.'

As she watched him go, Elena reflected that his garb was also a bit strange compared to the other reporters she'd encountered. None of the journalists, as far as she could remember, had ever turned up in an ankle-length coat or had their hair in a combed-out ponytail. Was outre the right word for it? She thought to herself once again, well, that's the French for you.

Sixteen

The Narcotics Division to which Detective Sergeant Charlotte Plennard had been attached, was housed in one of the many police buildings located in the centre of Paris. It was a baroque, fin-de-siecle edifice in the 7th Arrondissement, in a narrow street off the Boulevard des Invalides.

Charlotte was late for the morning conference, and she drove way over the speed limit down the narrow street, screeching to a halt where a pair of unfriendly-looking Gendarmes, armed with sub-machine guns, stood by the courtyard entrance. She flashed them an enticing smile, receiving not even a flicker of interest, as they made no move to raise the barrier.

She leaned out. 'What's the best way for a girl to get in? Show her knickers?'

The taller of the two, spoke: 'Identity, please, Sergeant.'

'You see! You said "Sergeant", so you know who I am!'

They both remained deadpan. Charlotte sighed and dug her pass out of her jacket, waving it at them with a sardonic, sexy, wristy action.

The barrier went up, and as she drove in she yelled at them: 'Any more of that and you're off my list of possibles!'

They gazed after her as she shot into a parking space, jumped out and dashed up the elegant, curved steps.

'You reckon that tough bitch is as big a tease as she seems?' asked one.

'Give me one night with her and I'll tell you!' said the other, their faces cracking in lascivious grins.

Inspector Blasson gave a nod to the young detective at a computer, who keyed up a shot of Joussier, the bookseller, on a big screen.

A dozen or so drug squad officers were gathered in the Briefing Room, the walls of which were adorned with lots of photographs of people and places, and several maps with flags and ringed areas on them. There were also one or two blackboards with diagrams.

Blasson pointed to the bookseller's picture. 'Someone known to most of you, I expect,' he said. Vincent Joussier, dealer and fixer in cocaine and crack, under cover of his piffling books. His time is nearly up. We've let him operate freely to see who – or what – we might catch sight of further up. We got lucky...'

A shot of Tabard joining Joussier at the riverside, now appeared on the screen.

During this, Charlotte crept in, slipping into a seat next to the fat cop whom she'd rowed against the day before. She gave him a sideways look, holding out her hand. He shrugged and handed over the five euros he owed her.

If Charlotte thought her lateness had gone unnoticed, she was mistaken. Just as she was preparing to light a cheroot: 'Glad you could make it, Sergeant Plennard,'

'Sorry, Concorde was jammed solid.'

'You don't mind that we started without you, I hope?,' Blasson said with heavy sarcasm.

Charlotte gave a bright smile. 'I can catch up.'

'No, I've got a better idea. You can personally fill the team in on our friend on the screen here.'

As she nodded and moved up front to address the squad, Blasson pointed sternly at the cigar in her fingers.

'Without smoking, if you please. We wouldn't like the Chief to come in and find us breaking our new health laws, would we?'

She put the cheroot away, slipping off her jacket, facing the gathering to give them a run-down.

Charlotte explained: 'He is Raphael Tabard, and he came as a big surprise, because we know him in Martinique as an outwardly respectable businessman.'

'In perfumes, and yet your JIBOC bureau never smelt a thing!' sneered Blasson, and for the first time she realised that the Inspector, even as a cop, had the same smugness and arrogance that she found in so many Parisians.

'How about you lot?' she countered defiantly. 'Did you know about him? As we now gather, he's been in Paris at least a dozen times in the past eighteen months. Did your investigations reveal that?'

'Okay, okay,' Blasson admitted. 'Can you tell us anything more about Tabard?'

'I spoke with my boss, Inspector Carmona, last night. They're doing further, urgent checks and hope to e-mail us something on him in the next twenty-four hours.'

'Good,' said Blasson. 'Though we may not need it. Tabard is staying at the Crillon and we're sticking to him like puke to a blanket. We understand a large consignment of cocaine was landed last week by this Dutch banana boat, the *Onno van Noort*, at Rotterdam last weekend.

As they looked at a photograph of the berthed cargo ship, Blasson continued: 'Interestingly, on the ship's manifest, drums of perfume essences crop up, loaded aboard in the Caribbean. The perfume company is called "Herald Industries".'

'Tabard means a herald's waistcoat!' exclaimed Charlotte's rowing companion, Sergeant Cassal, looking pleased with himself for his quick deduction.

'Ten out of ten, Cassal,' Blasson congratulated him. 'We also have reason to believe that at least half the cocaine has already been delivered to Paris. Put up the picture of the farm,' he ordered the young cop.

On the screen there appeared a photograph of a small farm in a remote setting.

'Belvedere Farm, Marne-la-Vallee,' Blasson announced. Only a stone's throw from EuroDisney would you believe? But there's nothing fucking Mickey Mouse about this place.'

Now the computer showed shots of Joussier getting out of his car and going into the farmhouse.

'Joussier's place. Where we believe he's stashing the cocaine.'

'You aiming to go for a bust?' asked Charlotte.

'Maybe. Meanwhile we're intrigued by this man,' said Blasson, as Caubec's image took over the screen, shots of him strolling alongside Tabard in the botanic gardens.

'Maurice Caubec. He looks like a ponce, but he's a dangerous bastard, make no mistake. So what, we ask, is his involvement with the drug scene? We don't know. But we've got a file on him. It reveals that he's a former Legionnaire, a trained killer, suspected of being responsible for several murders in different parts of France.'

Blasson looked at Charlotte. 'Still turn you on, does he, Sergeant?'

Seventeen

The subject came up when they were playing chess.

Harper considered himself to be an above average player, but he found Sir Walter a tough, wily opponent. After three checkmates, Harper played stealthily, then made a move to take a majority of Sir Walter's scattered pieces. But suddenly, in a deft sequence in five by his White Queen's rook, inside the Black King's defence, the Prime Minister beat him.

Sir Walter got up and poured another malt scotch for his bodyguard, a neat coke for himself. 'You can do me a big favour, Harper,' he said, putting his glass down beside him.

Harper glanced up from the chessboard. 'Sure, what's that?'

Sir Walter walked to the open window and gazed out at the lights twinkling over Maida Vale and Little Venice. He could just see a bit of the canal in the distance, and was remembering how, as a student, he sometimes used to work all day Sundays, collecting tickets on one of the launches that ferried people to and from the London Zoo in Regent's Park.

'Did you know I had a sister in London?'

Harper frowned. 'They never told me.'

'Her name's Dulice. I haven't seen her for over ten years.'

'Surely you've been in London lots of times? Commonweath Conferences and so on?'

Sir Walter sat down with a sigh. 'If you must know, we had an unfortunate quarrel long ago, so we never spoke again. It was you talking about your family that set me thinking about her. She's had a hard life, I know. Her man ran out on her, left her with three kids.'

'You want to phone her?'

'Better than that, Harper,' he said, 'I'd like to see Dulice.'

Harper shook his head firmly. 'You know that's not possible. This isn't the moment to make things up with your sister. You'd be breaking cover. Even a phone call is risky.'

'And if I don't pull through the operation?'

Harper looked at him. He was being put on the spot.

'Exactly,' said Sir Walter. 'There won't be another chance.'

It had been difficult for Harper to argue against the Prime Minister, and Sir Walter was in any case a forceful character. He owed his success in politics to that. From his luggage he found a tweed hat that Emilie had thoughtfully packed for him, and he and Harper left around eight-thirty the next morning.

As they got into his Saab, Harper was still very unsure about giving way.

'I don't like disobeying orders, I don't like it one bit,' he said, looking nervously around the courtyard in front of the hospital.

'It's my hide, Harper,' said Sir Walter. As well as the hat, he'd donned dark glasses.

'Yeah,' Harper replied, 'and what happens to me if something happens to you?'

'Shepherd's Bush Market,' Sir Walter instructed him amiably. 'That's where she works. As you probably know, its shoppers are at least fifty per cent West Indian, so I'll hardly stick out in the crowd, will I?'

'Are you sure she'll be there?'

'Somebody sent me a magazine article about the market only last month. She was in it. They asked her if she was really sister of a Prime

Minister. She said, "Sure, I run a market stall, he runs a country, so what's the difference?'" Sir Walter chuckled. 'I liked that! Dulice, she could eat a banana sideways!'

As Harper drove off, another car started up in the section of the courtyard marked 'Nursing Staff Only.' It was a hired Focus, and Caubec, wearing gloves to avoid fingerprints, was at the wheel, with the satisfied look of someone who had second-guessed them. That was another of his dangerous attributes.

Harper found a metered parking bay in Lime Grove, a street with no trees whatsoever. He knew the Shepherd's Bush area well, especially the market. His parents often used to shop there, indeed his mother still did occasionally. And brother Lennie's first professional soccer club, before a £3m transfer to Spurs, was QPR, at the Loftus Road ground, just around the corner. Sir Walter was visibly impressed when Harper pointed out the tall floodlights that dominated the area.

As they walked along Uxbridge Road towards the entrance to the market, they were totally unaware of the Focus that had also found an empty kerbside space.

Caubec got out and followed them, not even bothering to lock the car. He'd hired it in a fake name with a fake passport, and if somebody stole it, so what?

Besides, if he was successful, he might not have any further use for it.

The market was a noisy conglomeration of stalls, shops and lock-ups. You could buy fruit and vegetables or jerk chicken at one end, all kinds of clothes and footwear in the middle, and elsewhere everything from pirated DVDs and music CDs, carpets, mirrors and gruesomely bad pictures, to travelling clocks and trunks, fashion wigs, and ghetto-blasters hot off the backs of lorries. You could be told your fortune, tattooed, or drawn by a lightning artist.

Since, as Sir Walter had forecast, it was thronged with Afro-Caribbean customers on another hot and sunny day, it could have been a colourful market in the West Indies, except for its rather forbidding location, a littered concrete strip with the rear of office buildings on one side, and an elevated section of the Metropolitan Underground on the other.

Harper and Sir Walter wandered among the clothes stalls. In the jolly, bustling atmosphere, Harper felt a little more relaxed. Though he knew they had an endless pickpocket problem in the Bush, things seemed safer in a crowd. Just the same, he kept close to his charge.

At length, looking down an aisle between two rows of stalls, Sir Walter grabbed Harper's sleeve and drew his attention to a lock-up with a painted sign above, which proclaimed: *DULICE'S WARDROBE – FASHION IN VOGUE*. Standing in the doorway, holding up a garment for a customer's scrutiny, was a huge, beaming woman in a brightly patterned cotton shift. Dulice was almost as broad as she was tall, but she had the same noble features as her brother, and although a few years his junior, the same greying hair.

'My little sister's lost a few pounds since I last saw her, but not many,' he said with a grin.

Harper couldn't help grinning as well, wondering if Vogue, as a magazine of haute couture, had ever thought of suing under the trades description act. The lock-up was hung with all kinds of gawdy dresses, blouses, skirts and sweaters. It also managed to fit into its crammed display, accessories like tights, gloves, shawls and hats.

She was cajolling the customer, a teenage girl, to buy. 'Now I'd say you and that blouse were just made for each other! Why don't you just come on in and try it on?'

She ushered the girl into a changing booth at the back of the lock-up, pulled the curtain, and turned to find Sir Walter, who'd removed his hat and glasses, standing there. Harper hovered a few paces behind him. For a few seconds Dulice was in shock.

Then she said quietly: 'Well, fuck me, isn't this a funny old day?'

'Isn't it just. How are you, sweet sibling?'

'Walter!' Shrieking and sobbing at the same time, she hurled her arms around him. They held each other tightly, and Harper could see that Sir Walter could scarcely control his own emotions.

He felt a trifle embarrassed to be there, an intruder, like he'd been made to feel at the hospital.

Sir Walter detached himself from his sister. 'Meet my bodyguard, Sergeant Buchanan.'

Harper nodded. Dulice stared at him, then at her brother. 'First you turn up here, of all places, a man in your position! Out of the blue, after all them years! No letter, no phone call?'

'I can explain, Dulice.'

'Then you announce you have a bodyguard? Where's Emilie? What the hell is going on, Walter?'

'Look, why don't I leave you two alone for a while?' said Harper, who'd noticed a small cafe nearby with a service counter where he could stand and keep an eye on them.

'Thanks, Harper, much appreciated,' said Sir Walter.

'I'll be over there,' said Harper, indicating the snack counter. He walked towards it to order himself a coffee.

Caubec had had no trouble catching them up. He watched the reunion between brother and sister, and saw Harper move away to the greasy spoon.

When he'd observed Harper coming out of the hospital with Sir Walter, he'd sussed him out instantly as a cop. Just the way that Harper had walked, even the gestures in the unheard conversation between them, suggesting somehow that a Head of State was taking orders. The big question was, was this cop armed? It was a chance Caubec had to take.

Very quickly he made an assessment – that was another thing the Legion had taught him – and found no difficulty in reaching the vantage point he decided was best. It was at least fifty yards away, and the landing on the fire escape at the rear of an office gave him perfect height.

As he climbed the metal staircase and casually stepped onto the first-floor landing, he was also already working out an escape plan.

The rifle, a Czech Super Posny 101, a sniper's choice model, one of his favourites, had been obtained from a dependable dealer in Kilburn – a former supplier to the IRA – whom he'd contacted before leaving Paris. Short and exceptionally light, he'd hidden it in the hemline of his long coat. It had been tricky keeping his gait looking natural, as the coat swung behind him like an ankle-length kilt.

Now, with the rifle in his gloved hands, he quickly brought out the telescopic sight from a pocket and snapped it into place. He knelt down and took aim.

In the sight, which he adjusted to near-perfect focus, he first of all got Dulice, as she talked, still misty-eyed, with her brother outside her stall. He could actually make out the mole just above her right eyebrow.

He switched immediately to Sir Walter, who'd donned the dark glasses and tweed hat again. There was sunlight glinting on the glasses, flaring out, which proved a problem until Caubec lowered his aim and professionally found the Prime Minister's heart.

His finger hovered on the trigger. Just as he was about to squeeze, Sir Walter turned his body away. Caubec's eye lifted from the rifle sight and he saw that Harper had walked back from the cafe, holding his plastic coffee cup. He was talking to them both, pointing to the inside of the lock-up, probably advising them to step inside for safety's sake.

Damn! He'd have to do it now, or wait for another chance, and when would that be? He pressed his eye back into the sight and quickly took aim at Sir Walter. His sister's arm was draped across part of his chest, but there was just enough space for a bullet. Hold. Steady. A soft, easy pressure on the trigger...

It was at that moment that the girl who'd been trying on the blouse, and decided she didn't want it after all, left the changing booth and came out to speak to Dulice. The girl was running late, she had to get back to her office, so she interrupted, holding out the garment.

'I'm sorry, but I'm afraid it doesn't------'

She never finished her sentence. Even as he pulled the trigger, the blouse draped itself between the assassin and his target, screening Sir Walter's chest.

Nevertheless, the shot hit him. Sir Walter spun round with the impact, and amid screams from Dulice and the girl, Harper caught Sir Walter as he staggered with blood spurting from his chest, and hauled him down to the ground. He drew his gun.

Caubec was fairly certain that his aim had, as usual, been lethal. But Sir Walter was lying sideways, presenting a perfect target for a second shot, as Harper was bringing out his revolver.

The Frenchman took aim again and fired. This time it was Harper, crouching down protectively beside the Prime Minister, who was in the way.

He was hit in his left shoulder, though the bullet only ripped the top of his sleeve and grazed him. By this time lots of people in the market were hollering and running for cover.

But Harper, almost subliminally, had seen the flash and the source of the second shot, and now he glimpsed the fleeing figure of Caubec, desperately clattering down off the fire escape.

As Harper fired a shot at him, he caught a glimpse of the man's face, his blond hair and pony-tail, and the long coat, for just a fraction of a second. The shot missed, and Caubec disappeared, as he'd planned, into the crowd.

Harper started running after him, through a wall of curious shoppers, most of whom didn't really comprehend what had taken place. Was it some TV drama or candid camera sequence? Or a scene in a film? Where were the stars? That's what most people seemed to think these days whenever there was a street incident – a nightmare for the police.

Caubec was using a lane behind some lock-up stalls for his getaway, but he knew he had to dispose of the gun. Spotting a folded tarpaulin beneath one of the stalls, he stopped, thrust the rifle in and covered it. Then he walked on, hoping to make an unobstrusive, unhurried exit from the market. So far he'd managed to give Harper the slip.

But what Caubec hadn't seen was that he was being closely watched by a young man, Errol Duffy, sitting on a wall drinking a can of beer, keeping well out of sight of any work and his mother, who ran a lingerie stall. Errol was eighteen, but his height and build made him look a good deal older. He could hardly believe what he saw – a guy stashing away a rifle!

He watched Caubec make his getaway, and was about to slide off the wall when Harper came charging round to the back of the stalls and saw him.

'Police!' said Harper, brandishing his I.D. 'You see a man in a long coat back here?' he asked. 'White guy, hair in a pony-tail,' he added

Errol decided to tell part of the truth. 'Yeah, he took off in that direction,' he said, pointing. He didn't mention the rifle.

Harper ran swiftly to the Goldhawk Road exit. But by then he knew he'd lost his man. There was no sign of Caubec in the street, busy with traffic and passers-by. And the market at this end was even busier. He scanned the faces in the crowd for a few moments, then turned and urgently made his way back to Dulice Julien's stall.

There was a ring of gawpers around Sir Walter. Someone had already called an ambulance, and a doctor who happened to be in the market, was trying to staunch the flow of blood from the Prime Minister's wound. He was still alive, but only just, by the look of him.

Dulice was on the ground beside her brother, holding his hand and murmuring 'Shit, shit, shit,' over and over again.

Harper told himself bleakly that he was the one who was about to be in deep, deep shit.

Eighteen

Caubec had decided to abandon the hired car. He bought a ticket instead at the neighbouring Goldhawk Road Underground tube station. He just missed a train and had to wait at least ten minutes for the next one. When it arrived he got into a carriage with relief and, as it happens, took a seat on the side that gave him a clear view of the market as the train rumbled across the viaduct.

Two police cars, with overhead lights flashing and sirens screeching, were driving straight into the market from a side entrance. He could see there was an ambulance already there, and before his view was cut off, he watched two ambulancemen lifting the inert figure of Sir Walter onto a stretcher.

Harper didn't want any fuss made about his shoulder wound, but the doctor had insisted on having a look. Meanwhile a police doctor, who'd arrived in one of the cars from the nearby police station in Uxbridge Road, was supervising the lifting of Sir Walter into the ambulance. They were desperately transfusing blood Dulice, weeping, waited to get into the ambulance after the stretcher. Uniformed men strung their crowd control tapes around the scene of the shooting.

As Harper, his wound dressed, put his torn jacket back on, another car pulled up and Chief Superintendent Norris jumped out. He went straight to the ambulance and had a brief word with the police doctor, then turned and marched in Harper's direction. He looked even more stricken than Harper.

'You bloody fool, Sergeant!'

Harper shrugged. 'It was Sir Walter who insisted,' he began, but shrugged again, this time wincing with the pain in his shoulder. 'Okay, I know I can't shift the blame.'

'You're too damned right, you can't. You've really landed us in it. There'll be a fucking nuclear explosion in Whitehall,' said the Superintendent.

'I'm sorry,' said Harper lamely. 'He's still alive, isn't he?'

'Only just. They can hardly feel any pulse.'

'I saw the guy with a rifle,' Harper told him. 'I couldn't catch him, he was a professional,'

'Of course he was, Buchanan!' said Norris angrily. 'Assassins usually are! He outwitted us. Pity you didn't see him earlier.'

'He must have followed us from the hospital,' said Harper.

Norris glared at him with ill-disguised dislike, and if Harper had ever had any doubts about the Special Branch man's deep hatred of black officers, they were now dispelled. 'That was your first fucking mistake, Sergeant Twilight,' said Norris coldly, using a racial-sounding name tag that Harper hadn't heard before.

The uniformed officers and two local CID men had already started to clear the area completely for white-overalled forensics' usual on-their-knees minute comb-through, and Harper was needed to give a full description of the gunman, where he'd stood, the angle of fire, and so on. Norris went to talk with an Inspector.

Errol Duffy left the fringes of the crowd watching the police, trying to decide what he should do about the rifle. Should he should try removing it now, in case the police search widened to the whole market, or leave it where it was and hope to collect it later? Errol wondered if the gunman intended to return and reclaim it. He thought it unlikely.

He was round the back of the stalls gazing at the tarpaulin, when his mother's voice cut across him like a whip.

'Errol, there you are! Where have you godam well been!'

Jamaican, and an unmarried mother of seven kids, she had beaded hair and a legendary temper. She ran her own lingerie stall, and though Errol was almost six feet and she only came half way up his chest, he was terrified of her.

'What you doin' back here anyhow?'

'Nothin,' Mammie.'

'Ain't that right, you lazy little good-for-nothin!' Well, how's about you moving that idle ass of yours and helping me pack up?'

Errol knew he'd have to wait before he could get his hands on that rifle. From what he saw, he thought it it had telescopic sights, and he reckoned it could worth a lot.

And he badly needed money for his drug habit.

Nineteen

It was just after seven-thirty when Frank Van Molder arrived for work at the headquarters of the UPP, a solid stone-built office on the shore road at Merton Bay, a small island township that had been one of the main sugar ports in that industry's heyday.

The office, white-washed, with a couple of tall cabbage palms on the gravel terrace facing the sea, looked a bit like one of the country's three Customs Houses. In fact, it had been put up at the turn of the century by the same builder who was responsible for Excise establishments. But its more recent owners had been the British Cable and Wireless company in the pre-satellite days when telegraph and telephonic communication depended on an undersea cable, laid across the Atlantic to the company's receiving station near Penzance, Cornwall. Indeed the West Indies building was still called 'Penzance House.'

Van Molder was always first to turn up, since every morning at crack of dawn, he did a twenty-mile cycle journey from his beach house on the windward side of the island. He liked to avoid motor traffic, particularly in view of the general level of driving skill in the Caribbean. Pedalling his route in a skin-tight, Tour-de-France-style lycra outfit, he carried his clothes in a rucksack. Then he would change and be properly dressed, ready for his office duties, at eight o'clock.

Unlocking the main door, he followed his usual routine, which was to check his e-mails before shaving and showering in the men's washroom.

The first message, sent from some casual Parisian cyber-cafe sent a shiver through him, despite his body sweat. It said cryptically:

TARGET LOCATED. BELIEVED BULLSEYE. It was unsigned, but he knew who'd sent it because the wording had been prearranged.

Van Molder started to print it out, at the same dialling a number, and Harbinson, en route in his car, answered on his hands free mobile. 'Yes?'

'An e-mail just arrived,' said the Dutchman. 'It says "Bullseye".'

Harbinson, gripped the wheel tightly, but remained composed. 'So our man succeeded?'

'Apparently.'

'I'll reach you in thirty minutes,' said Harbinson. 'You know the list of people to ring. Tell them to get over as quick as they can for an emergency meeting.'

'Shouldn't we wait for confirmation?' Van Molder queried.

Harbinson said: 'No, I don't care if Julien's only half dead.'

'You intend to begin the takeover straight away?'

'Yes, and that includes the Army,' Harbinson told Van Molder. 'Colonel Marcel is on the UPP's side anyhow.'

'I'll start phoning around immediately,' said Van Molder. 'Will you leak the news?'

'Yes. The point is, Sir Walter's not here. He may be dead, and we have to ensure stability and peace on the island,' said the Opposition Leader, who had been rehearsing for weeks the sincere speech he would make on television after the coup.

In an ante room to the operating theatre, Harper waited with Norris and Jonathan Walmsley, who had arrived from the Commonwealth Office in an agitated state. As well as his dismay at what had happened, Walmsley was worried about Dulice being there, but Norris assured him that nobody else knew who the victim was.

Dulice was in a corner, still in shock, a WPC sitting with her. Through an observation window a team of doctors and nurses, led by Hardwicke, could be seen working urgently around the operating table in an effort to save Sir Walter's life.

Walmsley said: 'They wouldn't spend all this time, would they, if there wasn't a chance?'

'He doesn't seem to be reviving, though,' Norris observed.

It was, in Harper's book, a brutal thing to say in Dulice's presence. He touched Norris's sleeve, reminding him that she was seated a few feet away.

The Special Branch man's only response was to glare at him, leaning close and saying under his breath: 'Listen, Sergeant, don't start giving me bloody lessons on etiquette! Not in your situation.' And then, threateningly: 'I'm coming to you next.'

Hardwicke opened the door of the theatre, tugging his mask down, standing on the threshhold to avoid having to sterilize himself again. Oddly enough, in his jaycloth surgical hat and green gown, without his smart suits, he looked even leaner and younger, less like the polished Harley Street money maker.

'Still hanging on, is he?' asked Norris, who was always intrigued by the way these surgeons wore wooden clogs.

This time, Harper didn't even bother to remind him that Sir Walter's sister was there.

'Put it this way,' said Hardwicke, 'we are hanging on to him. We've got the bullet out, but I'm afraid he's still critical.'

'Just do your best,' said Walmsley.

Hardwicke said caustically: 'Oh, we're doing that alright, it's you lot who've been a bit less than your best looking after him.'

He turned and went back in to rejoin his colleagues. Harper was the one most affected by his remark.

'Well, at least they haven't put up the shutters yet,' said Norris.

'I just hope the media don't get onto it,' said Walmsley.

Norris shrugged. 'We've issued a cock and bull story about gang warfare, to cover the shooting.'

Harper said: 'Fine. But whoever was behind it will know the truth.'

Walmsley nodded in sombre agreement. 'Yes, that's what worries us. His enemies may have already decided to make a move whether he's dead or alive.'

Twenty

Around about lunchtime the first bulletins had been broadcast on radio and television on the island about the coup, which naturally wasn't described as that, but with full political spin as 'an emergency procedure designed to maintain law and order following the reported assassination of the Prime Minister.'

Maitland Harbinson duly appeared on TV, accompanied by Colonel Theodore Marcel in full combat gear (and a chest of medal ribbons), to explain to the populace that they were being 'protected against certain revolutionary and violent elements by the speedy intervention of the UPP.'

The Army showed off, troop carriers and trucks rushing all over the island, headlights on, with whippy radio masts, giving them a sense of power and urgency. It was a kind of military event, though nobody actually felt that anything was really changed.

But Emilie Julien would. Late morning she'd gone for a swim, and stayed on the beach for a snack lunch. She was reading a good new novel. It was about three-thirty by the time she returned to the house. She hadn't watched television, nobody had even phoned to warn her about what was taking place.

The first thing that happened was that she found Louis Machin, the P.M.'s Secretary, outside the private suite. He asked her to prepare herself for bad news, then made her sit down while he told her of the unconfirmed reports that Sir Walter had been assassinated in London.

Emilie thought she would pass out, but she just sat there numbly, wishing that at least a couple of her older children were with her at that moment.

Machin comfortingly tried to convince her that nothing should be believed until he'd spoken with the Commonwealth Office, but so far he hadn't been able to contact them as the phone lines from Government House weren't working. They'd had trouble with the phones recently, but Machin didn't tell her that in fact phone lines and internet services had been cut and mobile phones rendered useless in the area by blocking the satellite signal.

When she was alone, Emilie broke down and cried. She also got to her knees and prayed that Walter hadn't in fact been murdered.

It was then that she heard the sound of the tanks. Drying her eyes, she went out onto the balcony and saw four tanks (the island's entire armoured strength) drive up and sit facing Government House. An hour passed, and still they squatted there. And then the phone rang.

But it was an internal call, and the caller was Maitland Harbinson. He was downstairs, he said, informing her that since her husband was believed dead, there had been a change of leadership, indeed of regime. Hence the tanks. He could have said 'on the lawn,' but realised it sounded too political.

He came to the private quarters shortly afterwards, accompanied by Van Molder, whom Emilie loathed. They had also brought several Army officers and a military detachment, who had searched the house and found a scared George Cotter, the double.

Cotter was arrested for impersonating the Prime Minister, though nobody knew if this was really a crime that you could pin on someone when they'd been hired by the man he was impersonating. Machin was charged with complicity. Sir Walter's two bodyguards, who'd lounged around playing cards, just being themselves, doing the job they were officially paid to do, were clapped straight into gaol, though it did cross Harbinson's mind that if they were any good, maybe he would hire them all over again to protect himself.

Emilie faced Harbinson and the detestable Van Molder, in the elegant Drawing Room.

'You treacherous, scheming bastards!' she said with earthy venom.

'Don't talk to us about scheming, lady,' said Harbinson.

Emilie spoke coldly: 'Lady Julien to you.'

'But no longer First Lady,' Harbinson countered. 'You thought you could fool the people, however you didn't fool our party.'

'You're not a party,' said Emilie contemptuously, 'You're a bunch of plotters. There is a difference.'

Van Molder spoke for the first time: 'Be careful with these insults, if you want to be allowed on a plane to London.'

In spite of herself, Emilie's voice faltered: 'Is it true about my husband? Is he really dead?'

'We believe so,' said Harbinson. 'But this sad event had nothing to do with us,' he insisted.

'Liars and murderers!' she shouted.

'As far as the UPP is concerned we have taken over government to ensure national stability,' said Harbinson.

Van Molder nodded agreement: 'Peace on the island will be maintained.'

'So long as we don't need to use force,' Harbinson added.

Sir Walter was still putting up a fight in intensive care when Harper left the hospital four hours later with Norris and Walmsley, whose mobile phone shrilled the Eton boating song in the lift. It was from the Commonwealth Office.

Walmsley's face was grim as he listened.

'Right, yes, I've got that. Update me when I'm back in the office,' he said, ringing off. He put the phone back into his pocket with a solemn gesture. 'Well, it's damn well happened. There's been a short, sharp coup. Virtually over.'

'That was all they needed to know – that the hit had been made,' said Harper.

Norris shook his head. 'My God, those coons must think British coppers are nig-nogs letting it happen!'

Harper's face remained impassive. 'That's a tautology, sir,' he said with heavy irony. 'Coons and nig-nogs...'

As the lift doors opened and they crossed the reception, Walmsley said: 'We're not yet sure of the make up of this takeover group. On the surface, it's the UPP and the Army, but it also has all the hallmarks of the crime syndicate behind it.'

'How about Sir Walter's wife?' asked Harper.

Walmsley said: 'Oh, they're allowing her to leave straight away for London. Apparently she thinks her husband's dead, as they are all presuming he is.'

At the exit, Walmsley suddenly stopped. 'You know, that might be an idea. I wonder what my Minister would think of it?'

'Think of what?' Norris asked.'

'If this coup by the UPP doesn't have the wholehearted approval of the people – and we don't think it does – Sir Walter could return to power.'

'If he survives,' Harper vouched.

'And if they find out he's still alive, mightn't they want to kill him for sure?' Walsmley pointed out.

Norris frowned: 'You mean to guard his life, we confirm he's dead?'

'No, in a coma, brain-dead, that sort of thing,' Walmsley shrugged.

Harper stared at them both: 'Hang on, what about his wife?'

'We'll make her part of the secret when she arrives. One way or another, the Prime Minister's definitely going to be safer out of it,' he said.

Walmsley's chauffeured Jaguar was waiting outside. As he got in, he seemed a lot happier. 'And if he does live, he turns up later and sweeps back into office, by popular support. Bye for now.'

They watched the sleek car drive off. 'He's devious enough to become Foreign Minister himself one day,' said Harper drily.

'How's your shoulder?'

'Bloody painful, but I'm okay. I want to help track down this gunman.'

'Sorry, Buchanan, but as of this moment, you're off the case. Suspended from duty,' said Norris.

Harper was shaken. 'Shit, that's not fair, Inspector. Surely I'm the officer most involved?'

'What do you expect? A medal for failing to protect your man?' Norris shook his head: 'You broke the rules. Your station's been informed. In due course there'll have to be an inquiry. Meantime, I repeat… you're on suspension. Is that clear?'

Twenty-one

About twenty-five miles East of Paris, with the early morning mist still rising from the fields, Inspector Blasson parked the car in a small wood near a village. Charlotte Plennard sat beside him, yawning.

She'd been to a dinner party that had dragged on into the small hours, then had to fend off the advances of an American painter, who gave her a lift home. His wife was in hospital having special prenatal care for a baby due any day. Bizarrely, he claimed, he was only being very French and wasn't it acceptable behaviour? He also said that for a cop she was unworldly. If only he could have guessed her own complicated world before she did this job, and some of her past was in New York, at that. No, come to think of it, that would simply have made him more of a nuisance.

She finally got rid of him around three a.m., reflecting once again on the difference she felt by hailing from Martinique. All that talk about being French didn't cut any ice. That was Parisian bullshit. Anyhow, she supposed that if you were from her part of the world you were, in France at any rate, a provincial.

She yawned again. Blasson produced a flask of of coffee and poured her a cup.

'Thanks. Just what I needed. It's way past my bedtime,' she joked, but it was true, she hadn't bothered to go to bed at all, because he'd arranged to pick her up at five-thirty.

They had driven out to Marne-la-Vallee, where the bookseller Joussier had his farm.

Just off the main motorway to Reims, the agricultural land on both banks of the River Marne had soil the consistency of brown putty. The terrain was devoid of much interest. Until of course they built EuroDisney in one of the most boring bits. In fact, on the horizon, through the mist, they could just see the tops of such wonders as The Sleeping Beauty's Castle, Thunder Mountain and a candy-floss pink hotel.

But Blasson's interest, as he adjusted his his binoculars, was Belvedere, the quite substantial, red-roofed farmhouse set in a slight dip half a mile away, with various barns and outbuildings surrounded by several hundred acres. In one field there was a herd of beef cattle; in another, two or three white Charollais bulls grazed. Around the farm were droves of chickens and geese.

Apart from the dull roar of the nearby motorway, it was a tranquil scene.

'Joussier has a farmer and his wife running the place, though they don't live here,' said Blasson. Outwardly he's a credible figure in the countryside.'

Charlotte took a look through the binoculars. Joussier's car, a Renault Espace, piled high in the back with books and prints, stood outside the front door. There was smoke coming from the kitchen chimney.

'If you think there's a big haul of coke in there, why don't we just go in and arrest him?,' asked Charlotte.

'Tomorrow.'

'Why wait till tomorrow?'

'You ever read your horoscope?'

'No, I don't believe in all that shit,' she said.

'Well, I do, and my stars said yesterday that Jupiter will be in conjunction with Venus, spelling complete success the day after tomorrow, and that I should be patient today. My wife read that out to me. She was very excited.'

Charlotte grinned crudely at him. 'Maybe she wasn't talking about your work?'

As Blasson was about to make some equally crude riposte, they both saw the car approaching the farm along a track.

It wasn't diffult to recognise the driver as the ponytailed Maurice Caubec. He hooted his horn as he got near, and as he drew up outside the house, Joussier emerged. They shook hands and went inside,

'Maybe your astrological advice was right,' said Charlotte. 'I wonder what Caubec's been up to?' Charlotte mused.

In the kitchen, as Joussier, despite the hour, poured them both a generous pastis, Caubec held out a copy of *Le Monde*, which carried a front-page story about the shooting of Sir Walter Julien and a report of the coup in the Caribbean.

'I bought this on the way. Thought you'd be interested.'

'Thanks.' Joussier handed him his glass, setting a jug of water and a saucer of ice cubes on the kitchen table. He took the newspaper to scan it. 'Everything went according to plan then?'

'More or less. He's in a coma and on a life support. He's not expected to recover.'

'What if he does?' asked Joussier.

'Look, my task was accomplished,' Caubec argued, pouring water into the pastis. 'Sante,' and he swallowed most of the contents of his glass as if it was the milk it resembled.

He splashed some more water over the ice. 'Suppose you tell me why I had drive out here for my money?'

Joussier looked up from the paper. 'My instructions from my principals' he said. 'You're to be paid the rest of your fee from an offshore account.'

'Offshore? What the hell are you talking about?' Caubec demanded suspiciously.

Joussier said: 'It's safer to pay you abroad. The money's in Credit Lyonnaise in Martinique. Your plane ticket will be waiting in your name at the Air France desk at the airport.'

Caubec got up from the table. Without asking, he went to a dresser where the drinks were and helped himself to another triple Ricard. 'Look, I had a deal that said the balance would be paid in Paris when I'd done the job.'

Joussier nodded. 'Things have changed, we've had an alert. A reliable source, warning us to watch our step. It seems there could be an informer in our organisation.'

'You mean your drug ring?' Caubec came back to the table holding up another glass of the milky fluid.

'This may be one of my vices,' he said, 'but drugs are not included. Count me out of your set-up. I'm not into that scene.'

Joussier leaned over and said ominously: 'No, but whether you like it or not, you are now involved in our business. We think it wiser for you to disappear from France for a while,' he said, helpfully spooning some ice into Caubec's drink.

Caubec stared into his glass, at the ice going a jaundiced yellow and thought about his debts, his recent slack period workwise, not to speak of the crummy apartment he'd been forced to rent.

'Don't you like the sun? The taste of rum …and pretty girls?' asked Joussier.

Twenty-two

Errol Duffy walked towards Shepherd's Bush Market, trying to stay calm. He'd been very restless, waking up several times during the night, wondering whether he should sneak out of the house and go and retrieve the rifle. But a black guy in the street in the small hours, even if he had a fucking crucifix around his neck, would end up at the nick, arguing his innocence. Moreover, his eyes would betray that he was still a little high on the crack he'd bought down the club the night before.

Now, around six a.m., when there were still only milkmen and dustcarts about, he carried a Puma sports bag in which to hide the rifle. Errol reckoned that he wouldn't be stopped by the cops then. This time in the morning he'd come over as a nice, law-abiding young man, on his way to make a healthy start to the day with a workout in the gym.

People used the market as a short cut from one main street to another, so he had no qualms in walking through, then detouring around the back of the lock-up stalls where he'd seen the guy hiding the rifle. He reached the stall, checking that the coast was clear, and searched in the folds of the tarpaulin. His hand felt the wooden butt of the rifle first, then cold steel. It was still there!

He hauled it out, instantly ramming it into his bag, relieved that it was short enough to fit in. He zipped up the bag quickly and strolled away.

But Errol wasn't the only early bird.

On the third floor of one of the offices that backed on to the market, a tired Security Man shuffled on his final round of punching time clocks on the landings, to prove he hadn't been fast asleep all night.

His feet were killing him. Even more, as he told his wife repeatedly, the bloody job was killing him. He was fifty-six-years old and had been made redundant by his pest control company a year ago, with only a few months' compensation. Now he had to wear this uncomfortable itchy uniform, work unsociable hours for low money, and had another nine years before he could draw his pension.

He stopped in the corridor and opened a window to breathe in one of the few pleasures of his all-night stint: the soft, sweet morning air that pervaded, however briefly, even an area like this. And so he saw, down below in the empty market, the young black man collect the rifle. Watched him stuff it in the bag.

Errol, who had been the only witness to the gunman getting rid of his weapon, had now himself been witnessed.

But not only that, the Security Man, who also shopped regularly in the market, believed he recognised Errol Duffy. Wasn't he the cheeky layabout who sometimes helped his mother on her lingerie stall? The reason he remembered was because once, when he was walking past the stall, Errol had lifted a pair of frilly silk knickers and teased him, in front of several customers, about whether he might like to wear women's underwear under his uniform? The joke didn't go down well at all. Yes, he was sure that's who it was, and the sight of the weapon alarmed him.

Moreover, the bloke who took over his job at the pest control firm when they made him redundant, was black. And he really resented that.

As soon as he was awake, Harper phoned a special number allotted to Sir Walter's private suite at the hospital to check on his condition. He was relieved to hear that he'd recovered consciousness and was stable, though still under intensive care.

Harper didn't bother to ask whether he could see him. He knew there was bound to be a 'strictly no visitors' instruction, and they were sure to have posted another plain-clothes man to guard him. He wondered if he'd be the same colour as himself.

Harper decided to drive over to St John's Wood. At the hospital reception desk he flourished his wallet with his I.D. at Elena

Saplimides. When she'd come on duty half an hour earlier, she'd been told that the patient called Ballantyne was under police protection following his emergency operation the day before.

No one had explained what had happened, but she remembered Mr Ballantyne leaving the hospital in the morning with the detective who was now talking to her, only she didn't realise then that he was a cop.

Harper smiled at her. 'Like a word with Mr Ballantyne, please,' he said. He'd pocketed his I.D. card before she'd actually been able to read it, and now he added: 'I'm Superintendent Norris, Special Branch.'

Elena rang and spoke first with the man on guard. 'It's one of your lot,' she said. 'From the Special Branch, Superintendent Norris. He wants to talk personally to Mr Ballantyne. Right.' She indicated a house phone across the foyer.

'Take it over there, sir.'

As Harper went to pick up the phone, Elena frowned and chewed her lip. She was thinking about the odd looking radio reporter who'd come in, trying to fix the interview with someone called 'Sir Walter Julien,' who wasn't registered. It had crossed her mind he could have been describing Ballantyne, but she'd followed the rules, refusing to give him any information.

Elena hadn't told anyone about the Frenchman. She'd acted properly and sent the man packing. Yet although, like the other receptionists, she was in the dark about it all, it worried her.

The council flat where Errol lived with his mother and five of her brood – the others were married, shacking up, or in prison – was on an upper floor of a high-rise block It was one of four tower blocks built alongside the Westway flyover in the sixties.

They stood like gaunt, ageing tombstones, marking a dead era of municipal architecture. Graffiti scarred almost every visible surface, the lifts seldom worked, and stank of urine like the staircases. The seedy shops at the base of each block had permanent metal grilles over the windows.

Surprisingly, Zienia Duffy and her children kept the local squalor at bay. Their cheap but comfortably furnished flat had three bedrooms and a boxroom, which Errol had commandeered for himself. It had no window, just an air vent that Errol had removed and replaced with the top of a plastic container, which he took out when his pals came round and the ganja fug got too much for even them to breathe.

By the time he got back from the market there was nobody at home except two of his sisters who were finishing their breakfast and were late for school. They were surprised to see Errol come in. Usually he'd still be fast asleep in the boxroom. They eyed his sports bag curiously.

'What you got there, Errol?' asked eight-year-old Samantha.

'I'm in training,' explained Errol. 'Working out.'

'When did you ever do anything that had 'work' in it?' said Vanessa, echoing her mother. She was fourteen, almost as tall as Errol, and had her hair cut, topiary-like, in what seemed to be the shape of a Greek patriarch's hat.

Errol grabbed a slice of their toast and went into his room, locking the door.

A few minutes later he heard the girls leave. By now he'd got the rifle in his hands, examining it with great excitement. But he became cautious when he discovered it was still loaded with four bullets.

Slipping them gingerly out of the magazine, he put them in an old tape cassettte box, removing a collection of Bob Marley numbers. He placed the box among his other tapes beside his ghetto blaster and, unlocking the door, wandered around the flat with the rifle, striking various firing poses and peering from the window through the telescopic sight at unsuspecting targets nine floors below.

He kept speculating how much it was worth, and decided he'd need to take advice. That meant he'd have to hide the rifle for a few days. Not in the flat, though. Far too risky. No, when he'd had a cup of tea, he'd take it round to the mews garage that his Mother used as a stockroom. He was sure he could find a safe place there, amid the clutter of crates and boxes that filled the loft above.

After having a word with Sir Walter on the phone, Harper went up in the lift to the penthouse. He had explained he was suspended, hence his deception. The Prime Minister was immediately indignant on Harper's behalf. He agreed to go along with the subterfuge, and the young DC on duty didn't even bother to ask for Harper's I.D., even if he thought it odd that Special Branch had such a senior black officer.

Sir Walter was wired up to a heart monitor, and was on a drip. He looked weak, but defiant. Harper closed the door of the bedroom, excluding the DC. A stout red-haired nurse, whose job was to check Sir Walter constantly, said she couldn't leave him even for a minute and whisperingly urged Harper not to talk too long. She sat down at a desk to make some notes.

Harper pulled a chair close to the bed. 'How are you feeling?'

'Not the best preparation for a heart operation,' said Sir Walter ruefully. 'What's the news from back home?'

Electing not to tell him about the coup, Harper ducked the question. He said: 'I gather your wife's on her way.'

Sir Walter's face lit up. 'Emilie!'

'Her flight was due in at Heathrow an hour ago,' said Harper.

Sir Walter frowned, shaking his head. 'Then it's all out in the open – on the island, I mean – they know that I'm here in London?'

'She'll fill you in on events. I'm sorry this happened. I should never have allowed you to put a foot out of here.'

Sir Walter attempted a shake of his head. 'Nonsense, I'll make it quite clear it was entirely my own fault.'

'It won't make any difference,' Harper shrugged. 'I disobeyed orders. If you hadn't been a Prime Minister, I probably wouldn't have been persuaded, but it's too late to speculate.'

'It seems damned unfair on you, Harper,' Sir Walter said. 'How the hell did they find out I was in London?'

Harper leaned closer. 'You know who they are?'

'I've a pretty good idea. Was the marksman …our colour?'

'No, he was white. The betting is he was a hired hitman.'

'You saw him, then?'

Harper nodded. 'Just a brief look at him, after he fired the first shot. His second bullet hit me in the shoulder, but it's only a graze.'

'So that's all the police have to go on?'

'Whether I'm part of the investigation or not, I intend to find the bastard,' said Harper determinedly.

Sir Walter looked at him worriedly: 'Promise me one thing, Harper. Don't do anything rash on my account.'

'It's as much for myself,' Harper replied. At that moment the phone on her desk rang and the nurse answered. She put down the receiver and walked over to the bed.

'Your wife is here to see you, sir.'

Harper left as quickly as he could. But as he stepped into the sitting room the DC was already opening the door to admit Emilie Julien, accompanied by Jonathan Walmsley and Norris, who reacted with total astonishment as he saw Harper.

Emilie looked at him curiously, and Harper half expected Norris to introduce him as 'This is the man who allowed your husband to get shot,' but before anything could be said, Walmsley deftly steered her towards the bedroom.

Norris waited for a second, then vented his fury in no uncertain manner. 'Just what the fuck do you think you're doing, Buchanan!' he hissed.

Harper said: 'I came to apologise. No law against that, is there?'

The young Constable by the door was looking confused and distinctly uneasy.

'How did this bastard get in?' Norris barked at him.

'I'm sorry, sir, but I understood he was from your---'

'Cool it, don't blame him,' Harper intervened. 'So I tricked my way past the desk. But since you're here maybe can I ask you to reconsider-'

'Sergeant, I'm warning you,' said Norris, the boiled blue eyes blazing with almost laser-like malignancy. 'You'd better leave smartish. Fucking well get this clear: you're out of it! Take a holiday!'

As Harper stepped out of the lift the reception area was filling up with patients and he found himself face to face with Hardwicke's secretary, Sally Ivenhaugh.

'How's the patient?' she asked, carefully choosing her words in case she was overheard.

'I'd say your surgeon has done a pretty good job,' Harper told her.

'Let's hope 'Mr Ballantyne' pulls through.'

He assumed Hardwicke would have told her the reason for Sir Walter's emergency surgery, though she wouldn't necessarily know about Harper's suspension.

Harper was about to move away to let her enter the lift, when Sally gave him a confidential look, beckoning him to one side and dropping her voice: 'Sergeant, I was going to tell my boss later, but since you're here, there's somebody I think you'd better talk to.'

Harper was surprised, intrigued. 'What about?'

Sally turned, pointed out the Cypriot receptionist at the desk. 'Elena, just told me. Apparently there was someone here enquiring about Sir Walter, by name. Trying to find out if he was booked in.'

Harper took Elena for a coffee in the hospital cafeteria, where she explained that she hadn't really connected the two things together until this morning: the emergency operation on 'Mr Ballantyne,' and the Frenchman who came asking questions.

'A Frenchman?'

'Yes, he said he was from a Caribbean radio station.'

Harper stared at her, scarcely concealing his immediate reaction. 'Was he thin faced, blond hair in a ponytail, long coat, in his thirties?'

'That's him!' said Elena. 'Funny sort of bloke.'

'He give his name?'

She shook her head. 'No, just said that he wanted to interview Sir Walter something-or-other, a West Indian VIP. Only we had nobody like that listed. Our only patient from that part of the world was a Mr Ballantyne.'

'How about the name of his radio station?'

'I saw a sticker on the tape machine he was carrying,' said Elena. 'It was RCF, Radio Carib or something..you know, in French. Oh, and there was an airline tag on the strap, and I definitely remember it was Air France.'

Twenty-three

The overnight Security Man at Shepherd's Bush didn't go straight to the police. It was his habit every other morning, on being relieved by the day-shift, to have an 'early risers' swim and sauna at his local municipal leisure centre. The ticket was at a reduced price until nine-thirty, and it enabled him to keep going till lunchtime, and thus maintain a sort of social life with his wife before he went to sleep in the afternoon.

He turned up at the desk in Uxbridge Road police station, pink and a little dizzy.

Possession of firearms is always guaranteed to set alarm bells ringing in any police station. But the reaction to the security man's statement about what he'd seen, was faster than normal in view of the shooting.

While a team of marksmen from the Specialised Firearms Unit, CO19, was being summoned, the CID detectives on the case were round the market like a shot, confronting Zienia Duffy as she opened up her lingerie stall.

She knew all about the incident the previous day, but she was stunned when they questioned her about her son Errol, and told her about the hidden rifle. She was fairly certain that Errol would still be at home. He usually stayed in bed until around mid-day when he got hungry.

As she closed up her stall and got into a police car, armed response officers in navy blue jumpers and bullet-proof jackets arrived in a Range Rover. They were instructed to follow the car.

Ziena felt a mounting panic, especially when she saw their Heckler and Koch MP5 automatic rifles.

With the rifle back in the sports bag, Errol left the flat and headed along the street towards the mews less than a few hundred yards away. He was in a state of rising exultation, having had the last of his supply of crack, boasting to a friend on the phone about the surprise acquisition he would show him later in the day.

He'd been walking for a couple of minutes when he heard the police siren, and because of what he had in the bag, he stopped, instantly tense, and turned his back to peer in the window of a video shop.

In the reflection he saw the police car, followed by the Range Rover with armoured shield, travelling along the other side of the street, blue lights flashing. They passed by, and he resumed his walk. Suddenly there was a squealing of tyres and looking back, he saw both vehicles turning. Errol, knowing instinctively that they were coming for him, started to run.

Ironically, it was his Mother who pointed him out in the street, and just as quickly wished she'd kept her mouth shut.

Errol's long legs got him to the mews fast. He thought he might have made the turning without them seeing him and dashed for the garage, fishing the keys out of his pocket. Hastily unlocking the padlock on the door, he dragged it out of the hasp. He still had the Yale lock to deal with, but even as he inserted the key, he saw the leading cop car tearing into the cobbled mews.

Pushing the the door open, he went in and slammed it shut, working the snib so that it couldn't be opened. He stumbled through the gloom of the downstairs stockroom, climbing the stairs to the loft, which had a window overlooking the mews.

Peering out, he saw the car pulling up cautiously about fifty feet away, and the Range Rover parking just behind it. Police officers were jumping out of the car and he stared with consternation as the doors of the Range Rover flew open and the armed marksmen came out with their rifles.

But the real shock was seeing his mother get out of the car. A moment later another police car arrived and he saw two more plain-clothes fuzz emerge. One of them, a burly figure with short grey hair, was obviously senior and immediately started taking charge. Errol could see him talking urgently to his mother.

He knew he was in for it. They'd never believe he'd simply found the rifle.

Maybe he could pull that stunt he'd seen recently on TV, where the fugitive put the gun to his head, threatening to blow his brains out unless they let him walk away free? He couldn't remember what actually happened in the film after that, but it might be worth trying. He unzipped the bag and hauled out the rifle.

Twenty-four

Harper was returning his revolver to his station arms officer when he encountered his boss. The way things were, he was hoping to avoid colleagues, at least for the time being. But just as he was leaving, DCI Carol Smart arrived in a squad car, a young DC with her.

'Harper! I wondered when you'd put in an appearance. Come and put me in the picture,' she said. 'How are you?'

'I'm okay,' said Harper. He noticed the DC at her side didn't say a word, and Harper thought: I bet the bastard is enjoying the shit I'm wading in.

'By the way,' said DCI Smart, as Harper followed her back into the station, 'we just heard on the radio that there's a siege going on over near Shepherd's Bush. Young bloke with a rifle. Could that be connected with your shooting match?'

For half an hour, some distance from the garage, Norris and Zienia Duffy had pleaded with Errol through a loud hailer to throw the gun down onto the cobbles and come out. He was promised he wouldn't be harmed. Errol had opened the window of the loft and occasionally they could see the rifle in his hands.

The marksmen were crouched behind the Range Rover and police cars in the mews, and two of them lay on the back-slope of a roof opposite.

To begin with, Errol had tried to do a deal. He shouted to them that he'd pull the trigger on himself if they didn't let him go. But

Norris refused, pointing out that if he was innocent of gunning down the man in the market, he had nothing to worry about.

Zienia was appealing to her son yet again: 'Errol, you listen to me! Don't be a fool, throw the gun away. Where did you get it from anyhow?'

'Do as your Mum says, for your own good!' Norris shouted in support.

But Errol was too scared now to answer.

Harper got there as quickly as he could. The mews had been closed off to the public, but he showed his I.D. and they let him past the tapes. As soon as Norris saw him he was livid.

'What do you bloody well mean by showing up here, Sergeant?'

'I thought I might be able to help' said Harper.

'Look, the only way for you to help is to obey orders and keep away,' Norris snarled.

'It's my son, Errol,' Zienia said to Harper, drawing comfort from the fact that he was black.

'My Errol's no killer,' she wept.

'What age is he?' asked Harper gently.

'Only eighteen,' Zienia told him. 'It's them drugs. I think he's had some stuff already today. Mister, he don't know what he's doing.'

Harper turned to Norris, imploring: 'Let me try and talk to him,' he said. 'What's there to lose?'

Just at that moment, Harper caught sight of Errol looking out of the open window and reacted.

'I recognise him!' Harper exclaimed. 'He was sitting on a wall yesterday in the market, when I gave chase after the shooting. He told me which way the gunman ran.'

'Maybe he pointed you in the wrong direction?' said Norris cynically. 'How do you know he wasn't in on it – an accomplice?'

Before there could be any further argument, Harper walked along the mews, straight up to the garage and stood under the window, calling up.

'Errol! I'm Sergeant Buchanan. You saw me yesterday, running after the man who fired the rifle. Can you hear me?'

Harper glimpsed Errol's profile, just visible by the window-reveal to one side. He was listening.

'You were seen collecting the gun in the market. It isn't yours, is it?'

'No.'

'Then don't take responsibility for it, and the shots that were fired. If you know whose it is, tell us.'

'I just saw this bloke hide it, then he ran,' said Errol. 'Then I went back to pick it up.'

Harper sensed he was on the verge of getting a surrender.

'Alright, Errol, let's bring this to an end. Chuck the rifle out of the window and come out and talk to me some more.'

'How do I know you won't shoot?' Errol asked.

Harper insisted: 'I'm unarmed, and no one's going to shoot if you do as I say.'

There was a pause, then Errol moved into view at the window to get a better look at Harper, almost as if he was seeking confirmation for a stand-off from the cop's face.

But he didn't release his grip on the gun, indeed the barrel of it it seemed to swing ominously in Harper's direction as he leaned out. Harper fluttered a hand behind him to warn the others to do nothing. But as Errol came into full view, with the rifle apparently raised, there was a staccato of shots from the marksmen, who thought they were saving a fellow police officer.

Errol, who took at least three bullets, fell right out of the window, dead before he hit the cobbles.

Zienia was screaming her head off.

Harper felt sick.

It was two weeks later that one of Errol's sisters found the four bullets in the Bob Marley cassette box.

Twenty-five

The apartment Charlotte Plennard was temporarily renting in Paris was on the fourth floor of a tall, narrow building in the Mouffetard, the crowded, originally Arab market area beside the Pantheon, above St. Germain.

As she went up in the lift from the gloomy entrance hallway, she was thinking that she wouldn't be here much longer. Operation Hurricane was likely to be concluded soon, then she'd be on her way back to the Caribbean.

She'd collected just one letter from her mailbox downstairs, addressed in a neat, but childish hand – her daughter Angeline's. That was one bit of her background she had avoided telling Inspector Blasson about – that she was an unmarried mother.

The father of Angeline, born ten years ago, was a New York photographer, Paul, whom Charlotte had met in Martinique. She was still a convent schoolgirl, just turned sixteen. When the Mother Superior found out about her liaison with Paul, who was a Puerto Rican aged twenty-three, she was expelled.

As far as Charlotte was concerned, it was the second time she'd been expelled. The first was from home, when her mother died.

She was only eight years old. Despite the fact that her father, Jean-Pierre Plennard, was rich and had servants, he felt unable to cope with looking after a small daughter, and put her in the convent. Her brother, Leon, fourteen years older, stayed at home.

Charlotte had never forgiven her father, and after her expulsion, she rebelliously went to live with Paul in Manhattan, where he had a studio loft on the East Side.

For a time she was happy, eventually becoming pregnant when she had just turned eighteen. But then the blow fell. Paul was arrested on a drugs charge, and she discovered that he'd become a heroin addict and worse, a dealer.

As he was being transferred from gaol to a court hearing, he managed to escape. He phoned her once or twice and told her he was hiding out in New Jersey with some friends, fellow junkies, she guessed. Charlotte had pleaded with him to turn himself in for his own good, but he wouldn't. In a few weeks he was found dead from an overdose, and there was a police suspicion that it hadn't been self-inflicted.

Two months later, Angeline was born and Charlotte was deported back to the Caribbean. She lived in a hostel, under the supervision of social workers, where they let her keep the baby. Jean-Pierre Plennard visited the hostel several times, but she refused to see him.

She learned shorthand and typing and began working as a temp, and eventually got onto a panel for police secretarial replacements. It was one of her social workers who first suggested the police as a career, pointing out that they might be interested someone with her sort of experience. After all, she hadn't committed any crime herself.

Rather to her surprise, she was accepted for training at the Police College in Guadeloupe. It was a shock for her father with all his old French aristo hang-ups. He died without seeing her again, a week before she graduated.

Charlotte lit one of her cheroots, poured herself a glass of wine, and sat down by the big windows overlooking the street, to read Angeline's letter. Immediately she became quite homesick. She was longing to see her daughter again.

Ironically, Angeline was in the very same convent, St Claire la Bienfaitrice, that Charlotte had left so ignominiously. Nuns never held grudges.

She knew she couldn't phone and speak to her daughter direct, so she did the next best thing and rang her brother Leon, who had loyally offered to make regular visits to the convent.

Leon, who looked like Louis Jourdan in his prime, ran the estate, with its old-established banana plantation, mahogany forest and timbermill. He had always been on her side. Even closer in recent years since he and his wife, Nadine, had divorced after endless bickering and flying objects.

'Lottie!' How are you, little sister?'

'I'm fine, Leon. Maybe I'll be heading home very soon. And you?'

'Terrific, but we've had too much damn rain for this year's banana crop,' he complained, and Charlotte thought: he sounds just like our father, who always said the same thing every year.

'Is Angeline okay? Have you've seen her this week?'

'Only yesterday. Listen, she's missing you, but she's very perky. Mother Superior obviously adores her.'

Charlotte smiled. The same lady who kicked her out. And yet she still loved Mother Superior. 'Leon, what's going on in the other island?' she asked, having read in the French press the latest stories about the shooting of Sir Walter Julien in London, and the subsequent political coup.

'Heaven knows,' said Leon. 'We're all sitting here looking across there, wondering how it is at the moment.'

His housekeeper, Claudine, a faded blonde in her mid forties, whom he fucked every other night, in a clinical way, rather like having a shower, brought him his regular sundowner, a large tequila chilled near to near freezing with salt around the rim of the glass.

'And you? What's going on in Paris?' Leon asked.

'Maybe I'll tell you one day,' she replied. Charlotte had a strict rule: she never disclosed the nature of her police work to outsiders, even her brother.

She was sure he'd be astonished if he learned that one of their targets was now Raphael Tabard.

The report on Tabard, sent by Eddie Carmona from JIBOC, said he ran a successful company from a laboratory in Fort-de-France, on Martinique, had no criminal record, belonged to the best clubs, gave generously of his time and money to charity, and was rumoured to be in line for decoration from the Elysee Palace in recognition of his contribution to the French island's economy. In other words, an esteemed *Beke*, a pillar of society.

But Charlotte Plennard now knew otherwise.

On the neighbouring island, Government House and Yellow Ribbon Beach looked towards Martinique. Maitland Harbinson, who never drank anything but undiluted fresh lime juice, stood on the balcony, sipping at his glass, satisfied with the way things had gone in the last forty-eight hours. He was about to have a celebration dinner with a small group of people who had supported the UPP power grab.

There were hundreds of bright stars scattered right across the sky, dominated by a full moon reflected in the bay. He could hear the thin rustle of waves on the beach.

Harbinson, whose father was a fisherman, remembered his Christmas present when he was about ten years old. It was was a small telescope, and he used to sit out on the verandah in the small hours, with the telescope set up on a wall, a pillow behind his back, staring at the awsome infinity of space.

Even then his ambitions were aimed a lot higher than any of his friends. But what he recalled now, quite calmly, was an incident on one of those star-gazing, moonlit nights. He had been sitting out on the verandah for nearly four hours when his older brother, Gladstone, drove up on his motorbike with his girlfriend.

He didn't come near the house, but leaned the bike against a palm tree, and took his girl down onto the beach where he screwed her. Maitland delicately kept his telescope skywards, but when an hour later, Gladstone came home and saw the telescope on the verandah, he was convinced that his young brother had been spying on him. He smashed the instrument to pieces.

To a ten-year-old it was vandalism of an extreme sort. And Maitland Harbinson plotted revenge. It came about a month later when Gladstone bought his own fishing boat which had an old flywheel engine. Young as he was, Maitland had a technical mind and he fixed the driveshaft bearings so that when the engine was fully heated the shaft would shear off.

Gladstone was about half a mile out to sea when his engine blew up, the snapped-off shaft creating sparks and igniting petrol that poured from a severed fuel pipe. Poor Gladstone, unable to quench the flames, had to jump for his life, and only just made it to the shore.

Because his brother didn't drown, Maitland soon got over his guilt.

'Your dinner guests have arrived.'

Harbinson turned to see Simeon, whom he had just installed as his personal manservant. One of the perks of being acting Prime Minister. Simeon was wearing white ducks and a maroon monkey-jacket, white shirt and bow tie. Maitland thought he looked quite fetching in his outfit.

Simeon was his boyfriend, and it was a usefully discreet appointment to the household.

Twenty-six

By now, following reports of the Caribbean coup, Sir Walter Julien's shooting in London and his comatose condition was front-page and television news. Harper sat watching ITV News, with a stiff scotch in his hand.

There were pictures of Maitland Harbinson taking over as acting Prime Minister at Government House, the scurrying troops and token tanks under Colonel Marcel, and the usual interviews with pundits on the general effect of the attempted assassination of Sir Walter on the West Indies political scene. Even the Hon. Jonathan Walmsley made a contribution of behalf of the Commonwealth Offfice.

Harper considered the lie about Sir Walter's real state was a pretty heavy piece of baggage for a few people, including himself, to have to carry around.

Then came the story about Errol being shot down by the police marksmen. The circumstances of his death were given no special emphasis by a black newscaster, as if bending over backwards not to show any colour prejudice. But Harper could detect in the newscaster's dry delivery, unspoken question marks about the manner in which the youth had been arbitrarily, ruthlessly, and possibly needlessly, killed. At one point, he used the old standby phrase, 'reliable sources say,' to suggest that no bullets had been found in the rifle.

Officially there was no tie-up between the Shepherd's Bush shooting and this one, though the point was made that it was the second gunshot incident in the area in two days. Unfortunately the story was backed by video footage taken by a passer-by with a mobile, and Harper sat upright as he saw himself standing with the others in the mews, shortly after Errol died.

Within what seemed like ten seconds the phone shrilled and it was his Mother demanding to know all the details. Harper turned the TV sound down and told her it was sub judice, and he couldn't discuss it, even with family. It was just something that had happened in the line of duty, he said, and everyone was sad about Errol and very sorry for his distraught mother and family.

'Oh, sure, I bet they were,' said Lucy Buchanan, sardonic and unconvinced.

Supportive though she had been over Harper's career, she'd never really come to terms with it. She found it hard to distrust her own son, but she'd never liked policemen, and she certainly hated the dangers he regularly faced.

Harper's second call was from brother Lennie. As a star footballer, Lennie was also recognised as a good ambassador for black players in the sport. He sometimes had to take plenty of stick from racist yobbos at certain grounds, yet he always showed dignified patience. But a black youth being slain like this wouldn't help community relations much – or Lennie for that matter.

Sympathising with Lennie, Harper nevertheless kept up the lie about Sir Walter being in a coma, explaining about his role as a bodyguard and his current suspension. He also added that Norris and Special Branch were determined to believe that Errol may have been part of the gunman's getaway strategy, collecting the weapon in order to dispose of it as evidence.

As he rang off, arranging to meet his brother in a few days, Harper didn't dare tell Lennie that he had decided to make further investigations on his own, strictly against the rules.

His decision was made when – faced with Norris's needling behaviour – he instinctively and deliberately withheld the information from the hospital receptionist about the Frenchman who'd posed as a Caribbean radio reporter.

Taking a chance, a few hours earlier, he had sought the help of an artist whom the police regularly hired to draw suspects. He didn't reveal that he was acting unofficially when he took Elena Saplimides round to the artist's studio, and she gave a detailed description of Caubec.

The problem would arise later when the man put in his bill for the drawing. By then, Harper hoped he might have found some positive lead.

He had scanned and e-mailed the portrait of the wanted hitman to Gerard Dercourt, a personal friend in the Paris police, whom he could trust. Asking Gerard, a detective sergeant like himself, to check it out, Harper hoped to get lucky and uncover someone in French criminal records – which might include a Caribbean dependency – who looked like this and had form.

After he switched off the television, Harper, in a sombre mood, selected a CD of one of his classical pieces, Mendelsson's Concerto in 'E' for Cello, the solo played by his ex-wife, Tessa, and conducted by Zubin Mehta.

He poured himself a second large Glenmorange and settled back in the Swedish posture chair he'd bought last year for Tessa, listening to the music, almost feeling her vibrations as she sweetly coaxed the notes from her hundred-year-old Vuillaume. It was the highly expensive instrument that he gave her as a present for her twenty-fifth birthday four years ago, but it seemed to him like only yesterday.

He fell asleep, tired, listening to the normally therapeutic music, but his dreams weren't relaxing ones, and just as he was about to be cut up by a chainsaw, the phone rang as if with a screech like the saw. Sweating, he reached out and lifted the receiver.

'Harper, you old chocolate drop! How are you?' It was Gerard, full of good cheer, despite the fact that he'd phoned his wife and said he'd be spending the evening in records, on the hunt of a murderer, and he might not get home in time for the late night sex film on Canal Plus.

'Any luck?'

'Yes, the portrait you sent me was almost a perfect likeness.'

'So you found him! He has a record?'

'He certainly has. His name is Maurice Caubec, and he doesn't originate in the Caribbean. Don't know what that connection is. He flew back to Paris the day before yesterday, under his own name,' said Gerard, taking a puff of the huge, curved briar pipe clenched in his mouth under the heavy black Gallic moustache.

'Gerard, you're a genius!'

'Not quite, Harper,' said Gerard. 'I had to bribe a colleague to give me the computer password to access the files. Imagine me, having to do that! This info I'm giving you is strictly off the record.'

'What do you mean? What's happened?' Harper asked.

'A little heart murmur six months ago, that's what happened. They moved me to an exciting new job in Premises Maintenance,' said Gerard with a sad sigh.

'Yet you're still smoking that foul chimney you call a pipe?'

Gerard chuckled. 'You're one hell of a detective, Harper. But perhaps you can explain something. Why did you ask this as a personal favour when it's routine police work?'

Harper told him about the shooting and his own predicament, and then announced that he'd be coming over to Paris. He wanted Caubec – badly. Gerard argued that one cop, even a suspended one, shouldn't try to deal single-handed with a ruthless killer, like this man's record said he was.

'Can you come up with an address for him?' Harper queried.

As soon as Sir Walter had agreed to be reported as virtually dead, an ambulance transferred him to an exclusive health clinic outside London that had a medical wing. Carl Hardwicke, who wouldn't be able perform the heart operation for some time, offered to pay regular visits to his patient.

Before she left, Emilie had arranged for their younger children to stay with a sister in Barbados, and asked her to explain secretly to all the family that the report was an expedient lie. Their father was conscious – alive, if not exactly kicking. But they must not reveal what they knew. She was about to add 'on pain of death,' but decided it would be dreadfully inappropriate.

Briddstock Grange was a sprawling, late Victorian mansion near Alfriston, on the edge of the Sussex Downs. Since many of its clients were figures in public life, especially celebrities suffering any number of addictions, they tended to keep to themselves as much as possible. Thus the privacy of such a place was ideal. Just the same, the guest list was thoroughly checked by Special Branch.

Jonathan Walmsley arrived at breakfast-time to make sure the Prime Minister and his wife were comfortable in their suite. It had been decided that a bodyguard would only attract attention in a place like this, and in any case there was no reason to protect a man considered to be almost dead anyway.

There was a bundle of morning newspapers on the bed, beside Sir Walter's breakfast tray. He rifled the papers, observing wryly: 'I'm having a hell of a struggle getting used to these stories about me. Next step's my obituary!'

'Makes me quite queasy, Walter,' said Emilie with a shudder.

'Perhaps it won't be too long before the regime of those gangsters in Government House collapses, Prime Minister,' said Walmsley.

'I'm teetering on being an ex-Prime Minister,' joked Sir Walter.

'Oh, I'm sure you'll make a come-back from the edge of the grave,' Walmsley assured him, then wondered, as he so often did, if such a remark was in bad taste. 'If you know what I mean,' he added hastily.

'What about this youth with the rifle, who was shot by the police?' asked Sir Walter. 'Was he part of it?'

Walmsley shrugged. 'Seems he might have been. One thing's certain, though, it was the rifle that fired the bullet into you.' And again Walmsley instantly regretted phrasing it like that. 'Sorry, but it's a forensic fact,' he said apologetically.

'My husband is very concerned over Sergeant Buchanan's suspension,' said Emilie.

'Can't you do something?' asked Sir Walter.

'I'm afraid it's a disciplinary matter, entirely for the police. We can't intervene,' said Walmsley.

'It's wrong, though, that he should take the rap for me,' said Sir Walter. 'If I hadn't been so pig-headed about seeing my sister, it wouldn't have happened.'

Walmsley said: 'I can understand how you feel. But I shouldn't worry about Buchanan. He'll get a reprimand. Meanwhile, I believe he's on a spot of enforced home leave.'

Twenty-eight

Stepping off the plane at Charles de Gaulle Airport, Harper felt vaguely like a criminal with a fake passport. It was a curious sensation for a cop, to be arriving in another country, conducting an investigation when he was strictly unofficial, and even paying his own fare.

And he was black into the bargain.

France had a strange, almost disingenuous approach to the racial question. Immigrants from former French-administered territories like Senegal, were tolerated, but there was no great influx. Some, from other West African countries that used to salute the Tricolor, had become part of French society by way of the military forces or the police, but mainly *les negres* sold leatherware, beads and carpets on the boulevards.

Just the same, liberal Frenchmen, particularly in Paris, told themselves that there was decent integration, even a multicultural model for the rest of the world. The trick, of course, was to keep the numbers down, apart from EU rules about Eastern Europe. They had a different view, of course, about those from Algeria and Morocco living in their ghettos just outside Paris and other main cities. The Islamists, as they were elsewhere in the world, were breathing down France's neck.

Travelling along the conveyor from the arrival gate, Harper couldn't help remembering that the last time he'd made the trip to Paris it was with Tessa, when the orchestra played at an outdoor concert at the Palace of Versailles three Summers ago.

Their marriage was still okay then, and the city cast its usual romantic spell as they stayed on for a few days after the concert, living in an attic room in a small hotel in the Rue Maitre Albert, just across from the Notre Dame.

The thunderous bells, forever associated with the Hunchback, were only allowed to ring up till midnight and after six a.m, but so far as Harper was concerned, he wouldn't have minded hearing them at intervals all night long. That was in the days when they enjoyed the sleep of the contented.

After passing through a long tunnel from the satellite, the conveyor now descended through one of the perspex tubes that feed passengers up and down to the main airport concourse. Harper had only an overnight bag, so he would shortly be in a taxi headed for the centre of Paris.

As the conveyor neared ground level, and he was still thinking about that last visit, Harper failed to notice an eccentrically dressed passenger being borne upwards in a neighbouring conveyor tube. A man in an ankle-length coat with his blond hair in a fluffed-up ponytail.

Maurice Caubec was on his way to join an Air France flight to Martinique, where he'd been told he would collect the rest of his contract killer's fee.

Also in Paris, meanwhile, the final stage of Operation Hurricane was about to take place.

In the Briefing Room, Inspector Blasson addressed his team – all of them, including Charlotte Plennard, dressed in combat gear.

'We're now ninety-nine per cent certain the latest delivery of cocaine is present in Joussier's farmhouse,' he said, indicating Belvedere Farm on a blown-up section of an Ordnance map that had strategic markings on it, detailing how various units would surround the place.

'Are we sure we'll catch Raphael Tabard in the net?' asked Charlotte.

'Why? You want them to pin a medal on you back home in Martinique?' Blasson joked. Everyone was very tense and he felt it best to lighten the atmosphere.

'I won't win any friends for helping to arrest a man like Tabard,' said Charlotte. 'He belongs to a favoured clique, to which I and my family used to belong.'

'We all know where drug barons like him belong, Sergeant. Behind bars, cleaning out their own shit!'

He pressed the play button on a tape machine. 'This was recorded late last night.'

The team heard a phone tap of a conversation between Joussier and Tabard, in which the latter said he would come to lunch the following day, bringing with him two of their most important clients.

'One way or another, we might have an interesting haul at the farm,' said Blasson.

As he spoke, he glanced out of the window into the courtyard, where jeeps and a couple of police buses were parked, filled with extra cops drafted in for the operation.

When the drug officers had been fully briefed and, being French, everyone had partaken of an early lunch and a glass or two of wine, the convoy would head for Marne-la-Vallee to be in position just after noon.

A taxi ride on the Paris Peripherique was guaranteed to wake anyone up if they arrived on an early flight and had to be in the city centre quickly. Shake them up, more like.

Harper was reminded that Parisian drivers don't believe anyone should come between them and their personal grand prix on the ring road, indulging in duels which have won them the biggest road accident rate in Europe, presumably a matter of pride. If, of course, they lived to enjoy such a reputation.

Relieved at last to arrive at the headquarters where his demoted friend, Gerard Dercourt, worked, Harper paid off the taxi and showed his I.D. to one of the two Gendarmes on duty at the barrier. His name checked out with their visitors' list and he walked across the courtyard to the entrance, contrasting the period splendour of the building with his mundane copshop in South London.

He also found the paramilitary display of vehicles and men in combat gear intriguing. They weren't riot squad, no visors or shields. Was it a training exercise? Or were they off on some big crackdown?

He had to show his I.D. once more to the female officer on the reception desk, who told him he'd find Gerard on the fourth floor and indicated the lift.

As he got in, he shared the lift with a stout high-ranking officer in a gold-braided uniform, and a rather striking girl in a flak jacket, smoking a small cigar. She had her dark hair piled up, held by a black velvet bow, the only real concession to her femininity, except for a worn pair of shapely tan leather boots. Slung over her shoulder was a satchel. With all due deference to his female cop colleagues in the Met, there weren't any who were quite as attractive as this, Harper thought to himself.

Charlotte was nearest the lift buttons. She looked questioningly at the portly senior officer and at the tall, handsome ethnic guy, who was presumably a cop, but somehow had an un-French appearance. Then, in the same moment, she noted his overnight bag bore a British Airways tag.

'Which floor?'

'Third,' said the officer brusquely.

'Fourth for me, please,' said Harper in surprisingly perfect French, and Charlotte wondered if he was actually a countryman, and she'd been wrong about his nationality.

As the lift ascended, she brought a revolver from under her flak jacket to check it, and Harper was impressed. But the officer was more concerned with her cigar, pointing to a vivid *No Smoking* sign stuck to a mirror.

'That's the new rule in public buildings, officer,' said the braided uniform man sternly.

'Yes, Chief,' she replied, making a contrite gesture that she'd get rid of it. But as soon as he'd stepped out and they continued to the fourth floor, Charlotte's eyes flashed defiance and she puffed at the cigar even more luxuriously.

'What's the world coming to?' she said. 'Can't even fucking kill yourself, can you?'

Harper reached out a hand towards her, gently putting the safety catch on her revolver to the *On* position. 'Better not to kill yourself by accident, though,' he cautioned her.

'You never answered my question. Oh, you don't need to. You're a non-smoker, correct?'

Harper smiled and gave a shrug. 'It's a free world,' he said. 'You mind telling me which direction I take for the Administration section?'

Charlotte pointed along the corridor. As he thanked her, she went the other way and he looked back and saw her stick her cigar firmly between the cold marble lips of a Tallyrand bust.

If there was a non-smoking rule in the headquarters, it was certainly not observed by Gerard Dercourt in his small office, which neverthe-less did have a view of the Eiffel Tower. Gerard, puffing enough smoke for a Pope's election, warmly greeted his old friend.

'Harper, it's wonderful to see you again. How many years is it?'

'Too many.' Harper looked around. 'So this is Premises Maintenance?'

Gerard shook his head in mock sorrow. 'I think we are both finished, you and me.'

'Balls,' said Harper. 'Listen, I'll have a word on your behalf with your President Sarkozy if you promise to speak to the new guy in Downing Street about me,' he joked.

'It's a deal,' Gerard said, but then he became serious: 'Harper, I'm not sure I should give you this bastard Caubec's address... for your own damn good, you know?'

'Yeah, I know. But who made you into the top English student at Lille?'

'Who coached you in postgraduate French?' Gerard countered. 'Okay, I'll give you the address. Tell me, how is Tessa?'

'She married another guy in the orchestra.'

'Oh? Too bad,' said Gerard.

He chuckled. 'I hope he was piccolo, not trombone!' Then belatedly slammed a fist into a palm. 'That's not funny, is it, my old friend?'

'Caubec?'

'That nasty piece of work lives above a cafe in Billancourt. Sleazy area.'

'I just want to sniff around at first.'

Gerard shook his head and looked at him anxiously. 'Then you'll behave sensibly and promise to turn it over to the regular section?'

'Why not live a little dangerously and come over there with me?' Harper suggested.

'I only wish I could. Alas, my shift doesn't end till five-thirty,' said Gerard. 'But Yvette and I will expect you for dinner tonight. Is that a date?'

'Of course. I know how much she yearns for me.'

'You just keep your hands above the table tonight, Sergeant,' said Gerard grinning and puffing up like a steam train.

Twenty-nine

The Cafe Bonaparte was a run down establishment on a dreary boulevard. It was sandwiched between a tyre changing bay and a builders' merchant's. Harper sat at one of the badly-wiped, dimpled-zinc tables outside, waiting for a coffee, deciding that the ambience was just about as non Parisian as you could get. Even the people who walked by on the littered, chewing-gum-studded pavements looked as if they were from another planet.

The Patron, an unshaven Corsican in a singlet, his chest and arms covered with tattoos, came out with a café crème which Harper had ordered. Almost inevitably, the cup was cracked and the spoon dull and twisted. In an unsubtle gesture he rattled down the bakelite saucer with the bill, as if Harper might abscond. Harper put a fifty euro note on the saucer.

The man scowled. 'Haven't you got any change?' he grumbled.

'Maybe I'm not looking for any,' Harper replied.

His brow instantly creased in a wary frown, almost as if Harper was presenting him with a forged banknote.

'How come?'

'You rent a room upstairs to a man called Maurice Caubec?'

Now the Patron was openly suspicious. 'What of it?'

Wordlessly, Harper put down another fifty euro bill, and the Patron's co-operation was sealed.

Upstairs, Harper looked over Caubec's accommodation, which the Patron had rather grandly described as a 'studio apartment.' Admittedly, as well as the main room, it boasted a small adjoining kitchen and bathroom, but it was strictly basic comfort, threadbare and as cheerless and maybe worse than any seedy motel.

Harper quickly realised that there were, in fact, no traces of Maurice Caubec. All the cupboards were empty, there was nothing personal save for some TV magazines and a half bottle of Pernod. In the bathroom there was a worn toothbrush, an exhausted tube of toothpaste, some disposable razors, and an unused condom.

He turned angrily to the recipient of 100 euros: 'So Caubec lives without food or clothes? He isn't here any more, is he?'

The Corsican shrugged his psychedelic shoulders. 'The guy paid the rest of his month's rent and quit this morning.'

Harper sighed. If this had been a proper investigation, he'd have this bloke flat up against the wall, choking for breath.

'You forgot to mention it. Okay, you're a hundred euros up. You can go and buy yourself a nice new tattoo. So where's Caubec now?'

'He said he was going on holiday, indefinitely.'

'Did he say in which direction?' Harper asked.

'Caribbean… Martinique,' said the Patron.

Harper realised he was getting somewhere. He'd almost caught up with the gunman, and the tie-in with the West Indies was a definite breakthrough.

'He talk to you about his trip?'

'No, only that it was all paid for. Lucky for some.'

'Mind if I root around a bit more?' Harper asked.

'Help yourself. For another fifty.'

Harper extracted another note from his wallet: 'You'll be opening up an hotel on the Cote d'Azur soon.'

The Patron took the money and left him to it as he went back downstairs.

It turned out to be a fruitless search. Caubec had left nothing behind him except possibly his fingerprints, and Gerard Dercourt had those on file anyhow. Harper came out onto the shabby landing and was on his way downstairs when he spotted a payphone on the wall. Beside it was a discarded newspaper. He retraced his steps, picked up the paper and saw that it was the previous day's issue of *Le Figaro* with a front-page story and picture on the London shooting of Sir Walter Julien.

Just as he was putting it down again he saw the phone number, faintly scribbled in a margin. Harper looked at the number for a moment, then used his mobile to phone Gerard's office, and asked him to check out the number. He knew the Paris police like the Met could whistle up that sort of information in a few minutes.

'The number belongs to someone called Vincent Joussier, his address is Belvedere Farm, in Marne-la-Vallee,' said Gerard.

Harper asked him to repeat the name and address and he wrote it down. 'Can I take a taxi there?'

'Think of the risks you could be getting into on your own, Harper!' Gerard warned him.

But Harper assured him he was only intending to carry out a careful reconnaissance and rang off.

The Patron was busy collecting cups from one of the sidewalk tables as he came out of the cafe.

'You find anything?'

'No, nothing,' Harper replied.

'Mind me asking what you're investigating? Private eye, aren't you?'

'A hundred and fifty euros says it doesn't matter a fuck to you who I am, or what I'm doing,' said Harper, hailing a taxi.

'How come you speak such good French?'

Harper gave him a look. 'For a British guy, even a black guy, you mean?' he said drily.

Then, dropping into English, he added: 'Stunning yet, ain't it? And in case you don't know, that isn't even good grammar.'

Gerard checked his watch and got up from his desk. Around about this time it was his habit to take a stroll round to his favourite delicatessen for his lunchtime sandwich, peppery Ardennes sausage with chives on brown, with tomato slices, and one of their excellent Danish pastries to follow. He liked to go early before the hungry queues built up.

As he left the building he saw the Operation Hurricane team assembling in the courtyard for final instructions.

He didn't know anything about it, or where they were off to, but seeing them, he felt a pang of envy. Not so long ago he was in the thick of it himself, like a real cop.

While Harper was using his mobile on the landing, the Patron had been lugging in crates of beer that had been stacked by the delivery lorry at the rear of the cafe. He'd stopped at the foot of the stairs to listen to the conversation.

After he'd watched Harper leave in the taxi he went upstairs and found the newspaper with the phone number Caubec had written on it, and now he waited as the phone rang at the other end.

Joussier answered: 'Yes?'

'You don't know me, but I think I have some information that could interest you,' said the Corsican. He wasn't sure if he could make something out of it, but it was worth a try.

'Information about what?' Joussier asked guardedly.

'About Maurice Caubec.'

'Who? I don't recall knowing anyone of that name.'

'Oh, yes, I think you do,' said the Patron slyly, taking a gamble. 'Your friend who's gone to Martinique,'

There was a squeezed silence. 'What exactly is your interest?'

So the Patron said his interest was in a nice reward, and where he could send it. Joussier asked how much it was worth, and they settled on two hundred euros before he was told about the visit by Harper, who may have been a private investigator.

He also learned that Harper had written down a name and address, presumably his, which he'd apparently got by phoning someone in the police. His informant assumed this because he'd overheard Harper ask for 'Detective Sergeant Dercourt,' then address him as 'Gerard'.

But it was when Joussier was told that Harper was a West Indian, that he became instantly alarmed.

Raphael Tabard was having a drink with the two dealers he'd arranged to meet in the opulent splendour of the cocktail bar at the Crillon. One was already a major customer of the syndicate to which Tabard belonged. He and his associates specialised in supplying the Paris hotel trade, three stars and upwards, and the other was from the newly burgeoning drug outlet of Rouen and the Normandy holiday resorts.

Both men were interested in the new consignment of top-grade Colombian that they'd been told about, and were keen to effect an immediate deal. Tabard had offered to let them personally examine the quality of the cocaine.

A car was waiting to take them out to Marne-la-Vallee, and as they crossed the regally furnished hotel lobby, the head porter intercepted Tabard, telling him there was an urgent phone call.

He took the call in one of the plush booths, from Joussier, who was in a panic and was relieved to have caught him.

Tabard didn't waste a moment: 'Jesus, start loading the stuff up right now, and get out fast!' he said. 'Just make sure no one finds it there! Contact me later.'

He hung up and hurried out to the car to lie to the customers that they'd have to wait until the following day to examine the stuff. It crossed his mind also that it would be wiser to book out of the hotel at once.

He didn't trust anybody, not even at the best address in Paris.

Thirty

Harper travelled in the taxi anti clockwise around the Peripherique, until they exited at the Porte de Bercy, picking up the motorway towards Marne-la-Vallee.

This time he had a woman taxi driver, a fierce, middle-aged harpy who, if anything, drove faster than the last one. Shortly after the fare began, she announced that she and her husband, also a cab driver, intended to go and live in Tel Aviv, and she was learning Hebrew. Did he mind if she continued with her studies en route? Harper was mystified until she donned walkmans and switched on a language cassette, her lips framing Hebraic words as she maneouvred from one lane to another.

He leaned back, pondering on the safety of a deaf driver, recalling that he'd been told by a friend who lived in Israel that driving manners in Tel Aviv were worse than in Paris. Maybe this lady and her husband would fit in well.

Not long before they reached the junction where they would turn off the motorway, the taxi overtook a police convoy. He recognised the vehicles as the ones he'd seen earlier outside the headquarters, the dark green buses, jeeps and patrol cars. So the matter in hand was taking place some distance from the city, whatever it was. He wished his fellow cops luck.

The convoy dropped away into the background and they were soon on country roads heading for Joussier's farm. Harper noticed numerous signs for EuroDisney, and the lady driver, her Hebrew lessons now dispensed with, explained that the huge theme park, almost the size of central Paris itself, was just a few miles away.

The French, she said, thoroughly detested it, accusing Disney and the USA of cultural imperialism. Then she coyly admitted that she and her husband had had a day out there with grandchildren and thoroughly enjoyed it, except for the thrill-packed train ride on Thunder Mountain. Too scary, she said, as she hurtled into an S-bend and the Peugeot taxi made a sound that Harper could have sworn was metal fatigue.

As they saw a wooden sign, *Ferme Belvedere*, hanging from a wrought iron arm at the entrance to a private road just ahead, Harper asked the driver to slow down. He wondered whether they could risk driving in, claiming they'd merely lost their way if challenged. He'd already said he wanted the taxi for a round trip, and the woman was beginning to look at him uncertainly in her rear mirror.

She was cautious of black fares, though he had turned out to be English and French-speaking. And he was well dressed. He had explained where he wanted to go, and asked how much. When she quoted a price he'd opened his wallet and offered her the money there and then, but she said it could wait till the hire was complete.

Harper decided on his excuse. 'The farm's up for sale and I'm thinking of making an offer,' he said. 'But I want to give the place the once-over without the owner knowing.'

That seemed to satisfy her curiosity. When she and her husband made up their minds to sell their nice little apartment in the 13th, and move to Israel to be with their daughter, they had visited Tel Aviv to inspect a few properties, some discreetly. Jewish sellers and buyers waged a very special battle of wits, you had to play a crafty game. She understood Harper.

He told her to turn into the farm, and they drove for about half a mile along a rough, undulating road, through woods and fields until they reached a crest and saw Belvedere in the hollow below. It was a sunny day; the farmhouse and its outbuildings looked very attractive.

To Harper it was strangely like so many farms in Sussex, with mellow red brick and tiled roofs, green with lichen, as if smeared by a painter's brush.

There was no car outside the farmhouse, no sign of life. So he decided to a closer investigation.

They drove down into the courtyard by the front door porch.

Harper got out of the taxi and rang the doorbell. Nobody answered. Prudently, he rang again, but there was still no reply, so he wandered around peering through windows. The taxi driver had resumed her Hebrew lessons, now wearing a Tallit prayer scarf.

At the rear of the farmhouse Harper made an odd discovery. By the backdoor lay a large pile of old books and prints, in good condition, not the sort of thing you would leave out in the open. It looked like someone had abandoned them suddenly, and seeing tyre marks, he deduced they had been unloaded from a vehicle.

Harper found the backdoor unlocked. After calling out and receiving no answer, he decided to enter the house. Now he prowled about inside.

The phone had been listed in the name of 'Vincent Joussier.' Who was this man who had a peaceful farm and yet had a connection with an ex-Foreign Legion gunman?

The comfortable sitting room with its old beams and a fireplace filled with logs, bore no clues, except for a number of photographs, two of them showing a dark skinned man with silver hair and a pointed beard. In one of the photos he was wearing a beret and standing beside a bookstall with Notre Dame in the background.

If he was a bookseller it would explain the stack of books at the door, though not why they'd been dumped like that.

He walked into an adjoining study, found it lined with crammed bookshelves. There was a desk with computer leads including a modem on it, but no computer, although a printer and scanner remained. Littered around were invoices for the sale and purchase of books and prints. Clearly that must be Joussier's occupation.

Making a quick tour of the rest of the house, Harper found nothing else of interest; he returned to the study desk, searching through the drawers.

Thirty-one

The police convoy had arrived almost silently. The buses, parked furthest away, disgorged a small army of officers, who quickly took up their positions on the fringes of the farm. The cars and jeeps moved to prearranged points, blocking all exits.

Inspector Blasson and Charlotte were both in a jeep that was driven into the cover of a copse with a good view of the farmhouse. Everyone was in touch by mobile phone. The whole place was encircled.

Blasson scanned the house with his binoculars. 'Taxi and a driver parked outside,' he reported to the others. 'That means Joussier has company.'

He handed the glasses to Charlotte. She noted that the taxi driver was a woman, wearing a Jewish prayer scarf, and found it a bit odd that there was no sign of any other cars, particularly Joussier's own Espace. Maybe it was parked on the other side of the farmhouse?

Blasson made a check by radio, but the group who had a clear view of the rear reported that they couldn't see any vehicle. It was pointed out, however, that it could be garaged in a barn. The Inspector decided to issue the order to move in.

A few minutes later Harper heard the sound of vehicles approaching.

Slamming the desk drawers shut, he started to make for the kitchen and the backdoor, but even as he reached the door, there was a screeching of tyres all around the house, the sound of running feet.

In a panic, he hurried back into the sitting room to look out at the taxi, and what he saw astonished him.

Dozens of policemen from buses were converging on the farm, others jumping out of jeeps, and they were all armed. The Jewish woman was standing by her taxi with her hands up. She looked both comical and scared.

But a bigger shock was yet to come. As a jeep drove up and an officer jumped out with a loud hailer in one hand and a revolver in the other, he was joined by a tall, dark girl in flak jacket – the same girl he'd met in the police headquarters lift!

Now Harper knew where the police convoy had been going.

Blasson barked through the loud hailer: 'This is a police raid! You are completely surrounded! Come out with your hands up!'

As Harper opened the front door and apprehensively stepped outside, he found himself looking straight at Charlotte Plennard's revolver. At least twenty more weapons were trained on him.

He said: 'It's okay, I don't have a gun. And it looks like I'm the only person here.'

'Frisk him!' Blasson ordered her.

Harper grinned a trifle weakly at her as she stared at him with recognition. 'It'll be a pleasure,' he said.

'You were at headquarters!' Charlotte exclaimed. 'Who the hell are you?'

'You're not going to believe this,' said Harper. 'My I.D. is in my back pocket.'

She reached into his back pocket and took out his I.D. wallet to look at it.

Charlotte read out for the others: 'Detective Sergeant Harper Buchanan.'

'London Metropolitan Police,' Harper added.

Blasson and the rest of the drug bust team stared at him incredulously.

Harper gave them an apologetic shrug. 'I think we'd better swap notes,' he ventured.

Thirty-two

Harper returned to Paris in the back of a patrol car. Charlotte sat stiffly on one side of him, Sergeant Cassel, the burly officer who'd been her rowing companion, on the other. Harper was decidedly unpopular and they were treating him as though he was under arrest.

The farmhouse had been searched from top to bottom, but there was no trace of the major cocaine haul Blasson had hoped would be splashed all over the next day's newspapers, earning him personal kudos and maybe promotion.

Despite a conspicuous 'No Smoking' notice on the dashboard, Charlotte lit up one of her cigars. She looked challengingly at Harper.

'I need this, and if you mention that notice, I'll blow smoke in your face,' she told him.

'Are you always this rude?' he asked her.

'Yes!' she said, savagely. 'You completely ruined it all for us, you imbecile rosbif!'

'Rather amusing, in view of my complexion, to call me that,' Harper grinned. 'And it was all quite accidental.'

'You call that accidental? Shoving your nose in our operation?'

'How was I to know we'd get our wires crossed?' Harper protested.

'To think you came creeping secretly around our office for information!'

'Secretly? I didn't try to avoid you in the lift, did I?' he said. 'I doubt if anyone could avoid you,' he added.

'All those weeks of surveillance and planning, all of it wasted! Right, Claude?'

The paunchy cop nodded agreement. 'And two drug suspects go free. No proof, not a speck of cocaine.'

'Oh, come on, I didn't actually tip them off,' Harper pleaded.

'They must have got wind of trouble, thanks to your enquiries,' said Charlotte.

'Okay, so I blew it, I'm sorry.'

'Not half as sorry as you'll be when my Inspector is through with you,' she warned.

Harper shook his head. This dame wasn't going to let him off the hook. He still found her fanciable, though. 'What rank are you, by the way?' he asked.

Charlotte said: 'Same as you, Sergeant.'

'Well, if we're going to have equality – even without fraternity, Sergeant – would you mind opening your window?' said Harper.

She glared at him. Then pressed the button to lower the window. She flipped her cigar out and raised the window again, leaving a thick fug in the car.

'Catch a chill easily do you?' Harper enquired, a touch caustic.

'How did you guess,' said Charlotte, hunching back in her seat.

'Even with such a thick skin you get colds?' said Harper wryly. There wasn't even a flicker on her face. He remembered that the French seldom seemed to enjoy jokes delivered in French by foreigners.

The meeting with Inspector Blasson was short and to the point.

Blasson had found out about Harper's suspension. The two men faced each other in the empty Briefing Room with all the maps and photographs for the failed operation rather forlornly adorning the walls.

Harper tried once more to apologise. 'It's too bad things got messed up,' he said, 'but you have to understand I was after this guy Caubec, a fucking assassin. I never knew there was a link with your activities, Inspector.'

Blasson scowled. 'You had no right to act without authority here in France, especially when you'd been dismissed.'

'Not dismissed,' Harper corrected him. 'I was just taken off the case in London.'

'Well, whatever, Sergeant, I think you'd better keep away from us.'

Harper protested: 'Even though one of your drug barons hired a killer?'

'We know all about the connection, and also why they wanted the West Indian Prime Minister dead,' Blasson replied.

Harper pointed out: 'Okay, but if I'd nailed Caubec, the people who've stolen power out there might have been exposed, along with the drug cartel you're closing in on. Your Operation Hurricane.'

But he knew Blasson wasn't prepared to listen to reason.

Blasson picked up a sheaf of papers from the briefing desk and headed towards the door.

'Look, Sergeant Buchanan, I hope I make myself clear. Just piss off, just take yourself off back to London and continue your suspension. You got that?'

As Harper was being conveyed to one of the satellite departure gates, holding his boarding card and overnight bag, he wondered if there might be someone shadowing him, to make sure he left Paris. But he decided he was being a little over the top thinking that, especially since they hadn't even supplied a car to take him to the airport.

The night before, he'd had dinner with Gerard and his charming wife, Yvette, and their two children. It was a jolly family meal, and although Gerard had been severely reprimanded for giving Harper assistance, he was quite relaxed about it.

'After all,' he joked, 'they can't exactly demote me from Premises Maintenance now, can they?'

Harper, who'd stayed the night with his old friends, knew precisely when he had decided on his next move.

He and Gerard were having a cognac before going to bed, and the latter was commiserating with Harper over his two unlucky experiences. First the shooting of Sir Walter Julien (Harper still felt he couldn't reveal the truth, even to Gerard) and now the drug bust fiasco.

'The only thing you can do,' said Gerard, pouring them both another hefty Hine, 'is to take advantage of your idleness and go and have a damn good holiday somewhere.'

And suddenly Harper knew just where that would be. He wouldn't even bother to go back to London, he could buy another ticket with his Visa card.

Which was why the boarding card he held in his hand was for an Air France flight to Martinique.

Part two

Shady men and twisted shadows

Thirty-three

Even before the plane began to lose height, Harper could swear he smelled the tropical heat.

It had been a rough night. Thanks to his fellow passengers he'd only managed a brief doze in eight hours.

They were mostly tourists bound for the Club Mediterranee on Martinique, where as well as the beach they would enjoy all the comforts of home, especially the food, and not for the first time Harper marvelled at the verbal stamina of the French. For them it had been like one long night at the brasserie. All the latest gossip about President Sarkozy and Carla Bruni, the politics of Europe and especially Brussels, everyone investing their views with the inevitable hint of greater knowledge than their neighbours.

Not even a good in-flight movie – Depardieu and Deneuve – could still their tongues. As they spotted small dots of green islands below, they grew louder and even more recklessly self-important by the minute.

From a few thousand feet Harper gazed down at the vivid scene below with rapt curiosity. To people on the plane, especially given his colour, he was doubtless considered just another local returning home. He had mixed emotions. On one hand he wondered vaguely how his spur-of-the-moment mission would turn out. After events of the past few days, he was strangely calm and, if he was honest, almost as much in the holiday spirit as the chattering tourists.

Presumably Blasson had asked his police colleagues in Martinique to search for Maurice Caubec. Maybe he'd already been arrested, in which case Harper's unofficial pursuit would be pointless. Maybe not.

His other feeling, deeper and more personal, was one of great anticipation on this, his first visit to the Caribbean.

He was indeed 'coming home,' and as the plane banked and headed towards its final destination, he saw in the distance the birthplace of his parents, an island somewhat smaller than the French one, but he recognised its shape immediately. It gave him a profound tug.

He decided that before doing anything else he would make it his first port of call.

On the flight he'd overheard a couple of stewardesses discussing the UPP coup following the shooting of Sir Walter Julien in London.

He wondered how Sir Walter was progressing, realising that the moment he set foot on the next-door island he would be harbouring a secret that could blow the new regime of Maitland Harbinson straight out of office. He would also put himself at risk if he revealed who he was and, more importantly, what he knew. But if he could, he intended to stay well clear of trouble.

It would be strictly a sentimental visit. Besides, there was one man living there whom he planned to see, who might help him trace Caubec if he was still at large.

In the early afternoon, Aimé Césaire Airport was like a furnace, humid air blasting its way in as soon as the aircraft's doors were opened. Harper slipped his tie off and carried his suit jacket and holdall, realising that he would have to buy some lighter clothing. He was the only long-haul traveller with no hold baggage. The Air France desk directed him immediately to an inter-island flight counter where he bought a ticket for his short onward journey.

As he was ferried by minibus to a smaller terminal, the rest of the transatlantic arrivals awaited at a carousel for their things.

Among them stood a tall, handsome figure who'd flown First Class and whose expensive luggage appeared with early priority.

Passing briskly through Immigration and Customs, he was met by his Creole chauffeur, Obe, with a Mercedes.

Harper hadn't known it, but he had travelled on the same flight as Raphael Tabard, the man at the heart of the drugs investigation that had brought him here.

Maurice Caubec had only just woken up, having gone to bed at dawn after finding himself lying stiff as driftwood on the beach.

He had an atrocious hangover from the rum of the night before, and only dimly remembered lying on the sand earlier with one of the prostitutes who frequented the poolside bar. He couldn't recall anything else, except she demanded her money in advance. He leaned out of bed and checked his wallet. At least she hadn't relieved him of any more dollars.

He was still waiting for the final pay-off promised by Joussier, but his phone calls to Tabard's office had so far been in vain. A snooty-voiced secretary kept fending him off, saying the owner was still in Europe.

He could think of lousier places to while away the time, but all the same he'd like to get his hands on the rest of the cash for the job. As soon as possible he wanted to take himself off to Miami for a spot of gambling. Maybe he would settle in Florida for a bit, till the heat was off. He couldn't forget that black cop in London who'd got a good look at him as he fled the Shepherd's Bush Market.

Worse than his hangover, however, was the terrible sunburn he was suffering on what seemed every inch of his body. It was always a problem, but in the Foreign Legion it was a punishable offence to get badly burnt. He'd forgotten how vulnerable his pale skin was.

Painfully, he eased himself out of bed and took a cold shower, then pulled on a pair of flour-bag shorts and a garish shirt. There was a nearly empty bottle of the hundred percent rum on the verandah. He finished it off with a couple of hefty slugs.

The Blue Heaven Beach Club was a run-down dump with a dozen rustically furnished bungalows around the pool, a restaurant and reception desk in the shabby, clapboard hotel nearby, containing more rooms. Caubec had chosen this low-profile place to stay in discreetly, passing himself off as a Marseilles croupier in need of a break.

He walked over from his bungalow to the circular bar by the pool, where the wizened Chinese bartender with teeth the colour of old piano keys gave him a knowing wink.

'You sleep well? You sleep a long time,' he grinned, displaying the full keyboard.

'Gimme a white rum with lots of ice and coke. And the phone.'

The barman shoved the phone over to him and went to make his drink. Tabard's secretary answered promptly.

'Laboratoires Tabard?'

'Yeah, this is Maurice Caubec again. Your boss arrived from Paris yet?'

'Mister Tabard is due here at any moment,' she replied. 'I told you he'll be very busy,' she added haughtily, 'but your number's on my list.'

Caubec took his drink from the barman, clunking the glass clumsily against the receiver as he downed a mouthful.

'Make sure my name's at the top of that list,' he said abruptly. 'He and I have an important matter to discuss.' Hanging up, he swilled the entire contents, crunching on the ice.

'Fill it up again, Chinaman, and don't go so easy on the rum, huh?'

'You want to slay the dragon? Maybe you ought to have some lunch?'

'Just get my drink and cut out the fucking Confucious, okay?'

Though his mouth was still dry and foul, Caubec lit his first Marlboro of the day, squinting idly into the sun at the Twin Otter that flew low overhead towards a neighbouring island.

As he followed the plane's course it made him uneasy staring across at the home of the Prime Minister who had been his target a few days ago.

Harper was the only passenger in the Twin Otter, so he sat beside the pilot rather as if they were in a car together. He was a round-shouldered Irishman around fifty, with obvious contact lenses – not very reassuring – and a complexion that might owe more to Bushmills than the climate.

His airline cap was at a rakish angle and his short-sleeved white shirt with gold-bar shoulder tabs was soaked with sweat. But his big hands seemed firm on the controls.

'Fine steady breeze on the water today. I could float us over on a jar of poteen! We could do with some juice, I'm almost running on empty,' he announced in his cheerful brogue.

From his position, Harper couldn't read the fuel guage to check if he was merely joking. Maybe just as well. 'I'm amazed this airline pays its way when you take off with me as your only fare,' he said.

'We're a scheduled taxi service between islands. One passenger's the same as eight.' He'd immediately noted Harper's accent, which had only the slightest West Indian tinge to it. 'That's a very English voice you have there.'

'I'm from London,' Harper vouchsafed.

'So why not fly direct from Heathrow to where you're going? Why come in on Air France?'

'I had some business in Paris,' Harper explained cautiously. He had to be careful of island-hopping pilots who liked to ask too many questions.

Confirmed, when the Irishman queried: 'And what business would that be?'

'Sports equipment,' Harper lied, grabbing at the first thing that came into his head. 'But this is more of a combined holiday trip, visiting a relative.' he added.

'I expect you've been out here before?'

Harper shook his head. 'Actually, I've never been to the Caribbean.'

The pilot, trimming his throttles, glanced at him with surprise. 'Now there's a fine thing! A native who isn't!' Then, hastily, in case

Harper was offended: 'Foreigner like myself, if you get my meaning. You'll be in for a bit of a culture shock, then.'

'No doubt.' Harper decided to ask a few questions himself for the remaining few minutes left of the flight.

He heard the latest on the coup and Harbinson's 'caretaker government,' and the general shock at the news of the popular Prime Minister's fate. 'Fancy a thing like that that happening on the streets of London!' said the pilot, tactfully excluding the former IRA activities.

'Nobody's safe anywhere in the world nowadays,' remarked Harper blandly.

The Irishman brought the plane around in a tight turn and began his approach, changing the subject. 'So who's your relative?'

'My uncle,' said Harper uncommunicatively.

The pilot, touching his wheels delicately down onto the runway, reacted. 'Hey, wait a minute, your name's Buchanan. Would that make him Jimmie Buchanan by any chance?'

Harper nodded and decided he could afford to give that much away. 'That's right, my Uncle Jimmie,' he admitted.

'Well, I'll be damned!' the pilot exclaimed. 'Even I know the great Jimmie Buchanan! And I'm Irish,' he added, as if it was something Harper might have failed to detect.

Thirty-four

The offices of 'Laboratoires Tabard/Parfumes Tropiques' were as exotic as the firm's name, with its eye-catching logo of neon frangi-pani and hibiscus blooms sprouting from a giant test tube over the entrance of the steel and glass building in Fort-de-France. Tabard had plannned the interiors himself. The floors were cool marble, with lots of potted plants, the elegant modern furniture imported from Paris.

Raphael Tabard had come straight from the airport to catch up at his desk after his fortnight's absence. His secretary, Camille, a sleek girl in her thirties, and a former Miss Martinique, followed him into his private cloakroom with her notebook, as he shaved and changed his shirt.

'How was the flight?'

'Good food, boring movie. Can't stand that ugly mug of Gerard Depardieu's. What the hell do women see in him?'

Camille didn't tell her boss. She admired him as a shrewd businessman, but found him, despite his good looks, deeply unattractive. He fancied himself too much. A week after she started work, he asked her out dinner, making it fairly plain what he was after. Nothing doing, she told him.

Two years later she was still in the job. She was highly efficient and needed to be, because he made frequent sales trips abroad, mostly to Europe. She wondered if he might have a mistress in Paris.

'That was a terrible thing to happen to Sir Walter Julien,' she said. 'You heard all about it, I assume?'

'Yes, appalling. A good man, serving his country well,' said Tabard, shaking his head with a show of regret as he moved to his desk. 'What's the latest from our neighbours?'

'Maitland Harbinson's been sworn in as Acting Prime Minister. He's promised his party will run things pretty much as before, until there's an election. Seems there hasn't been much of an upheaval, thanks to the Army.'

'How about our warehouse over there?'

'There's a report on your desk. It says everything's secure.'

'That's a relief. Okay, what's urgent?'

Camille briefed him. 'Our Portugese agent wants a word. Chicago still hasn't acknowledged our invoices on the last batch....would you phone Lentheric in Grasse? And a guy called Caubec keeps ringing you.'

Tabard tensed slightly, hoping she wouldn't notice. He feigned a mystified frown. 'Where's he calling from?

'Some tacky beach place in St Pierre.'

'Right, I'll deal with it.'

She looked surprised. 'I didn't think you'd know him. He sounds like a drunk.'

As she turned over a page of her notebook, Camille didn't see the expression that flickered momentarily on Tabard's face. This time the frown was genuine.

He left the laboratory half an hour later, Obe driving him to Flamingo Bay where he moored his sleek yacht *L'Imperatrice Josephine*, a tribute to the girl born Marie Joseph Tascher who left the island to become Napoleon's wife and Empress.

As Obe, an expert sailor as well as chauffeur, busied himself preparing to sail, Tabard went below with his mobile phone and called the the Blue Heaven Beach Club.

Summoned from his stupor under a poolside umbrella, Maurice Caubec was in a bad mood.

'So you finally got here?' Caubec complained. 'Nobody said I'd be kept hanging around like this.'

'A couple of days is hardly an ordeal on Martinique.' Tabard replied evenly.

'Look, the sooner I'm out of here the better,' said Caubec. 'I want paid what I'm owed – and I want it now.'

'Don't worry, you'll get your money. Just give me a few hours.'

'Sorry, I won't take any more fucking delay. I'll be at your office later this afternoon,' Caubec threatened.

'No! Whatever happens, we can't be seen together, not here.' said Tabard curtly. 'Besides, I'm just on my way to a meeting on another island. I'll see you with the money tonight.'

'I'll be waiting,' Caubec snapped.

'Meantime, stay cool,' said Tabard, ringing off, nearly adding, 'and for God's sake try to stay sober.'

He could almost smell the rum over the phone. Maybe it hadn't been such a good idea to bring Caubec to the Caribbean.

Charlotte Plennard had arrived in Martinique on an earlier flight from Paris, immediately transferring to the neighbouring island where her workplace was.

Because she was attached to JIBOC, she had an apartment near their headquarters, behind the market place in the capital. After freshening up, she drove over to the Bureau in her battered old jeep, a relic from the American invasion of Grenada that had somehow found its way across the archipelago.

Inspector Carmona allowed her to use it, even though it still bore a faded US Army star, plus a busty blonde that some GI had painted on, when presumably normal military discipline had disintegrated like the failed CIA-inspired operation.

Parking the jeep outside the old warehouse building, she noted that Eddie Carmona's reserved space was empty. As indeed was the office, except for Yolande, the secretary, and a new recruit, a skinny young detective from St Kitts, Ben Thomson, who announced that Carmona and the rest of the squad had gone to attend a one-day seminar on arms smuggling being held in Trinidad, at Port-of-Spain.

'The seminar was yesterday, but they won't be back till late tonight,' said Ben. 'Delayed by the cricket,' he grinned, reminding Charlotte that it was the final day of the Trinidad Test, with Chris Gayle past his century at the Queen's Park Oval, and the West Indies needing only another hundred or so runs to win.

Bringing them both some coffee, Ben explained that the change of regime hadn't affected them yet. The Bureau, after all, had a kind of sovereignty since all the island states were the sponsors of JIBOC. Even so, Ben told her, Carmona was worried about potential trouble with Harbinson, who was known to favour the island's own police having sole control over crime, including narcotics.

As they talked, Charlotte reclaimed various items of equipment, including her computer, that colleagues had pinched in her absence. In JIBOC's underfunded establishment, they always plagiarised each other's things when they could. From her satchel, Charlotte withdrew the framed portrait which normally had pride of place on her desk.

Ben glanced with interest at the colour photograph of a pretty little girl of ten, in tennis gear, with light brown skin, sparkling blue eyes, her hair held back by a white head band. 'Cute kid,' said Ben. 'You must've missed her a lot. Looks just like my young sister, 'cept for the blue eyes.' he added, then wondered if Sergeant Plennard would appreciate such a comment. He'd heard about the Puerto Rican guy she'd shacked up with, and the rotten deal she'd had before she became a cop.

Charlotte smiled. 'Angeline's lucky. Her father was a hell of a good looker,' she said, checking her watch, which reminded her that she had a couple of hours to spare before she visited her daughter at her convent, when school was over.

She lit one of her cigars, set her desk fan going, and got down to work at her computer, writing a long report, including an account of Raphael Tabard's activities in Paris.

Although the Bureau was now aware of his involvement, she had tossed a surprise hand grenade from Europe in their lap. Until now, nobody had considered the French island to be that close to the drug trade, yet here was strong evidence that Martinique was part of the web.

The end of her report was an angry summary of the last-minute failure of Operation Hurricane. In particular, she described in harsh words how the foul-up had been caused by the crass, unofficial interference, for his own aims, of a London detective under suspension, called Buchanan.

Thirty-five

The Test commentary blared loudly from the radio as Harper headed in from the airport in a taxi, the driver's shoulders opening to every delivery, expressing glee as a back-in-form Chris Gayle despatched four successive balls to the boundary off a hapless bowler. Throughout the journey, he also added his own knowledgeable, if biased, commentary.

For all his own close interest in cricket, Harper only half listened to him as he studied the passing scene with wry detachment, gazing from side to side, captivated by the sights and sounds of a busy Caribbean capital – it was barely a city in size – that was completely foreign to him, yet oddly familiar.

It was even hotter than when he had landed, but the streets were a jostling melee of activity, thronged with colourfully dressed people, hurrying about their business, arguing, shopping, sitting at café tables, working in open office windows, packing the yellow municipal buses, enduring traffic jams in overheated cars, and cursing points policemen with white gloves and pith helmets, who stood atop upturned concrete filled oil drums, imperiously blowing their whistles like demented football referees.

He couldn't help thinking about his parents at that moment. He knew they had married here and lived in a house that they shared with his mother's cousin and her family. He'd seen pictures of it. It looked squalid, but it was all they could afford, and they seemed happy in the photographs.

Somewhere, a few miles out, was the shoe repair shop where his grandfather and his father worked. He would like to track down both these places when he had time. Uncle Jimmie, his last remaining relative, would know where.

The driver tore himself away from the cricket. 'Gimme that address again?'

'Ensign Parade, number seventy one. '

They were leaving the better part of town and now the man took a closer look in the mirror at his passenger. Educated, nice suit, cool customer. He'd reckoned on a good fare. So what's a guy like that wanting down this end?

A mile or so on they were in Grand Severn Harbour, situated on the West side, a crumbling area of disused warehouses and shanty dwellings. Its name was a legacy from the days when half the island had been covered by cane fields, the stench of molasses around the port the only the air people breathed, as ships plied back and forth from Tate & Lyle's English refineries. Now the world trade in sugar had been spooned off by synthetic stuff or easily created from other crops in Europe and the Middle East.

The driver told Harper there was a grandiose plan to demolish all the old property and build smart new hotels, berthing for cruise liners, and a yacht marina to add to the island's tourist attractions. Indeed, it was one of the Prime Minister's pet projects, like Margaret Thatcher's London Docklands had once been.

Now, with Sir Walter Julien's reported condition, his life uselessly suspended in a coma, like the former Israeli Prime Minister, Ariel Sharon, it looked as if there would be a long wait for the Grand Severn Harbour redevelopment.

So far as anyone knew, it didn't come high on the UPP agenda, though nobody knew exactly what did, and what island improvements they would be striving for. Except, as the driver drily observed, in a side-of-the mouth whisper, as if somebody might be listening on his call set, the usual fucking improvement in the politicians' own bank balances.

He spun his wheel and bumped across some rusty tracks of a disused railway that once ran the flatbed trucks of sugar cane to the portside mills.

They approached a roundabout, where a rocket launcher and a troop carrier were parked in the parched circle, thoughtlessly crushing the grass and flowers, the soldiers lounging around their vehicles, drinking cans of beer and listening to the cricket commentary like everyone else.

Harper, lost in his thoughts about his family background, was surprised to be reminded of the coup and his reason for being here. Apart from a heavier than usual military presence at the airport, he hadn't seen much sign of Harbinson's bid for power and the military alliance.

The taxi turned around into Ensign Parade, a long boulevard made two-way by a row of bedraggled sago palms down the middle. Halfway along, Harper indicated an old fashioned red and white barber's pole on a shopfront, just ahead. 'That'll be the place.'

The driver pulled up at the kerb, where a dozen, mostly elderly, men were clustered on the sidewalk around an open window. They were either leaning against the walls or seated on chairs and boxes, eagerly watching the Test on a portable TV, balanced precariously on the window ledge, angled so that those outside could watch the cricket as well as whoever was inside.

'Hey, mon, why didn't you say you wanted Jimmie Buchanan?,' the taximan grinned at Harper, as he got out. 'Great guy for a haircut. But you've sure travelled far for it!'

'Truer than you think,' said Harper, collecting his bag and paying him.

As the taxi drove off, he walked past the close scrutiny of the cricket fans to the open window, glancing inside. At one of the two chairs in the shabby barber's shop, a scrawny apprentice was employing an electric cutter with all the enthusiasm of a sheepshearer, his victim, a fellow teenager, staring glumly into the mirror at his cover sheet festooned with a mass of his shorn locks. Nearby, a roly-poly regular, who hadn't bothered to remove his hat, his feet up on the washbasin, was being shaved by a tall figure, only slightly stooped despite his seventy-six years.

In his crisp barber's smock, with his curly, snow-white hair and and handsome features, Jimmie Buchanan resembled a distinguished surgeon performing an operation, wielding a cut-throat razor like a delicate scalpel.

Harper realised it must be twenty years since he'd last seen his uncle, his mother's brother, who was a legend in the family. One of the best calypso singers in the business, before calypso became overshadowed by reggae, rap and raga, Jimmie and his steel band had played all over the Caribbean and in Europe in the sixties and seventies.

Harper remembered the pride he'd felt at school one year when the great Jimmie Buchanan was the big attraction at the Notting Hill Carnival. He'd gone there with his mother and father, and Jimmie had let him join in a number, beating on one of the drums. He hadn't done badly, either, he recalled, the rhythm that seemed to seep through all West Indians' veins giving natural grace to music and dance.

Around the walls of the shop were framed photographs of Jimmie in company with international celebrities – film stars, famous cricketers, even Royalty.

He'd heard all about how Jimmie had made a pile of money from concerts and record contracts, but like so many entertainers, he could never hold on to it. Apparently, he'd squandered his wealth on drink, drugs and an endless succession of wives. A notorious womaniser, he'd been married five times, on the last occasion to a dazzling Venezuelan model who left him when the cash ran out. Though highly critical of her brother's lifestyle, Harper's mother had always adored him.

Now Jimmie was back where he started, in a humble barber's shop. But looking at him fondly, Harper guessed his uncle's reputation for being a popular, happy-go-lucky figure was still intact. Still famous in his own backyard.

As a loud appeal for lbw blasted from the screen, Jimmie glanced over towards the TV set and caught sight of Harper at the window. For a moment the old man's face showed puzzlement, followed by the shock of recognition. He whisked the razor away from his customer's throat in a wide, if dangerous, gesture.

'Harper…?'

'Uncle Jimmie.'

'Well, I'll be jiggered! It is you!' Jimmie hollered, moving across to greet Harper through the window, the cut-throat still in his hand, the TV set rocking perilously as the two men hugged each other. 'Man, you've really shaken me!' said Jimmie. 'Why the hell didn't you let me know you were comin?"

'Last minute thing, Uncle. Mind if I come in?'

Ten minutes later, after the shop had been closed, the apprentice dismissed, and the cricket fans had moved on grudgingly to some other venue, Harper sat in one of the chairs having his hair clipped for free. Jimmie was enthralled to hear the reason for his nephew's first ever trip to the West Indies. He promised solemnly not divulge any of their conversation to a single soul.

'So you're hot on the trail of this French feller who did the shooting?'

Harper nodded. He had decided not to tell him how the Prime Minister had survived. It was too risky.

'Maurice Caubec flew to Martinique forty eight hours ago. He'll have gone to ground, either there or on one of the other islands.'

'And you want me to help you find him?' Jimmie beamed enthusiastically.

'Not so fast, Uncle. I'm supposed to be a visiting relative, but how many people actually know what I do for a living?' Harper asked cautiously.

Jimmie shrugged. 'Only my closest friends. It tickled them to hear my sister Lucy's boy was a real live detective!'

'Well, I might not be alive much longer if it gets around in certain quarters why I'm here. This has to be low profile stuff. I'm working strictly incognito, you understand?'

'I got you.'

'That means keeping my job to yourself,' Harper warned.

'You can depend on me.'

'Thanks for your offer of a room, Uncle, but I'm going to check into a hotel.'

'Under a false name, of course,' said Jimmie, warming to his involvement in the subterfuge.

'No, I can't do that because of my credit card and passport, which luckily, doesn't give the holder's occupation. For your information, I'm a salesman for sports goods.'

'Right, I'll remember,' said Jimmie. 'By "certain quarters" I take it you meant Maitland Harbinson and his mob?'

'The British authorities are convinced they hired the hit man.'

Jimmie nodded gravely as he rubbed a bay rum lotion briskly into Harper's scalp. 'Right now things are quiet. People are scared, still getting over the shock. But it won't last, there's bound to be trouble ahead. Harbinson heads a bunch of rogues, with plenty more shady men behind them. And them shady men throw some twisted shadows.'

Harper grinned. 'My mother used to say you weren't only the best calypso singer in these parts, but one of the best informed.'

Jimmie looked pleased. 'She told you that, huh?'

'What she actually said was you were the island's greatest gossip.'

Jimmie took it as a compliment. 'Oh, she did, did she? Well, happens as I do know a lot about folks hereabouts.'

'That's what I was counting on, Uncle,' said Harper.

'Besides, Walter Julien was a good friend of mine. I'll find that bastard for you, Harper, never fear.'

Thirty-six

Harper booked into the Trade Winds Town House, a 5-star international hotel in the centre of the capital, where Jimmie had suggested most businessmen might be expected to stay. With its plush lobby and uniformed staff, it was an expensive choice for the sake of anonymity.

At the reception desk he was aware that in his now slightly crumpled suit, with only a small holdall as luggage, he had attracted an unmistakeable flicker of a question mark from the big eyes of the chic, red-blazered girl who checked him in.

However, a combination of the Air France ticket protruding from his English passport and his accent and general demeanour, seemed to satisfy her he was a guest who made the grade. Harper realised that although there might not be such thing as racial prejudice in this part of the world, there was definitely a pecking order, if not sometimes outright snobbery, and then he thought, why be surprised?

His room, at the most modest rate available, was small, with only a mere glimpse of the sea over rooftops. An immediate cold shower would have been welcome, but he decided first to go out and buy some things to wear.

Directed by the head porter to a shop on Shaftesbury Boulevard, where the more upmarket men's outfitters were located, he bought cotton slacks, Bermuda shorts, a couple of shirts, fresh underwear, and a pair of sandals. He paid by credit card, asking for his purchases to be sent round to the hotel.

Harper was impressed to be served by an elderly assistant, attired in black jacket and striped trousers, in an establishment that bore an air of Savile Row grandeur.

In his turn, Henry Aitkens would have been astonished to learn that his firm, Aitkens & Jeffrey, was connected yet again in some way with the sad affair of the Prime Minister, a burden he had carried heavily, if privately, since the dreadful news.

Though jet lag was catching up with him, Harper decided to wander around the centre of the town, enjoying the atmosphere, especially in the noisy, covered market place, listening to the bright badinage of the locals. He tried to picture his mother as a young housewife, arguing over the prices. Pausing at a stall where a dazzling balancing act of exotic fruit made Harrod's food store display look like a corner shop by comparison, he noticed one particularly unfamiliar fruit, a sort of pear with yellow skin. Curious, he lifted one off the pile.

'You mind telling me what this is?' he asked the buxom stallkeeper.

'Why, ambarella, 'course'

'Amber -- what?' queried Harper.

The woman stared at him. 'You ain't never had no ambarella?' she said with disbelief, and a degree of suspicion that she was being sent up. 'Hey, where you been, mon?'

'London's where I've been,' said Harper rather tamely, replacing the fruit and moving on, wondering whether his mother ever bought ambarella in Shepherd's Bush Market. He felt a bit like the Bounty Bar he'd often been called in London.

Out here he knew they would also call people like him 'coconuts,' especially when they were cops. Same old joke.

He bought a day-old copy of *The Financial Times*, the only English paper on sale at a newspaper kiosk, and sat down gratefully with a cold beer at a pavement cafe. Rifling through the pink pages, mostly devoted to the downturn in global finance, he found just one small follow-up news item about the shooting of Sir Walter Julien, which announced that the British Government, "whilst much regretting the incident, was awaiting developments after the coup" and, being the FT, the report suggested that Commonwealth trade links were uppermost in the mind of Whitehall.

There was a smokescreen quote from the Foreign Minister at Prime Minister's Questions: "We are still studying the situation that has arisen," and mention of a "full ranging" internal police inquiry about security.

Harper smiled wryly, speculating about whether the Hon Jonathan Walmsley and Chief Superintendent Norris were aware that he had failed to return to London after messing up in Paris. Presumably, if they learned he was right here, on the hot spot in the West Indies, they'd go apeshit. Well, it was Norris who'd ordered him emphatically to 'take a holiday.' Serve them right.

As he glanced through the rest of the paper, three young English holidaymakers sat down at the next table, two men and a girl. They spoke in affected, lazy monotones that immediately marked them down as London smart set. Probably something in the media or the City, thought Harper. In the latter case they could now be unemployed thanks to the credit crunch and the banking fiasco. The taller of the two men was a chinless wonder wearing a huge hat of plaited palm fronds, the Caribbean equivalent of the giant sombreros tourists proudly lugged back from Spain.

'Christ this is rather a slummy place, isn't it?' said Big Hat.

'Native reserve, positively primitive Nigel, but I'm shagged,' the girl protested.

Harper resumed reading as they ordered drinks from the tiny, smiling waitress tending the pavement tables. It was then that he got an unmistakeable whiff of marijuana, and out of the corner of his eye he saw that all three were smoking joints, probably bought from one of the many ganga traders on the beach.

A moment later he heard one of them remark in a loud whisper: 'Not such a slum after all, chaps. One of the locals is reading *The Financial Times*. Well, they say it makes the best toilet paper out here!"

'Asshole!' said the girl, with a stoned snigger.

When the waitress brought their drinks and gave them their bill, they kept up their rude repertoire. First the girl claimed that her orange juice wasn't fresh, though only after she'd drunk three quarters of the glass.

'Just got squeezed at the bar, Miss,' argued the waitress.

Then the chinless one took a long swill of his Piton lager and pulled a face. 'You call this beer? It tastes like donkey's piss and just as warm!' He and his friend drank some more, to within an inch of the bottom of their glasses, just to confirm their complaint.

'Disgusting,' said the other man.

'You want to see the manager?' the waitress offered.

'No, don't bother, we're going some other place,' said Nigel, rising from the table, signalling to the others.

'Hey, how about your bill?' asked the waitress, growing upset.

'Sorry, it's called customer satisfaction, sweetheart.'

Harper couldn't stand by any longer. He got to his feet, barring their path. 'You aren't going anywhere till you pay,' he said menacingly. 'Fetch your boss,' he told the waitress.

'And just who the hell do you think you are, Afro boy?' the tall one said, feigning toughness and pushing back the brim of his ridiculous hat, cowboy-style.

'I'll tell you what I am,' said Harper in a steely voice. 'Firstly I'm an Englishman like you, though I'm ashamed to say it. Secondly, you're smoking dope, which is against the law, even here. And thirdly, here's the manager.'

To Harper's relief, the boss was a big guy, and he had brought an even bigger barman with him, with biceps like a Olympic weightlifter.

Harper walked back in the direction of his hotel, wondering why on earth he'd bothered to get involved. Police habits died hard, wherever you were, except here he was supposed to avoid revealing his true identity. He decided he'd been foolish to intervene, but knew it was just as much the tourists' taunts about his colour, as their treament of the waitress, that had wound him up.

Little did he know, however, that he was about to get himself into an even more tricky situation.

As he crossed an intersection with a quiet cul-de-sac, he glanced sideways and saw something that instantly took his attention. A tall youth with a Mohican haircut was lounging innocently against a smart VW Golf GTi, whose front door hung open, and another youth could be seen crouched inside the car by the dashboard.

Harper guessed what was happening. The boy inside was either trying to make a hotwire to start up the car and steal it, or dismantling the radio. With a cop's reflex action, Harper turned and headed towards them. Immediately, the lookout spoke to his friend, who jumped from the car, a ripped-out radio in his hand, the wires dangling.

Harper started running. 'Hey, you!' he shouted. The youth with the stolen radio bolted for the dead-end, hurling the radio over a wall and vaulting after it. But the Mohican, panicking, started to run down one side of the cul-de-sac to get past Harper, who veered over to the other sidewalk to block his escape.

'Hold it!' Harper challenged him, standing his ground.

As he skidded to a halt the youth glared at him. 'What's it to you, mon?' he said.

Again Harper was on the point of saying he was a police officer, but checked himself. In the momentary pause, a flick knife suddenly appeared in the Mohican's hand, its blade pointed dangerously close to Harper's chest.

This time there was no hesitation. Using his combat skill, as he'd done so often, Harper swayed to one side and with the heel of his hand, chopped down on the knife arm, at the same time bringing his knee up into the youth's groin.

The knife clattered to the ground. With a loud howl of pain, the youth bent double, and Harper finished him off with a vicious, scything blow to the back of his neck.

Panting with the exertion, Harper bent down to pick up the knife. As he straightened, he heard a loud screech of brakes. To his relief, a cruising patrol car had pulled up at the entrance to the cul-de-sac, and the two policemen in front were staring at him holding the knife, and the boy on the ground, and in a flash they were out of the car and racing towards him, drawing their revolvers from their holsters.

'It's okay,' Harper shouted, alarmed 'I just disarmed this bastard.'

'Drop the knife, Mister!' said one of the patrolmen, a Sergeant. 'Nice and easy!'

'Anything you say,' Harper replied, tossing the knife back on the ground. 'But stop pointing those guns at me and let me explain.'

They did nothing of the sort, of course, as Harper tried to tell them how he'd seen the two youths thieving and intervened, and how one of them had got away, but he'd dealt with this one. If they checked the car, they'd see it had been broken into. Its radio was somewhere over the wall.

'And just who the hell are you, Mister?' asked the Sergeant. He could tell that they were suspicious over both his accent and appearance. Although Uncle Jimmie had cut his hair, he hadn't had a shave or a shower, his shirt was grubby, his suit even more creased by the fracas. The way he looked, he couldn't really blame these cops for being dilligent.

'I'm a visitor,' said Harper cautiously. 'From England.'

'Doin' what?' asked the Sergeant.

'I'm a sports salesman,' Harper replied, wishing to God he could tell them the truth and clear up matters straight away. But that could land him in even deeper trouble. Maybe even cost him his life.

'Let's see your passport, Mister,' the Sergeant demanded.

'I'm afraid I don't happen to have it on me. It's back in my hotel.'

The Sergeant nodded to his colleague, who was hauling the semi-conscious youth to his feet. 'Right, get him in the car.'

He turned to Harper. 'You, too, Mister.'

'I was trying to help the law and now you're arresting me?' Harper complained, keeping up his pretence of being a plain civilian who believed in having a go.

'We're taking you to the station for questioning,' growled the Sergeant. And if you are telling the truth, let me give you a word of advice. Leave this kind of rough stuff to the cops.'

The only concession to his possible innocence was that he rode in the front with the driver, while the Sergeant accompanied the Mohican in the back.

As they sped towards the centre of town with the siren wailing, they shot through a set of red traffic lights, causing motorists crossing on green at the intersection to curse and swear as they braked sharply, nearly ramming into one another.

One of the vehicles was a battered old American Army jeep.

'Too many goddam American films!' Charlotte shouted.

If she had glimpsed the front-seat passenger in the offending patrol car, she might have given vent to an even louder oath.

Thirty-seven

Charlotte took her jeep over on the ferry to Fort de France, then drove the short distance along Martinique's West Coast to Point Simon, where a minor road, originally hacked out of the tropical rain forest by Jesuits, spiralled upwards into the mountains, past a church that was a startling, small-scale copy of the Sacre Coeur in Paris. The only snag was, apart from its scale, it had suffered from the excessive humidity, and had a permanently mildewed facade that made it just another jungle folly. Its huge, flaking wooden doors were forever bolted.

A mile or so uphill, amid the deep greenery and the colourful splashes of bougainvillea, pink bells and yellow hibiscus, the Convent of St Claire la Bienfaitrice was something entirely different. Even negotiating the hairpin bends and avoiding several tourist coaches by inches, Charlotte felt relaxed and happy, both at the prospect of reuniting with her daughter and returning once again to the place she had lived for almost half her childhood.

Whatever else the Plennard family owned on this French Caribbean island, the convent represented home and, like most homes, however disliked at various stages, it always had a strong, unexpected atmosphere of stability.

She reached the entrance to the road that led to the convent, surmounted by an arch with a crucified plaster Christ with His beard and surprisingly luxuriant chest hair, and a beatific grin, despite the rusty nails in His palms and His painful crown of thorns.

Charlotte remembered how it was always repainted by nuns on ladders, in a ceremony each year, after the rains, giggling as they touched up His loin cloth in pale blue, giving Him a handsome tan, daubing an even deeper blue in His eyes. There was love in the scented air, and the girls always had a picnic by the gates as they watched and said their prayers.

Then they went back to their dormitories with the memory of Jesus, the hippiest man they knew, quite unlike the priests from the town who were fat, boring, somehow not to be trusted either, in word or deed. The clue was in their over-tactile manner, especially to pubescent girls.

Nothing seemed to have changed at the convent since Charlotte's day, not even the songs. As she drove up, the sound of children singing drifted from the music room.

With a 180-degree view of the sea, St Claire nestled on a gentle plateau, an odd conglomeration of Provencal-style buildings with a stark, no-nonsense chapel, living quarters and schoolrooms, surrounded by a playing field that dipped at least ten feet from one end to the other, a single tennis court, and a large, old-fashioned swimming pool.

The pool, whose sides were lined by vulgar, but seemingly indestructible mother-of-pearl tiles, donated by a millionaire French philantropist in the mid-Thirties, was always leaking, but was constantly replenished from a fresh mountain stream through a system of solar heated pipes.

Apparently this ingenious piece of engineering – for its time – had been done by a poor, local plumber, who was a keen Catholic, and the pool was subsequently blessed with much pomp by a visiting Cardinal. But on learning that the man was bigamously married, he quickly ordered his excommunication. The plumber, depressed, promptly murdered both wives and hanged himself at the gates, under his beloved Christ. So much for Christian charity.

Charlotte parked the jeep in a courtyard, and almost at once a familiar voice exclaimed: 'Charlotte! Is that you?'

Mother Superior stood in the chapel doorway. Small and skinny, she must now be in her mid-eighties, Charlotte reckoned, and yet her voice sounded firm and as sharp as ever.

She never forgot a face, not even from a dozen yards away, wearing her half-moon spectacles. She was also as spry and as quick on her feet as she'd always been, scuttling over to greet her.

The old nun kissed her warmly on both cheeks. 'Welcome back, my dear.'

'I should have phoned, but I wanted to surprise Angeline. I hope you don't mind?'

'Not at all. She'll be so happy to see you, as I am.'

Charlotte leaned into the back of the jeep to collect a gift. 'These are for you, Mother Superior.' Because flowers were so abundant in this lush paradise, Charlotte had decided to buy something special – a huge bunch of Moses bullrushes with creamy-white plumes like candyfloss, in a chalice-like pewter vase, a nice ecclesiastic touch, she thought, as she presented them to a delighted Mother Superior.

'How lovely! I know just where these will look their best' she said, leading Charlotte back across the courtyard, pausing for a moment to speak to a passing nun. 'Sister Therese, will you kindly bring Angeline to the chapel? And don't explain why.'

Inside the chapel Mother Superior selected an alcove with a shelf that was too high for her to reach. Charlotte took the vase from her, stretching up to put it in place.

'I'm afraid I shrink every year,' sighed Mother Superior. 'Do you remember when you were smaller and I was taller?'

'Of course I do,' said Charlotte affectionately, adding a tender note: But your face never changes a bit. I remember Angeline said to me, soon after she came here: "Mother Superior is so beautiful". Tell me, how has my daughter been behaving?'

'Oh, living up to her name. A delightful child, just like you used to be.'

'Until I broke the rules,' Charlotte pointed out sombrely.

Mother Superior laid a fond hand on her shoulder. 'And now you're an angel for good in a risky job,' she said gently.

'Maman!' A shriek from the chapel door was followed by running feet, and Angeline, forgetting where she was, and failing to cross herself, hurled herself into Charlotte's arms. If the convent head disapproved of the lapse, she didn't show the slightest hint. Instead her face wore a beatific smile, stepping back and watching mother and daughter hug each other with joy.

'Perhaps you'd like to take her off with you for the rest of the day?' suggested Mother Superior.

As Charlotte approached the front drive of the Chateau Maribeaux, an old man in a straw hat stepped out through an almost theatrical screen of tall sunflowers, hoe over one shoulder, water-hose over the other. Jean-Claude Baptiste, known to everyone as "Bappy", had been a gardener on the estate ever since Charlotte could remember. Though he strenuously withheld his age for fear of being fired, he was in his late eighties, thin and wiry as a Giocometti, still amazingly strong and active. He doffed his hat, a big grin on his lined face.

'Mm'selle Charlotte! Angeline, ma petite!' he exclaimed, in his Creole patois.

'Bappy!' Charlotte shouted, with so many happy childhood memories of this elderly servant, who had taught her to swim, told her all about the flora and fauna, warned her about spiders and snakes and what her bare feet should guard against when she went out into the surf.

'How are you?' she asked warmly.

'Just fine. All the better for seein' you again, Mm'selle,' he said. Angeline made a beeline for him, embracing him, and he swung her off her feet effortlessly.

Charlotte gave Bappy a kiss on his forehead. He held his earthy palms back respectfully, but she reached out and took one of them for old time's sake. His leathery hand felt more secure than her father's ever did.

'The plants are looking very healthy,' she said. 'So are you, Bappy.'

'Too much rain for the crops, though,' he complained, the weather cliché echoing Leon, and practically everyone else who ran banana plantations, where sustained heavy rainfalls could blight the fruit. 'Not like me, parched like hell, Mm'selle!' he added. And she wondered if his longevity still squared with a daily intake of a half bottle of cheap rum.

'Is my brother around?'

'M'sieu Leon's up at the sawmill,' he said. 'He ought to be back soon.'

Charlotte pointed to a bulky package in the back of the jeep. 'Can I ask a favour, Bappy? This is a present from France for Leon. Could you take it round to the rear terrace for me?'

'Certainly, Mm'selle Charlotte.'

'It's quite heavy,' she said, thinking of his age. 'You might need a wheelbarrow.'

'I got one right here,' he said, chucking down the hosepipe and his hoe. 'I'll carry it round there straight away.'

As he fetched the barrow, and Angeline excitedly ran off into the house, Charlotte sat down on the corner of an ornamental stone balustrade, lighting one of her cheroots and taking in the surroundings with a mixture of nostalgia and regret for the rift that had existed between her and her father.

The Chateau Maribeaux, although one of the most imposing mansions on the island, was a mock chateau, being entirely constructed on a wooden frame, with a facade of overlapping white timber tiles. Undeniably in the French style, with its black, mansard roof, pinnacled towers at each corner, elegant, shuttered windows, and pretty, iron lace balconies, covered in a tangle of bougainvillea, it would have been more at home in, say, New Orleans.

The house sat in the middle of a 300-hectare estate in the South-West corner of Martinique, affording a spectacular view of Le Collier Bleu, the beautiful, necklace-shaped lagoon, below. It had been built by Charlotte's grandather, Lucien, at the turn of the century.

When phylloxera wiped out the French grapevines, he gave up wine growing and came to the Caribbean to harvest bananas instead, naming the place after his home village and chateau in Bordeaux. Originally, Lucien Plennard had owned just a hundred hectares, but he had successfully cultivated a lot more land, and subsequently, his son, Jean-Pierre – her father – had added a neighbouring plantation and a mahogany forest to the estate, now under her brother Leon's management.

Sometimes she wondered if she should have gone into the business with Leon when he offered her the chance after their father had died. But the truth was she looked forward to her police career, the sense of purpose it gave her, and the deep feeling of companionship with other police officers that came from frequently risking their lives side by side.

Besides, she'd never really cared for the life of the bourgoisie in Martinique, their social pretensions and their endless gossip. Convent life had removed her from it, and being a cop had completed that divide.

Which reminded her, she must ask her brother a few questions about Raphael Tabard.

But she would have to be careful. Leon was, after all, one of the staunchest members of the French freemasonry on the island.

Thirty-eight

Harper sat alone in a room at Police Headquarters. It was the usual windowless interrogation room, designed to intimidate and dispirit suspects, with the usual crappy furniture – a table and a few chairs, the stale reek of nicotine encrusted in the walls.

They'd sent someone over to the Trade Winds Town House to collect his passport and no doubt to delve among the rest of his things. He was glad he'd kept his Metropolitan Police I.D. tucked in his back pocket. As soon as he'd been left on his own, he'd slipped it into one of his shoes in case they asked him to empty his pockets.

Back in the cul-de-sac, before they got in the car, the patrol Sergeant had frisked him to check if he had any weapons on him other than the apparently incriminating flick knife in his hand. But Harper guessed they might get round to a full body search, unless he could convince them he'd simply been an ordinary passer-by who'd rashly decided to stop the thieves.

After a while, the door was unlocked and a tall, balding detective, impeccably dressed in a cream linen suit, white shirt and tie, entered, holding Harper's passport. He silently motioned Harper to get to his feet. Harper obliged. Without saying a word, the visitor languidly removed his jacket, draped it over the back of a chair, smoothed the collar and checked that the cuffs didn't brush the floor. He undid the strap of his shoulder holster for greater comfort, pulled up another chair and sat down, allowing at least ten more seconds tick by before speaking.

Recognising the old softening-up tactic, Harper stood there, trying hard to suppress a smile.

At length, without inviting Harper to sit, he introduced himself as Detective Sergeant McGeakin, CID.

Same rank and age as himself, Harper reflected, but guessed correctly that any equality, albeit unknown to McGeakin, would end there. There was a glint in this guy's eyes that marked him down as a grade-one listed bastard.

'So, Mister Buchanan, you're from jolly old England?' he said. Harper nodded. McGeakin flipped the pages of the passport. 'With an English name – or should I say Scottish? – like so many of us have. Them Jocks got everywhere!'

Harper gave a faint grin, but made no reply. Two could play at the mute game.

'Were you born here in the Caribbean?'

Harper shook his head.

'No, you don't strike me as the real thing,' said McGeakin with deliberate insult. 'That makes you a foreigner. And foreigners shouldn't go gettin' themselves into trouble, should they?'

Harper just shrugged.

'Your passport says you're a "Representative". You say you travel for a firm making sports equipment. Correct?'

Another nod from Harper. He could see his continued unwillingness to speak was getting to McGeakin. His eyes showed his growing frustration, which he strove to control. 'And yet we find nothing in your hotel room to substantiate this, no catalogues, no order forms or invoices. That demands an explanation.'

Once again Harper merely shrugged. The detective's composure finally snapped. He slammed the passport down on the table. Leaning forward angrily, his eyes turned slightly bloodshot.

'When I ask you a question I expect an answer! A proper fuckin' answer!'

Harper took the opportunity, unbidden, to sit down. 'Alright, you want me to talk, I'll talk, Sergeant. 'I was brought in because of my involvement in a minor street incident, to help you fill out a charge sheet, I thought. Now you're grilling me as if I'm guilty of a crime. How come? What kind of procedure is this?'

Harper realised he'd talked a bit too much like a cop, but McGeakin didn't seem to notice.

'We're not entirely satisfied over the reason for your presence here,' he said.

'My parents were born locally, it's partly a sentimental visit,' Harper replied.

'You're aware of what's been happening on this island?'

'If you mean the political coup, yes.' said Harper. 'Doesn't interest me. None of my business, and I don't really understand it,' he lied.

McGeakin glared at him. 'Coup? Why do you call it that?'

'That's how the UPP takeover's been described,' countered Harper. 'In Europe,' he added, to be on the safe side.

'Well, over here we're rather less sensational about it, more circumspect. We call it a temporary administration due to the present situation regarding our unfortunate Prime Minister,' said McGeakin. 'And we don't want no outsiders comin' in to stir things up, especially the media,' he added suspiciously. 'You follow me?'

Harper gave a disbelieving shake of his head. 'Is that what you think I am? A journalist?'

'You could be. It's our job to assist the government in maintaining a peaceful state of affairs at this difficult juncture.'

His words sounded as if they came straight from a political briefing sheet to a police force co-opted, however unwillingly, into a semi-military role.

British governments, Harper thought to himself, had tried that, too, though it had seldom worked, except for a miner's strike. But in some countries it often followed coups and revolutions.

'I'm warning you, you'd better be who you say you are, Buchanan,' said McGeakin.

'You can rest easy on that account,' said Harper, attempting to introduce a different, less ominous note to the conversation.

'You look like a keen sportsman. Maybe I can interest you in one of our new First Strike cricket bats, handmade of best Kent willow, double spliced and centrally coiled, with a new, shock-insulated, solid grip handle?' he ventured, summoning up a show of professional sales patter derived from his own cricket playing days.

'You wanna know somethin?' I hate fucking cricket,' said McGeakin, getting up and putting on his jacket.

Leon Plennard had come down from the sawmill, driving a massive Canadian truck used for dragging logs. Even in tattered shorts, bush shirt and workboots, he still looked every inch the successful French colonial landowner, lean and fit, in his mid fifties, with a charm that could win him any woman on the island.

He was as handsome as his sister Charlotte was beautiful, and there was a strong family resemblance. Pulling up outside the warehouses next to the chateau, where the unripe green bananas were sorted and stored prior to auction and shipment to Europe, he saw his sister and Angeline laughing and talking with a group of estate employees in the picnic area he had built under the umbrella trees.

For a moment, he felt a slight irritation that everyone wasn't hard at work. Then realised that it was the end of their long day's shift, and jumped out of the snorting monster truck and ran to embrace Charlotte and her daughter.

'Lottie! Angeline!'

You look like a man who's put in a hard day's work,' said Charlotte, brushing dirt off his brow.

'Up in the forest since dawn. We've got a hardwood shipment going out tomorrow to a Dutch company in Curacao. When did you get back?'

'Early this morning. I had to go over to headquarters to file a report and then come back over here to collect Angeline from the convent.'

They walked arm in arm towards the house, Angeline aloft on Leon's shoulders.

'Sorry to leave Paris, were you?'

'Yes and no,' said Charlotte.

'But a successful mission?'

'I learned a lot' she replied non-commitally.

'It's bad enough having a sister who's a cop, but you never tell me anything about what you're doing,' Leon complained.

'I've told you before, Leon, I can't,' Charlotte pleaded. 'But maybe later you can answer a few questions for me.'

Leon looked mystified. 'Me, officer?' he mocked, joining his wrists together as if handcuffed. 'You got the wrong guy,' he joked.

Angeline intervened. 'Maman's got a lovely present for you,'

'Don't you dare say what!' Charlotte chided.

'That's right, keep me in the dark like she does!' Leon laughed.

'Any chance of a swim?' asked Charlotte.

Leon unwrapped the odd-shaped parcel as they sat on the pool terrace watching the brief crimson sunset, Angeline still splashing around in the water.

His present was revealed as a bronze sundial, surmounted by a Greek figure holding a spear that acted as shadow pointer.

'But this is exquisite,' said Leon with delight. 'There's been no sundial here since the old stone one was smashed by one of the hurricanes years ago, remember?'

'It's an antique, it came from a monastery in Limoges. You do like it, I hope?

'Formidable!' said Leon. 'I'll have a plinth built tomorrow, right here on this terrace.

As he held up the heavy sundial, admiring it, Charlotte exchanged a friendly greeting with Claudine, his plain, blonde-haired, middle-aged, French housekeeper, from Gascony, who had wheeled out a trolley with drinks, ready to pour cocktails.

'That's all right, Claudine, I'll mix them myself.' said Leon.

'Shall I prepare supper for three?' she asked. Although she was nowadays his mistress, she maintained a discreet air of subservience.

It always amused Charlotte, who'd secretly known of their liaison ever since her brother's wife had departed.

Charlotte said: 'I'm afraid we can't stay long. I have to get Angeline back to the convent by seven-thirty.'

'I'll make a light snack straight away, then,' Claudine offered. 'Omelette and salad, perhaps?'

Please can I have a hamburger and frites?' pleaded Angeline from the pool.

'Angeline!' said her mother admonishingly.

'Of course she can have a hamburger,' said Claudine, smiling. 'It's what all convent girls pray for!'

In the ensuing laughter, Charlotte ordered her daughter: 'Out of the pool and get dressed! Claudine will help you.'

Leon made them tequilas, salting the rims of two frozen glasses from an ice bucket, pouring soda and the Mexican spirit in heavy measure, squeezing in a dash of lime-juice. He handed her her glass. 'Here's to us, Lottie. Salut!'

'Cheers.'

Leon sat down, running a finger over the bronze Greek warrior on the sundial. 'You have such good taste, ma petite soeur. Now, what were those questions you wanted to ask me?'

'It's about someone I met here once, at one of your parties,' Charlotte answered casually.

'The perfume manufacturer, Raphael Tabard.'

'Is this in the line of duty?' Leon enquired.

'Of course not, I'm just curious about him.'

'You fancy him, is that it?'

'Not at all. He's married.' She sipped her tequila primly, annoyed with herself that she'd got into such a frontal conversation. She'd intended to be much more offhand.

Leon shrugged. 'He's French, like us all.'

'It's simply that I thought I caught sight of him briefly in Paris... at the opera,' she lied.

'Quite likely, since he's often over there. So you do fancy him?', said Leon with a knowing, slightly lascivious grin. 'Underneath that tough cop exterior there's a woman after all.'

She ignored this. 'What sort of person is Tabard? I mean, is he a close friend of yours?'

'Merely a business acquaintance,' said Leon. 'We meet occasionally at Chambre de Commerce lunches and such like. He's a wheeler-dealer, not the toiler-of-the-earth that I am. Very successful, trading in a real growth industry – perfumes, for both sexes.'

'You aren't involved with him, you know... companywise?' she asked.

'If only I was connected with the nouveau riche, Lottie! I could use them,' Leon smiled. 'This estate needs much more investment than the paltry subsidies I get from Paris. Bananas are competing with half the world and hardwoods are bound by strict quotas, thanks to the Green mob. All very ecological, but we're fighting a rearguard action financially.'

Leon finished his drink and went replenish his glass rather too swiftly, Charlotte thought.

'Won't you tell me exactly what it is you're after? These questions about Tabard. It's not personal at all, is it?' he challenged.

'Maybe not. But that's all you need to know.'

Sometimes, thought Leon, he truly disliked his sister being a cop. It put an odd distance between them.

Thirty-nine

When Harper returned to his hotel, the same girl who checked him in earlier was on the reception desk. There was no mention of the police visit to his room, but her expression was positively brimming with curiosity as he asked for his key. What reason had they given, Harper wondered? Probably none, which would only increase speculation among the staff.

'There's someone waiting to see you at the rooftop bar, sir,' she told him, handing him a folded note with the key.

He read it as he rode up in the lift: "Got some news. I think we're on to our man. Uncle Jimmie." So much for keeping things under wraps! Though he had to admit that Uncle Jimmie would have been less enthused if his nephew was selling cricket bats and tennis racquets.

The Trade Winds roof terrace, created as a tropical garden, afforded a panoramic view of the city and harbour. In the cool breeze of early evening, it was a popular drinks rendezvous, and a buzz of conversation from the bar and busy tables met Harper as he stepped out of the lift. To one side of the terrace, a pianist wearing shades was playing at a white baby grand piano, tinkling Cole Porter and Nat King Cole, occasionally vocally imitating the latter.

Leaning on the piano, chatting to him in between numbers, was Jimmie Buchanan. As he saw his nephew reach the bar, he waved and came over to join him.

'Harper, at last! You been takin' in some local colour?'

'In a manner of speaking,' Harper replied, deciding against describing to him events of the past two hours. If he knew the truth, Jimmie would probably turn it in to a shining anecdote to enthrall his barber's shop customers.

'Sorry you've been waiting so long,' Harper apologised.

'No sweat.' Jimmie indicated the pianist. 'Passed the time with my pal, Wilbert. We used to play calypso together.' He dropped his voice an octave. 'You got my note?'

'You could've skipped writing "we're on to our man." It's a phrase – the sort used in a police investigation – that's liable to interest other people,' Harper said drily.

Jimmie winked and led him with a conspiratorial air to a table in a quiet corner. 'We'll be okay here. Don't want us to be overheard, do we?'

'So what did you find out?' asked Harper, as they sat down.

'I got lucky thanks to my friend Murdo.'

'Who's Murdo?'

'Laundry van driver over on Martinique. He does a daily delivery and collection at a place called the Blue Heaven Beach Club, thinks he may have seen your man. Around thirty, mean-looking Frenchman, booked in two days ago.'

'Blond hair in a ponytail?'

'My informant – that's the right police language, ain't it? – well, he couldn't be sure. He's gettin' on a bit, like me. Eyesight ain't so hot these days, and he only saw this bloke with a cap on, so the ponytail could've been underneath,' said Jimmie.

But he added: 'He was drunk on the ruinous rum – you know, the strong-arm stuff. Murdo reckons he's more than likely fair-haired'

'Why?' Harper queried.

'Cos he says he'd suffered really wicked sunburn.'

'He could've been ginger-haired,' Harper suggested.

'Murdo isn't that short-sighted, Harper. He would have spotted red hair.'

Harper summoned a nearby waiter. 'Let me buy you a nice stiff drink, Uncle.'

Jimmie shook hands with the waiter. 'My usual, Eustace. How's the wife?'

'Twins, Jimmie.'

'Again!'

The waiter turned to Harper. 'Sir?'

'Gin and tonic for me, please, Eustace. And congratulations.'

As he left them, Harper shook his head. 'Is there anyone you don't know around here Jimmie?'

Jimmie grinned. 'Not many. Makes keeping – what was it you called it, a low profile? – a bit difficult. So what's your next move?'

'I'll take the ferry over to Martinique in the morning,' said Harper.

'Want me to come with you?'

'Thanks for the offer, Uncle. I'd rather handle this on my own.'

Seeing Jimmie's crestfallen expression, Harper added: 'But I may need you for some more under cover work, okay?'

Eustace delivered their drinks. He had another order on his tray, a bottle of champagne, a jug of fresh lime juice and four glasses, and moved on to a table some distance away. It was in a discreet position, screened off by a wall of foliage from the rest of the terrace and usually booked by such as offshore bankers, when they wanted to do some probably dubious deals, including the notorious Ponzi schemes that had cheated thousands of rich USA investors, and was just part of the dishonest dealing that had all but crippled the whole world financial system.

On this occasion, however, there were four occupants whose business was rather different. They were Maitland Harbinson; Van Molder, the Dutchman, now promoted in the new Administration as chief political adviser; in civvies, Army chief, Colonel Marcel; and their visitor, Raphael Tabard.

They paused in their conversation as the waiter opened the champagne. He poured three glasses from the bottle and a fourth from the jug.

Harbinson picked up his lime juice when the waiter was gone.

'Gentlemen, here's to the successful transition that's been achieved.'

'And to continued prosperity,' Tabard added as they drank the toast. He thought it quite bold for the Acting Prime Minister to choose an off duty venue like this so soon after the coup.

But Harbinson, in a confident mood, argued that the quicker people got used to the change of regime, the better. Besides, there were bodyguards strategically placed around the terrace, and Colonel Marcel had his armed military outside the hotel.

Tabard had been telling them about Maurice Caubec when the waiter interrupted, bringing the drinks.

'So this professional of yours is unfortunately in a holiday mood?' said Harbinson.

Tabard nodded. 'From all accounts sozzled since he arrived.'

'Some choice,' the Colonel remarked scathingly.

'A piss artist and a big-mouth,' Van Molder added, shaking his head. 'That's a bad combination. A security risk.'

Tabard protested, niggled by them: 'It looks like he did his job in London, even if Sir Walter Julien's not quite dead, but obviously finished. And while we're at it, who was handling matters over there, taking risks? I was! All you lot had to do was sit here and wait for results.'

'Alright, take it easy, and keep your voice down,' warned Harbinson. 'Personally, I would have settled his pay-off with Caubec when he returned to Paris.'

'It was wiser to have him quit France immediately, especially now we know there was someone on his tail,' Tabard pointed out. 'It was a damn close call. The shipment was only removed from the farm in the nick of time.'

'Well, you'd better get on and pay our friend Caubec his dues,' Harbinson said. 'We don't want him hanging around any longer, do we?'

Forty

Harper left the hotel early without breakfast, wearing shorts, sandals, and the more colourful of the two shirts he'd had delivered from Aitkens & Jeffrey the day before.

Deciding he didn't look enough like a tourist, he stopped at a gift shop on the way to the ferry, adding a cheap camera and a pair of plastic binoculars to his get-up. He also bought a map of Martinique, which he flourished on the ferry, and in the bus from Fort-de-France, and with the help of another passenger, found out where the Blue Heaven Beach Club was located.

After the driver dropped him off at a bus stop a couple of miles from St.Pierre, he went down a slipway onto the beach. Still too early for holidaymakers, it was deserted, save for a lone fisherman mending his nets by his boat, upturned on a trestle.

As Harper headed along the water's edge in the direction he'd been given, his sandals squelched in black volcanic sand. To his right he could just see the looming shape of Mont Pelee, the sleeping volcano that had erupted over a hundred years ago, spewing its lava down onto the coast, engulfing the old St Pierre, the island's original capital, known as "the little Paris of the West Indies", and wiping out thirty thousand inhabitants.

A few hundred yards on, Harper spotted a faded sign for the Blue Heaven Club, huddled among the palms.

He paused, training his binoculars towards the pool and bar overlooking the beach. Because he was at a lower level he couldn't see much, so he plodded towards a flight of wooden steps leading up to the pool terrace.

He was only a short way from the steps when he heard the loud sound of a police siren from the road above the beach. Moments later a second siren was wailing, and a third. Harper stopped in his tracks. There was the screech of the vehicles pulling up at the club entrance behind the main hotel building, followed by shouting.

Feeling too conspicuous for comfort, Harper swiftly crossed the sand, stepping into a clump of mangroves, where he had a discreet view of the terrace through his binoculars.

Around the edge of the pool stood a small crowd of hotel employees and guests, some of them pretty girls in bikinis. Harper couldn't see what it was they were looking at. A couple of Gendarmes were fixing a tape to keep them back.

And then a group of newly arrived cops exploded into the scene – a gesticulating Police Captain with other uniformed men, and a reddish-haired Creole in plain-clothes who looked like a senior detective, accompanied by a skinny young assistant, and a police photographer. Two ambulance men came hurrying onto the terrace with a stretcher.

Deciding he could join the people around the pool without being noticed, Harper sauntered across to the steps and climbed onto the terrace for a closer look.

It was then that he saw the cause of the commotion.

Floating face down in the pool was Maurice Caubec, in shorts and floral shirt, his blond ponytail bobbing behind his head, in which there was an ugly bullet wound, still oozing blood.

'Looks like the suspect you JIBOC people were searching for,' the Captain was explaining to the Creole detective. 'We thought you'd better come over to this island and see for yourself.'

Harper, on the edge of the crowd, frowned. Who, or what on earth, was JIBOC?

Who found him?' asked Inspector Eddie Carmona.

'Apparently the bartender did, about an hour ago' said the Captain.

Carmona barked a command: 'Alright, lift the body out of the pool. And get rid of the fucking gallery of gawkers,' he said with distaste. 'Except for anyone we need to talk to.'

As the Gendarmes started moving the spectators from the poolside, Harper retreated back down the steps onto the beach, cursing his luck. He'd come all this way for his man, only to find him a waterlogged corpse.

Caubec, the hired assassin, had himself bought it. So did that mean Harper's private mission was ended right there? He had some thinking to do.

Trudging back along the sand, he was sure of one thing, though. It was hardly the moment to reveal who he was and why he'd shown up.

Meanwhile, on the terrace, Carmona was questioning the elderly Chinese bartender, whose wrinkled face was two shades of paler yellow as he watched them haul Caubec from the pool.

'He must have been in there all night,' said the bartender.

'How do you figure that out?'

One of the bikini-clad girls, waiting to be interviewed, butted in: 'He was still sitting out at the bar when we went to bed.'

'Rat-arsed on rum,' said a second girl.

'What time was that?' Carmona queried.

'I closed up at one-thirty,' said the Chinaman. 'Earlier, he told me he was meeting someone, he never said who. But nobody showed up.' he shrugged.

Carmona nodded, ordering his young colleague: 'Take their statements, Ben.'

But the uniformed Captain intervened. 'I think that's our job, Inspector. He may be the man your Bureau was after, but he's a French citizen, murdered on French soil. We must conduct our own investigation, you understand?'

'Oh, sure,' said Carmona. 'Thanks for bringing us in on it.'

'I gather you have an officer who can officially identify him?'

'Yes, he was seen in Paris by one of my team,' said Carmona. 'Where the hell is Sergeant Plennard?'

She's on her way,' said Ben Thomson, as they walked over to where the dead man was being laid out on the stretcher, the photographer busy taking pictures for the record. Even in death, Caubec's face and arms were still a lurid red from his sunburn.

Carmona leaned down to inspect the bullet hole just behind his right ear. 'Shot from behind. A handgun at close quarters,' he said crisply. 'You can see the burn marks.'

'Killer could've crept up on him if he was that drunk?' Ben suggested.

'Careless for a pro. Or else he was talking with someone he knew, and he turned his back on them,' said Carmona.

As he straightened up, Charlotte Plennard came hurrying across the terrace. 'Sorry, I just missed you at the ferry.' She stared down at the body. 'Oh, shit,' she said.

'Maurice Caubec?'

Charlotte nodded. 'Yes, that's Caubec. Pity we didn't catch up with him sooner.'

'We'd have located him eventually, I expect,' said Carmona. 'But why was he plugged?'

'Maybe there was a row about money, or he was threatening blackmail?' Ben offered.

'They probably planned to kill him anyhow,' said Charlotte. 'Put him in this dump, and then dump him.'

'Well, whatever the reason, he's no bloody good to us now,' Carmona complained.

They walked together to the rail overlooking the beach. 'I read your report before we got this call. Feeling recovered from your journey?' he enquired solicitously.

'The flight from Paris was just like a day off,' she joked. 'How was your trip to Port-of-Spain?' she enquired, straight-faced, knowing about the cricket, remembering also that Trinidad was his native island. 'You manage to look up any of your ex-wives and family?'

'Fraid not, much too busy,' said Carmona evasively.

As Charlotte turned away to hide a smile, she caught sight of a solitary figure along the beach. Even at a distance, strolling away from them, she recognised Harper, reacting with shock.

'No, it can't be!' she exclaimed. 'Surely not him?'

Harper had taken only a dozen more strides when there was a shout behind him. 'You! Stop right where you are, hands in the air!'

He halted, stunned, realising the voice was familiar, raising his hands as ordered. Then, slowly, he turned to find Charlotte pointing her revolver at him. The young cop he'd seen at the pool also had his gun out. Harper and Charlotte stared at each other with equal astonishment.

'My God, you certainly get around!'

'That goes for you, too,' said Harper.

'What the hell are you doing in Martinique?'

'Mind if I ask you the same question?' Harper countered.

'This is my home territory,' she answered.

'You never told me that in Paris,' said Harper.

'Search him, Ben.'

Harper recovered from his surprise. He started to lower his arms.

'Keep them up!' Charlotte commanded.

'Couldn't you frisk me, like last time?' he said with a grin.

They marched him back to the Blue Heaven Club and shoved him into the middle of the circular bar for questioning. The others stood outside, with an armed Gendarme blocking the exit.

Harper wondered if he should offer drinks all round.

'Chief Inspector Carmona, JIBOC – Joint Investigation Bureau of the Carribean,' the red-haired Creole detective announced. 'Sergeant Plennard, whom I gather you've met before, is one of my officers.'

'I wish I'd known that,' said Harper, giving her an ironic look. 'I thought there was a curious lilt to her French accent, not to say a sunny complexion you don't often see in dames in Paris,' he added just for fun.

'You've got a lot of explaining to do, Sergeant Buchanan,' said Carmona.

'For a start, surely you don't think I shot the guy?' Harper replied. 'I wanted him alive, and you know damn well why.'

'We wanted him alive too, to find out who hired him,' Charlotte pointed out.

Carmona added sternly: 'Instead of which we have now ground to a fucking halt.'

Oh, come on, you can't blame me for finding Caubec floating in that pool!' Harper retorted.

'Maybe not, but it seems you messed up Operation Hurricane, and now you come threatening to louse things up over here,' snapped Carmona. 'Added to which, you're under a suspension! I understand you were told to mind your own business and stay in London?'

'Look, the bullet that hit Sir Walter Julien was my business! And my failure, if you like,' Harper argued.

For a moment, Charlotte felt herself in sympathy.

'We're fellow cops, we understand how you feel about that,' she said, a little to Carmona's annoyance.

Despite everything, she still found Harper attractive. He was cultivated, obviously unafraid of danger, even if he was a damn nuisance! She'd even enjoyed some of their verbal sparring in Paris – in remarkably good French in his case.

Then she thought: how dare he say he detected what he called some kind of presumably Caribbean 'lilt' in her own voice!

'Maybe we understand, but that doesn't give you the right to keep crossing our path,' she said brusquely.

Harper shrugged. 'As I see it, our paths have converged anyhow. Twice.'

'Listen, Buchanan, get it into your head. We're handling matters here in our own way,' Carmona told him sternly. 'I'm sending a report to London. For your own good I'd advise you to buzz off home. You got that?'

Forty-one

The health clinic was only a short car ride from the Sussex Downs to the coast. Although it had been recommended that he stay indoors, Emilie Julien had arranged to take her husband, who was recovering quite quickly from his gunshot wound, for a brief outing. An ambulance deposited them at Beachy Head, and Emilie pushed Sir Walter in a wheelchair along the grassy clifftop.

She found a bench where they sat looking out to sea. It was a blustery day, but they enjoyed the famous view over the English Channel, despite the fact that it was the choice location for suicides, and there was a notice from the Samaritans to try and save them at the last minute.

'The sea, even this choppy grey one, makes me feel quite homesick,' said Sir Walter. 'Nothing in the newspapers about our island?' he asked.

'Not a line,' said Emilie.

'Too much going on in the rest of the world to bother about our little corner of the Caribbean. The financial collapse, Obama's presidency and all that. Good luck to him. Have you found out from Barbados how the kids are making out?'

'My sister says they're fine,' said Emilie. Knowing you're alive is all that matters for now,' she reassured him, tucking a tartan rug around him, against the strong Channel breeze.

'I still have a heart operation to go,' he sighed.

'That's nothing after what you've been through, Walter,' she said briskly, intent on keeping his spirits up.

'Or what's going to happen if I suddenly come to life again,' he said glumly.

She was about to reply, when their peaceful idyll was interrupted by a shout from along the cliff path. Approaching them, in agitated strides, was the Hon Jonathan Walmsley. Since it was the weekend, he wore green wellies, a tailored check jacket and tweed cap. He had a large black Labrador on an expanding lead.

'There you are!' he said as he reached them. 'For heavens sake, what are you doing out here? You're supposed to be in hiding.'

'A breath of sea air can't do any harm,' said Emilie. 'To what do we owe the pleasure?'

Walmsley, who was rather put out to leave his family and Sunday lunch and drive to Sussex, sat down on the bench. The dog hauled his lead out to go and snuffle in a litter bin across a grassy knoll.

'We've had an alarming report from the Caribbean,' said Walmsley, removing his cap.

'Oh, nothing to do with Harbinson and the situation on your island. No, it's about your friend Sergeant Buchanan.'

'Harper?' said Sir Walter, sitting up, intent.

'Yes, the confounded fellow has turned up out there, causing no end of problems,' said Walmsley. 'Off his own bat he was on the trail of the hitman, an ex-French Legionnaire, who flew to Martinique. Now he's been murdered.'

'Oh my God, Harper's dead?' said Emilie, horrified.

'No, I didn't mean Buchanan, I meant the gunman,' said Walmsley. 'Snuffed out, we assume, by the people who paid him to come and take a shot at you.'

'But Harper is safe?' asked Sir Walter concernedly.

'Sergeant Buchanan is very unsafe, that's the whole point,' Walmsley said. 'He's the one man in the Caribbean who knows you're still not in a coma, very much alive.'

'He said he'd been told to take a holiday. Is that not what he's doing?' said Sir Walter.

Walmsley frowned, detecting a note of approval in the Prime Minister's voice: 'Did you know he'd left London?'

'No, but I believe Harper is a good man, and trustworthy. He won't spill the beans,' Sir Walter replied.'

'If he did, he'd be setting you up as a target again. For your sake, we want him out of there,' said Walmsley.

Forty-two

It was a glorious Caribbean morning, with a sky as blue as the sea, and barely a twitch in the palm trees. But Harper felt rather dejected as he ate breakfast on the hotel terrace. Apart from tracking down a killer, there was so much he'd wanted to see on his first visit here.

Now he had a seat booked on tonight's British Airways flight to Heathrow. He'd spent the rest of the previous day buying a few presents to take home, and arranged a farewell lunch with Uncle Jimmie, who expressed keen disappointment at his sudden departure. Explaining that his own investigation was effectively concluded with the death of Caubec, Harper omitted to mention that he was being kicked off the island, not just by JIBOC, but also by Special Branch.

Chief Superintendent Norris had personally phoned him, leaving him in no doubt what his future would be if he didn't obey orders and return to London at once.

He was ordering fresh coffee when, to his suprise, he saw he had a visitor.

Charlotte Plennard was wearing a loose white cotton trouser suit and high heels, her sleek dark hair set in a more feminine style than usual. A satin bag was slung casually over one shoulder, and he saw that her nails were painted, which he'd never noticed before. As she gave him a wave and made her way over to his table, he thought how much more glamorous she looked when she wasn't playing her tough cop role. So what the hell did she want?

He got to his feet. 'Don't tell me I'm in deep shit again with the local constabulary?'

'I checked and found out you were still around.'

'It's okay, you can stop worrying. I'll be gone by midnight,' he assured her.

She fished a pack of cheroots out of her bag. There was a pause while she searched for her lighter. 'Please, this is a friendly call. I haven't had a real chance to talk to you.'

'That so?' said Harper drily.

'I mean, I'm sorry the way things have backfired on you. Perhaps I've been a little less than polite.'

'You've been as sweet as pie.'

Finding her Zippo at last, she lit up. 'How about me buying you Sunday brunch?'

'I've just had breakfast,' said Harper. 'And I've arranged to have lunch with my uncle. You're welcome to join us.'

'Thanks, I'd like that. But I ought to tell you I have a companion in my car. My daughter.'

Harper tried to hide his surprise. Somehow he didn't think of her as a married woman.

She read his mind: 'Cops do have children, you know. Angeline is just ten. Her father, who was my boyfriend, is dead. Come and meet her. If you like, we could fill in the time before lunch by driving around the island.'

Harper said warily: 'Is this the white flag?'

'No, just the French flag,' she replied.

Charlotte had brought Angeline over for the weekend from her Martinique convent, as she always tried to do.

They went on brief scenic tour of some of the island's more beautiful bays and inlets. Harper sat in the front of the jeep, as she drove fast but confidently on the winding, pot-holed roads. In the back, Angeline sat with her Nintendo. Harper, who'd wanted children of his own, thought she was enchanting, like a little bon-bon and just as eatable.

'What's your game?' he enquired.

'Grand Prix,' Angeline beamed. 'I'm leading by one and a half laps.'

'So's your mother, I think,' said Harper ruefully, as Charlotte took a bend, tyres squealing.

'I'll have you know I did a police driver's advanced course in Paris,' she retorted. 'This uncle of yours…?'

'You'll like him. His name's the same as mine, Buchanan. Jimmie Buchanan.'

Charlotte turned her head with astonishment. 'You mean *the* Jimmie Buchanan?'

'As of today I can say yes, that Jimmie Buchanan,' sighed Harper. 'Before now, I've tried to disguise the connection when I could.'

'I have all his calypso records. He's famous. Okay, where are we going? Where's lunch?'

'Runaway Bay?'

'Oh, splendid! That's where the British fought the French for the ownership of this island.'

'Who won?'

'You did. Well, the lords and masters of the time.'

'We're due at some place called the Green Hat. I gather it's quite primitive.'

'Great! I know it. Nice and relaxed,' Charlotte enthused.

From the backseat there came a tinny sound from the Nintendo, a screeching of brakes and a crash. 'You alright?' Harper asked Angeline.

'Me? Yes, but Lewis Hamilton is out of it. He lost a tyre and crashed into the chicane.'

The Green Hat, a painted shack on a remote beach, with a few fishing boats hauled up on the sand, was busy, noisy, wreathed in barbecue smoke. A popular eating place at weekends.

A decking terrace, covered by a bamboo awning, served as the restaurant area. Charlotte pulled into the car park behind the shack, to the sound of a steel band.

Outside, a gang of youthful crap players were hunched in the sand over the dice, a row of rum bottles beside them. One of them made a throw, claimed a win, starting a loud argument. It quickly developed into a brawl, and as Harper got out of the jeep to watch one of the boys collect his winnings, he saw a switchblade flash in the sunlight.

Christ, not again!

'Nice and relaxed, did you say?' Harper reminded Charlotte.

He motioned for her and her daughter to stay where they were, and walked over to the group. The challenger had a knife wielded dangerously close to the throat of the winner, held by a muscled ape with a neck like Mike Tyson.

'Don't act foolish, put that knife away,' said Harper gently.

The knife-wielder swivelled his eyes at Harper in mock puzzlement. 'Beg pardon, mon?' he said

'You heard me, lay off with the knife.'

Now they all turned to study Harper.

Another boy said: 'Listen to the mon, Lindsay! Kindly remove your lethal weapon from Mistah Wallace's throat, mon!' provoking shrieks of laughter from the others, except for the guy with the blade at his throat, whose eyes were still popping out, bright with fear.

'Do as I say, if you've any sense,' Harper said sternly.

'Oh, do-do-do as he says, mon,' chorused two of them.

'What's it, with that fancy fucking English accent?' said the one with the knife.

As Harper was about to tell him, a voice cut in sharply. 'He means it... drop the knife. Police!'

Charlotte was on the edge of the circle, gun in hand. As they stared at her, she flashed her badge.

'He's a cop, too,' she said, indicating Harper.

Then she let them have it, verbally, in a torrent of fluent Creole, some of it, Harper could tell, really coarse language. The effect on them was immediate. The heavyweight dropped the knife to the ground and all of them shuffled back a few paces, looking sheepish.

Harper picked up the knife. 'Thanks, Sergeant,' he said to Charlotte, then turned to address the group. 'I'd say you guys are lucky this lady's in one of her better moods.'

Uncle Jimmie hadn't shown up yet, but he'd thoughtfully booked a table right on the edge of the beach where they could practically curl their toes in the sand.

The clientele, mostly families, was mixed, both in race and class, and there was a general air of fun and the smell of good cooking. Some people were dancing to the music. Benjie, the owner, wore a green bowler hat, hence the name of the place.

Angeline went off to play a pinball machine with a few other kids, and they listened to the band while they ordered a pre-lunch cocktail, a house speciality: crushed ice, pineapple juice and green chartreuse, generously spiked with rum, and called, for some reason Harper couldn't fathom, a Fish Outa Watta.

He raised his glass. 'From one cop to another, Sergeant. Here's to an unexpected send-off.'

'Shall we forget the cop stuff? It's Sunday, and I'm Charlotte down here on the beach.'

'Okay, Charlotte.'

'As I said, you've had a bit of a rough ride, Harper.'

'Your boss came over a bit heavy,' he said. 'After all, I was only trying to run down that bastard Caubec.'

'Eddie Carmona has a hot Creole temper sometimes,' she replied. 'Spanish blood, with a touch of Irish, in case you didn't know.'

'I wondered where the red hair came from. Chip on his shoulder because of his complexion?' Harper asked.

'We all have chips of one kind or another,' said Charlotte. 'But let me tell you, he's a gem of a man to work with. A little unorthodox maybe, but one of the best.'

'Well, you've cleared up a mystery for me – JIBOC,' Harper said. 'I couldn't quite fix you as a bunch of routine police. Carmona from Trinidad, a guy from some other island, and you, a home-grown product of Martinique. So what is this outfit?'

'We're island hoppers, backed by a federation of states, including the British, French, and Dutch administered islands, and the Americans,' she explained. 'Our team tackles the wider-based crimes, especially drugs. A bit like Interpol in Europe. That's why we were called in when they found Caubec floating.'

'You don't strike me as being the usual sort of cop, even from a French island, Charlotte,' said Harper. 'Seems to be a bit of extra polish to you. Were you born out here?'

'Yes, my family owns estates on Martinique and Guadeloupe.'

'Born rich? That accounts for it!' he grinned. 'So how come you-' but he broke off, realising from her expression that she wasn't amused.

'I'd rather not get into it, if you don't mind,' she said curtly.

'Let's order another Fish Outa Watta, since that's exactly what I feel like,' Harper said a little lamely.

They'd almost finished their second drink when Jimmie Buchanan arrived. There was much high-five hand-slapping with Benjie, who doffed and twirled his green bowler, then greetings from waiters and customers before he finally reached their table.

'Hey, sorry I'm late.' He gave Charlotte a winning smile. 'But I see you haven't been stuck for company, Harper.'

'Uncle Jimmie, this is Charlotte Plennard.'

Jimmie's smile became even broader. 'Plennard? Then you must be Jean-Pierre Plennard's daughter, the one who decided to become a cop?'

Harper gave Charlotte a shrug. 'Didn't I tell you? Nobody's safe – he has ears like satellite dishes.'

'And a voice like a heavenly hummingbird,' said Charlotte.

'My, ain't you got good taste, Harper!' said Jimmie, pleased. 'Just an old has-been now, though.'

'Won't you sing one number at least?' asked Charlotte, indicating the band.

'Well, now that you mention it, the boys did ask me to do something with them,' said Jimmie. 'Why don't you two go ahead and order lunch? You want me to work you folks into the lyric?'

Harper shook his head uneasily. 'No thanks, Uncle. But her daughter would like it, I bet,' he said, pointing out Angeline.

As they tucked into a bowl of fresh mahi mahi seasoned with spices and chillies, Jimmie, with easy professionalism, entertained the customers. Angeline, propped up beside him on a steel drum, clapped her hands excitedly in time, as he cleverly concocted verses rhyming with her name.

Charlotte's off duty mood and two cocktails made her an even more delightful companion. If she was in London, he thought to himself, I'd want to date her plenty. Yet sadly, this was a goodbye lunch.

She caught his look. 'One way and another you're full of surprises' said Charlotte. 'First your untimely appearance in Paris, then you show up here, and on top of that you turn out to be Jimmie Buchanan's nephew.'

'I enlisted his help. Sir Walter Julien is a good friend of Jimmie's,' Harper said. 'I wish I could have cracked the case for them both.' He wondered if he should tell her the truth about Sir Walter, then decided better not.

'We're banking on Maitland Harbinson getting careless. We're damn sure he's part of the drug syndicate among other things,' said Charlotte.

'How about this perfume merchant who doesn't smell so good?'

Chartlotte shrugged: We're pretty certain Raphael Tabard was responsible for Caubec's murder, but it's another matter proving it.'

Harper looked thoughtful. 'Tell me, have you tried getting right up close to them?'

If you mean do we have undercover informers, yes. We've a network all over the West Indies,' said Charlotte.

'No, I meant using somebody to draw them out. As you said, make them careless.' Harper paused. 'Somebody like me, for instance.'

Charlotte lit a cigar: 'What are you suggesting? That you become some kind of bait?

'It would make amends for Paris, wouldn't it?' Harper said.

Forty-three

After a long, convivial lunch at the Green Hat, Charlotte, accompanied by Harper, had returned Angeline to the convent, then they ferried back from Martinique. She used her mobile to make a phone call, and drove the jeep to Carmona's plantation bungalow in the middle of the island, explaining en route her boss's domestic arrangements. Since it was the weekend, his two "wives" would be there.

'Sounds nice and cosy. Some guys have all the luck,' said Harper.

Charlotte smiled. 'I told you he was unorthodox. *Vive le sandwiche!*' she said coolly, and rather sexily.

Once again Harper savoured the way she was willing to switch her manner today from being the tough, laconic cop, to a teasing, French femininity. He admired both, thinking to himself that he'd never share someone like her with anybody.

Carmona, though clearly dubious at being confronted by Harper on his own doorstep, greeted them courteously, introducing his two companions without a trace of embarrassment. Inez served them tea on the verandah, while Margot, a keen artist, got on painting flowers in the garden, looking every inch the schoolmarm at her easel.

'Let me get this straight. You're suggesting you pose as a drug dealer?' said Carmona.

'Why not? Caubec's the only person who could identify me, and he's dead.'

'How about this uncle of yours?'

Harper assured him: 'I'll keep the lid on Jimmie.'

'If you don't, they'll pick you off like Caubec,' said Carmona. 'What gave you this notion?'

'It was Harper's own idea,' Charlotte said firmly. 'He's willing to risk his own neck, which speaks for itself.'

'I have a score to settle, remember,' said Harper. 'All I have to do is put it about that I'm a new dealer, looking for a stash, with my own method of shipping the stuff back to England.

'Flush out and arrest Tabard, and you might do a deal with him to spill the beans on the others.'

'Suppose they don't swallow it?' Carmona said. 'They're bound to check you out.'

'If Special Branch agrees, they can come up with references from a couple of inside men, London drug dealers – Yardies – on the police payroll.'

'I think it could work,' said Charlotte.

Carmona frowned. 'Not so fast. How about the little matter of cash to pay for the drugs?'

Harper shrugged. 'Surely you can fix that?'

For a moment Carmona chewed his lip, then turned to Charlotte.

'Okay, let's say Harper tries to make an approach to the syndicate. He can't just present his visiting card!'

'Then it's a job for our special mole, isn't it?' she said.

Eddie Carmona's request for Harper to remain in the Caribbean for the time being caused a flutter in London, as Harper guessed it would. The Commonwealth Office and Jonathan Walmsley freaked out, of course.

But Norris pointed out that if Harper were to help undermine the new regime, it would be a feather in everyone's cap, including Walmsley's. Thus far, the truth about Sir Walter had remained a tight secret, even from JIBOC, so what was to be lost?

Twenty-four hours later, a taxi picked Harper up at his hotel and took him to the outskirts of town. The driver introduced himself as Joe Guarnac, a detective from the Bureau. They arrived at a small, brightly painted chapel, which was apparently Carmona's choice as a regular undercover meeting place.

Harper would be contacted here by their drug trade mole, explained Guarnac, who, for appearances, charged him a fare and drove off.

Harper glanced at the Pentacostal notice board outside the chapel, with "Jesus Saves – Have a Godly Day", painted on it, along with the name of the pastor, The Rev Eugene Gwilt. There was a notice tacked up for a special prayer virgil "for the recovery our dear brother, Sir Walter Julien", held the previous day. Through the open front door he could hear the sound of an organ playing.

Looking around in the street, seeing no one about, Harper decided to step inside.

At the organ sat a sparrowy little woman, singing a hymn softly to herself. There were vases of flowers all around her, and it looked like she'd paused in her floral arrangements to put in a bit of practice, pumping the foot bellows of the ancient organ with surprising stamina. As Harper sat down in a pew, she smiled at him and went on playing.

After listening to her for a few minutes, Harper decided that his contact was possibly waiting outside, so he got up and went out into the street. A few cars passed, but nobody stopped. Then a solitary figure could be seen jogging towards the chapel in a tracksuit. Bald-headed, with a fearsome black beard, he eyed Harper speculatively, running on the spot.

'You aimin' to pray, brother?' asked the man.

'Not at the moment,' was all that Harper could think to reply. Was this his man?

'Well, think about it,' the Reverend Gwilt recommended as he loped on into his chapel.

A few moments later Harper, seated on a wall, heard the sound of an approaching car and the increasingly loud waft of Country and Western music from its radio.

Heading along the street came a 1950s Pontiac open tourer, beautifully restored, cream and maroon, with shining chrome and white-walled tyres. At the wheel, dressed in jeans and a buckskin jacket, sat an ageing cowboy with long grey hair flowing from under his stetson. Chewing gum and talking into a mobile phone at the same time, he ended his call as he neared the chapel, pulling up in a cloud of dust.

Turning down the music, he leaned out: 'You Buchanan?' he enquired in a Texan drawl.

'That's me,' said Harper warily.

'Hop in. Ah'm the feller you came to meet,' he said.

As Harper got in, his contact gunned the Pontiac away without bothering to introduce himself or shake hands. He shot a ball of chewing gum into the car's slipstream.

'Word is you're lookin' hereabouts for some merchandise. That so?'

'Might be,' said Harper.

'All the way from ol' London Town, huh?'

Harper nodded. 'You know how to get this merchandise?'

'Ah sure do!'

'You can sell me some?' Harper asked.

'Hell, no,' said the driver. 'Me, ah'm just the go-between, the broker man, so long's there's commission in it. Name's Floyd Kinthly,' and this time shook hands.

'Let's go see a guy who knows another guy who handles the kinda stuff you're lookin' for.'

And he turned up the Country and Western again, whistling mournfully along with Kenny Rogers' *Don't Fall in Love With a Dreamer*, and saying not another word, as they drove southwards along a coast road.

About five miles further on, the Texan turned off the main road and headed inland, up a steep incline until they sighted what appeared in the distance to be a small cluster of colourful houses on hillside terraces.

As they covered the last half mile, however, Harper saw that it was a miniature township of the dead – a sprawling Caribbean cemetery of mausoleums and gravestones of all shapes and sizes, ornately decorated, mainly in chequered black and white, with photographs of the departed, wrought iron gates and roofs topped by religious statues and marble crosses.

'Welcome to Tombstone City,' Kinthly grinned.

He parked the car by the entrance gate, and they mounted a long flight of steps, climbing up through the cemetery.

It was hard going in the harsh, mid-morning sunshine, and as they paused for breath half way up, two men suddenly materialised from behind graves on either side of them. Both were levelling machine pistols.

But the Texan, unperturbed, greeted them cheerfully. 'Howdy, fellas! Rest easy, Charlie's expectin' us.'

The armed men escorted them up the steps and into a glade covered by an arched roof of two huge Jacaranda trees hugging each other, draped with liana creeper.

'Mornin,' Charlie.'

'Mornin,' Floyd.'

It took a moment or two for Harper's eyes to adjust to the contrasting greenish light in the glade.

And then he saw Charlie, a grotesquely fat character wearing only a pair of shorts, who must have weighed over three hundred pounds. He was like the genie out of the bottle, his vast bulk stretched out on an outsize hammock. A battery fan was cooling him.

'This is Harper Buchanan, the customer I called you about,' said Floyd Kinthly.

'Good day to you, Mister Buchanan. Come into the office and take a seat,' wheezed Charlie, gesturing to a flat gravestone near him.

Harper looked around with astonishment. In the glade, where there were more flat-topped graves, a complete out-of-doors "office", together with a portable generator and satellite dish, had been set up. A secretary was busy at a laptop computer, with files and printer beside her, and another girl was conducting a mobile phone conversation, various letters and invoices spread out on her "desk" before her.

On neighbouring gravestones there were coffee flasks and cups, food, beer cans in a picnic cold box, and bottles of rum.

'I understand you want to place an order?' Charlie said.

'Depends on what you've got,' Harper replied, sitting down.

Charlie lit up a large Havana, rocking gently in his hammock, which looked like it was made of marine nylon rope. 'Well, now, first of all it depends on a lot of things. Such as why you didn't get in touch with us in advance?'

I was down in Trinidad trying to do a deal, but it blew out,' Harper said.

Charlie took a beer from Kinthly, who also handed one to Harper.

'Listen, you don't want to do business with that lot,' he said. 'They're selling shit. We can supply the top grades, right up to the very best Colombian.'

'Yeah, that's what I heard.'

'However, you won't mind telling me who you were dealing with?' Charlie enquired evenly.

Harper gave him a cynical look. 'You don't expect me to reveal that, do you? It breaks the rules.'

'Fair enough, but you understand before we go any further, we'd need to test your credentials.'

'No problem there, Charlie,' Kinthly intervened. 'Here's two of his main London retailers, both of them known to us,' he said, handing over a slip of paper.

'Why not call them personally?' suggested Harper.

'I will, if you don't mind,' Charlie said, giving the paper to one of his assistants. 'My board of directors insist on clearance before any transactions.'

Harper nodded: 'Very proper.'

'You have the necessary funds?,' asked Charlie.

'I can draw immediately on an account in the Caymans, enough for the supplies I need,' Harper said briskly.

'By the way, I'm impressed by your office arrangements,' he added.

'Oh, I run several of these al fresco establishments. No overheads, you see, and it's a healthy, outdoor life.'

'Robin Hood must've felt the same way,' said Harper. 'Except you're built more like Little John.'

Charlie liked that. His chuckle grew into a deep, rippling belly laugh, almost tipping him out of his hammock.

Forty-four

Harper had managed to switch to another room at the Trade Winds, one with a verandah and sea view, but even so he felt cooped up. Two days had passed and there was no news, though he was confident the check they would run on him in London would give Charlie and his friends the right answers.

While they awaited the next move from the drug syndicate, Eddie Carmona ordered Harper that there should be no direct contact with JIBOC. Harper hadn't explained the latest development to Uncle Jimmie, who would assume he'd already flown home.

To break the monotony, he'd wandered around town twice, visited the museum, had several swims in the hotel pool. The rest of the time he filled in viewing the local television channel.

As he ate a room service supper of fried squid, he watched Maitland Harbinson delivering one of his frequent addresses to the public, live from Government House. Seated at a large desk in the Prime Minister's office, he appealed for continued calm and co-operation following, as he put it, 'the tragedy that has befallen our island nation.'

It was was the first time that Harper had actually seen Harbinson in action.

The UPP leader was giving a smooth performance, adopting his academic air, which meant occasionally removing his glasses and running his hand through his unruly hair – Harper decided he must have a regular date with the hot tongs – and leaning forward intimately into the camera now and then to invest his remarks with greater sincerity.

'The aim of our acting legislation is first and foremost to maintain stability, and especially to create, as soon as possible, an upturn in our economy for the benefit of all, but especially for the unemployed, the elderly, and those who are sick or disabled,' he intoned suavely. 'I know that this would be the wish of our much-loved Prime Minister, still, alas, in a coma. As we pray for his recovery, all of us must strive to do our bit for the common good, as he would wish.'

Harper was reminded of the way politicians back at Westminster spoke. Same old spin-stuff. He switched off and finished his supper, idly wondering what Charlotte Plennard would be doing at this moment.

After she'd driven him back to his hotel, she'd given him her mobile number and the phone number of her apartment. Just in case of any emergency, she'd said. But he recalled speculating at the time whether she might have meant otherwise. Should he take a chance and call her, maybe invite her out for a drink?

After all, if the JIBOC people were supposed to be undercover cops, what was wrong with meeting privately and discreetly like they did at the weekend?

He got out his book and reached for the phone.

Her recording machine answered, but as soon as he started to leave a message, Charlotte switched it off and spoke: 'Harper, how are you?'

'I'm fine,' he said, 'I hope you don't mind me getting in touch?'

'Not at all. Have you had any reply to your… business proposition?' she asked, choosing her words carefully, in case anyone might be listening on his hotel switchboard.

'No, not yet. Look, the truth is I'm bored out of my mind, and I wondered if maybe we could have a drink somewhere?'

'I'm afraid I can't tonight,' Charlotte replied. 'I already have an engagement.'

Harper felt a slight twinge of jealousy. It sounded like a date. 'Oh, right, I was just phoning on the offchance that you might be free.'

There was a pause, then Charlotte said: 'Tell you what, I've a day off tomorrow. Are you a good sailor?'

When his television appearance was over, Maitland Harbinson dictated some memos to a secretary and went to his private quarters to have dinner, prepared by his manservant, Simeon, who told him that Frank Van Molder had arrived.

'Alright, show him in, but don't suggest setting another place,' said Harbinson, who had never enjoyed sharing a meal with his political colleague. The sight of those pink eyes and pale albino lips always put him off his food.

Van Molder was full of praise for Harbinson's latest screen lecture. The daily telecast to the populace had been his idea.

'You were splendidly convincing, Maitland, particularly with that phrase about the wishes of our much-loved Prime Minister,' he said.

'I have to win an election soon,' said Harbinson drily.

'So everyone must be put in the picture! The UPP must create air of keen anticipation – what's on our agenda, and so on. And, of course, there are certain people who have to be kept sweet,' the Dutchman advised.

'We're still doleful about what's happened to Sir Walter.'

Van Molder nodded. 'Naturally. But they aren't. We owe them one. Without their backing, there would've been no coup.'

'They'll get their various perks in due course, as we'll get ours,' said Harbinson.

Simeon had brought a huge seafood platter to the table, oysters, flying fish, stuffed lobster and land crab, stewed conch and curried Bajan prawns, all of it nestling in a bed of crushed ice. Pointedly he'd set down only one plate, and as Harbinson tucked in heartily he enjoyed the sight of the other man salivating.

'The point is, our partners are insisting on an early meeting,' Van Molder said.

'Not on our island,' Harbinson replied firmly. 'We can't afford to take any chances at this stage.'

'Can I tell your secretary to look at your diary?' Van Molder asked.

'Do that,' said Harbinson, pouring himself chilled lime juice from a pitcher. 'You look thirsty. Can I order you a drink?' he enquired with total insincerity.

Forty-five

In perfect yachting weather, bright sunshine and a nice breeze, *La Moqueuse* was bowling along at a comfortable five knots. Earlier, as the 32-foot jade-hulled Westerly Consort slipped her mooring on Cinnamon Quay, Harper realised it was hardly surprising that a girl with Charlotte's temperament and background would turn out be a skilful yachtswoman.

Delegated the simple task of taking the wheel in open water, he stood in the transom watching with admiration the way she moved around nimbly, barefoot, expertly using the winches to trim the mainsail and jib, hauling in fenders, tightening one of the stays, and checking bits of deck equipment she hadn't used for several months since she'd been in Europe. She looked stunning. Her dark hair was held back in a piratical red headband, and she wore a white singlet and tattered beachcomber cut-downs that showed off her long brown legs.

'Bring her around a few degrees, gently, towards the shore,' she yelled.

Harper complied with her command, rather too sharply in the event, causing Charlotte to duck in the nick of time as the sail snatched at the the wind and the jib boom whipped over, nearly scalping her.

'Shit, I'm sorry!' Harper shouted apologetically. 'You okay?'

She came astern to join him, fetching a bottle of the finest rum from a locker. 'Don't worry, you'll get the hang of it,' she said, taking a nip from the bottle and handing it to him. 'Nautical medicine. Insulates you against all weathers.'

Harper grinned and had a slug. He sat back enjoying the view as she took over the wheel, lighting one of her cheroots. The mountain range, dominated by the Two Anvils, was to starboard, the whole coastline spectacularly beautiful, looking much as it must have done to sailors over three centuries ago.

Somehow the dangers of police work, political coups and drug trafficking seemed very far away at that moment. Even more so did the streets of South London.

'You're very quiet. I hope you're unwinding?' said Charlotte.

'Chillin' out, honey, just fine,' Harper replied jokily. 'I was thinking I don't know many cops who own a yacht.'

'Inherited from my father. My one and only luxury.'

'When I asked you the other day how you came to join the police force, you clammed up. Why?'

Charlotte gave a shrug. 'Oh, my past is no great secret. I expect you could've got a complete run-down on me from your Uncle Jimmie,' was her wry answer.

'Only I didn't ask him,' Harper said. 'I'd rather you tell me, if you want to.'

As they cleared the tip of the island and headed for Martinique, Harper listened while she filled him in on her childhood, her expulsion from the convent, her elopement to New York with the man who fathered Angeline, and the sad ending which forced her return.

'Now I know why you can dish it out, why you're such a good cop,' he said.

'Except when I disobey orders,' said Charlotte.

'Like I do, you mean?'

'Eddie Carmona would have a fit if he knew where I was right now! I've told you all about me. How about you? Are you married?'

'Divorced.'

'You must be good to reach your rank,' she said.

Harper smiled. 'Why don't you say it? You mean... for a West Indian in London?'

'Well, there aren't many detective sergeants there like you, are there?' asked Charlotte, giving him a level look.

'Maybe one less when I get back – when they bust me.'

Charlotte laid a hand gently on his arm. 'Harper, I want you to know something, I loved the guy I went to America with. I don't have any hang-up about skin colour, and I find you very attractive.'

'The feeling's mutual,' said Harper. He wanted to take her in his arms there and then, but instinctively he knew it might be the wrong move.

'If things were different...' she gave a little shrug, spontaneously reading his mind. 'If we weren't tied in on a case together.'

'And when it's over?' he queried softly.

'I expect you'll be on your way back to England.'

'I won't be hurrying,' he said calmly.

Charlotte made no reply, turning her attention instead to the tricky task of navigating the yacht through a narrow deep-water channel into Le Collier Bleu lagoon. On the way in, she pointed out the Plennard family seat on the hillside above.

Harper gazed up at the imposing Chateau Mirabeaux and surrounding estate. 'Don't you ever miss your little old homestead?' he asked drily.

Charlotte slung the kedge anchor over the side with a splash. 'Working cops are out of place in colonial mansions,' she retorted.

Forty-six

'A real fancy office you got here, Rafe. Not that I'd ever go in for this sort of luxury! What is it you say in French? *Jamais peter plus haute que votre derriere* – never fart higher than your arse.'

This was followed by a vulgar rumble of laughter that unnervingly also threatened an unpleasant trumpet of flatulence.

Tabard sat behind his desk, eyeing his visitor with some distaste. Among other things, being called Rafe annoyed him. Only his wife called him that, and he regarded this man as merely a sales agent.

Charlie, wearing a beaded, kaftan-style robe as big as a tent, and looking like the late African despot Idi Amin, had been seated as usual on the office couch, since he was far too large for either of the smart black leather and tubular steel easy chairs. Even so, his secretary, Camille, worried about the couch springs. Charlie was always introduced as a client, and if she found it strange that he should profess to be in the perfume essence business – especially with his repugnant body odour – she never remarked on it to her boss. She served two café filtres and left them to their discussion.

'So what kind of a deal did you want to talk about?'

'I gotta customer from England who wants a large consignment, on the spot. He says he'll arrange to take it off the island himself, by private plane,' Charlie said, helping himself to a Monte Christo from a box at his elbow, sniffing it suspiciously, which also annoyed his host.

Tabard lifted an antique silver Ronson from his desk and came over to light the cigar. 'Who is this dealer?'

'Name's Buchanan. Ready to pay cash. Our hillbilly friend introduced him.'

'Not so fast. What do we know about him? Have you made proper enquiries?'

'You think I just came in on the last hurricane?' said Charlie disparagingly, blowing out a huge cloud of smoke, then inhaling it, making his chest wheeze. 'I have infrastructure, man, even if I do live in the woods instead of a glass palace like yours.'

'Cut the crap, Charlie. What's the profile on Mr Buchanan?'

'He's a regular London dealer. Upmarket, celebrity clientele. He checked out okay.'

'How much is he prepared to pay?'

'Seven hundred thousand US dollars' worth.'

'Well, that's not to be sneezed at,' said Tabard.

Charlie chortled and choked on his cigar, his stomach wobbling under his capacious kaftan. 'You just made a coke joke!' he spluttered. 'Sneezed at!'

'Money up front?'

'No other way, Rafe.'

Tabard removed the filter from the top of his coffee cup and took a sip. 'Then the goods will be ready and waiting for your client,' he confirmed.

On the walk uphill, Charlotte told him about her grandfather's arrival from France and the founding of the family business, Harper couldn't help contrasting the lifestyle of landowners like the Plennards with the life that his own parents would have known in the Caribbean.

If he had been impressed from the shore, he was even more so when they neared the Chateau Mirabeaux in its lush surroundings, smooth lawns with sprinklers and well-tended flowerbeds spilling over with brilliant colours. Nearby, discreetly tucked amid the trees, were several long, low buildings of quarried stone, which Charlotte explained were the banana warehouses.

'You mentioned your brother is divorced. All this for a single guy,' Harper mused. 'No wonder he wanted his sister to share the place.'

'Oh, Leon leads a busy life running the estate, and he loves the Chateau Mirabeaux,' said Charlotte. 'He's a bit old-fashioned. You know, one of the plantocracy, but full of fun. You'll like him.'

Claudine came out to greet them as they arrived at the house. Charlotte introduced her guest, the housekeeper smiling and shaking hands politely, but Harper was conscious of a mild flicker of surprise that the hand she held wasn't quite the colour she'd been expecting.

Although she'd been told he was a visitor from London, and she secretly spoke a little English, she chose to talk in her own tongue, the consummate French snub.

'Your brother's upstairs in his office. He'll be down in a few minutes,' Claudine announced. 'Lunch is a barbecue on the terrace.'

Charlotte led Harper into the marbled hallway with its curving staircase, and they passed through a series of cool rooms, sparsely but elegantly appointed, like most of the chateau, with period French furniture, paintings and antiques.

Overall there hung the faintly damp odour associated with stately old houses in the tropics, mixed with the smell of wax polish. As she chattered about the various features, Harper tried to picture her as a child here, but somehow the two images didn't seem to fit.

They stepped through open windows onto the poolside terrace. Harper whistled in admiration as he took in the view. Claudine reappeared with a bowl of rum punch, then went to busy herself at the already-lit barbecue on the edge of the terrace. Charlotte poured drinks, dropping some of the exotic fruit into each glass.

Harper toasted her. 'Here's to what you sacrificed by becoming a cop.'

'When I did live at home it was like being in a museum,' Charlotte replied. 'Not out here by the pool, though. This is the bit I miss. Cheers!'

As they drank, her mobile phone trilled from one of her pockets.

'Where are you supposed to be?' Harper queried as she took out the phone.

'On my yacht will do.' She snapped the phone open. '*Plennard, oui?*'

The call was from Carmona. 'Sorry to bother you,' he said. 'I've tried to reach Buchanan at his hotel, but they say he's gone out for the day. You wouldn't happen to know his whereabouts would you?'

Charlotte shot a guilty glance over at Harper, who'd wandered over to watch Claudine placing jumbo prawns and a whole John Dory on the barbecue. The fish looked like it might've just been hauled out of the bay below, where Charlotte's yacht rode at anchor.

From the tone of her boss's voice, Charlotte could tell that he suspected she knew precisely where Harper was.

She decided to come clean, and said sweetly: 'As a matter of fact, Sergeant Buchanan is with me. I was just about to take my yacht out when I saw him strolling on the quay.'

'Oh yeah?' Carmona said sceptically.

'Well, I thought if we were out at sea it'd be perfectly safe to be with him. I mean, not to be seen. You want a word?'

'Just tell him the deal is on. Our mole's confirmed it with his friend Charlie. And Raphael Tabard will personally be delivering the consignment.'

'Exactly what we wanted. Right, I'll explain.'

Harper was talking to Claudine fluently in French. He enjoyed the slight bemusement this caused her after her initial reaction to his colour. Seeing Charlotte put her phone away, he rejoined her.

Charlotte lowered her voice: 'That was the Bureau. Our contact's been on. They're willing to sell you the stuff.'

'Now we're getting somewhere,' said Harper.

'Yes, where your head will be well and truly on the block,' Charlotte reminded him.

'Who do I make the purchase from? Charlie, the black-tyre Michelin Man?"

'Full details when we get back.' She spoke even more softly. Claudine was enveloped in smoke at the sizzling barbecue, but Charlotte was afraid that the housekeeper might pick up the name. 'As we hoped, Tabard's come into it as supplier.'

'How about the Texan?' Harper asked.

'He's done his job as fixer.'

'Nice work for him, then. Commission on the deal, and he gets paid by JIBOC for setting it up?'

'You've got it wrong,' Charlotte said. 'Firstly, nobody's meant to actually lay their hands on the money. Secondly, Floyd's an undercover agent for the U.S. Narcotics Bureau in Miami. He's FBI, one of us.'

As Harper was about about to express his surprise, Leon Plennard came out of the house.

'My sincere apologies! Some urgent business,' he said striding towards them.

'Leon, this is a friend of mine, Harper Buchanan.'

Leon smiled and held out a hand. 'Delighted to meet you, Mr Buchanan.' Once again Harper thought he caught a slight blip in the bonhommie, as with the housekeeper. Like his sister had warned, he was the old-fashioned plantocrat, a bit of a snob.

'It's Sergeant Buchanan,' Charlotte corrected him. 'Harper's in the same line of business as me.'

'Not here in the Caribbean, though,' Harper said quickly. 'I'm off my patch, as we say. I'm from London.'

'Ah, dear old London. Such memories! My wife and I honey-mooned there. We stayed at Claridges. Do the waiters still wear those Georgian wigs?'

'I wouldn't know,' said Harper. 'Not one of my haunts.'

'And how is the wonderful Metropolis looking?' Leon said affably, pouring himself a glass of punch.

'Depends on when you last saw it.'

'Oh, it feels like a lifetime ago. Viv Richards was the West Indies star batsman in those days,' said Leon ruefully.

'I think you'd find some big changes,' Harper told him. 'Like most cities in Britain, London took several steps forward in the seventies and eighties, then slumped backwards. The first few years of the millennium were promising, but then came street crime, rail and road transport problems, parking, rising council charges, and worst of all the financial recession and job losses. Most people dream of getting away from it all, especially to somewhere as magical as this,' he added.

'It may look like that to you, Harper, but we also have our problems. It's getting harder to earn a living running an estate like mine. We've severe unemployment. Our banana trade's being undercut by growers in other parts of the world, especially Africa. There's an irony for you: the descendants of black slaves thrown out of work by fellow Africans!'

Charlotte, fearing her brother, despite his charm, would stray into even more sensitive territory, broke in, changing the subject: 'This is Harper's first time in the Caribbean. He was born in London.'

'My parents were your neighbours,' said Harper, pointing towards the island across the water, almost at the same moment thinking to himself that "neighbours" might be an uncomfortable description to a landowning *Beke*.

Leon reacted diplomatically. 'Really? Well, now, this must be quite an experience for you.'

'It most certainly is,' Harper replied with equal applomb. 'Makes me a descendant of the black slaves, too,' he added. 'I feel at home amongst strangers.'

'Oh, I know just how that strikes you,' said Leon. 'Like the first time my father took me to France. Odd feeling of familiarity without actually belonging. But after a few visits, you get over it. Take my little sister, packing her JIBOC badge in her rucksack and cruising the mean streets of Paris! What brings you 'off your patch' then?'

'I'm nothing to do with JIBOC, I'm on a completely separate investigation,' Harper replied cautiously, remembering Charlotte had said she never discussed her police work with him. 'Routine stuff.'

'Here to arrest somebody? So what's the case?' he enquired enthusiastically.

Harper thought fast. 'It's a long story, involving a guy who fled to the West Indies after an armed incident in London,' he said truthfully, but vaguely enough to avoid any further details.

'Well, I hope you get your man,' said Leon.

Charlotte, who'd left them to examine her sundial gift, now given pride of place on a plinth on the terrace, said: 'It's one o'clock, *J'ai faime*.'

'Right!' said Leon. 'Claudine's barbecue smells delicious. Shall we have lunch?'

Forty-seven

They were half way back from Martinique, just off the small blob of an uninhabited island, when the squall hit them.

One minute the sea was placid and the skies clear; the next the wind came at them with the whoosh of an express train, an ugly mass of rain clouds suddenly billowing out of nowhere. The hull of the yacht twisted violently like a bent ruler, the sails snapping and screeching in protest against the force of the sudden gust.

The craft heeled over on her port side, her masts and rigging almost theatening to skim the water, the gunwhales seeming to be just inches above. They were being driven dangerously near jagged rocks. Harper, a helpless landlubber, held grimly on to a rail and watched Charlotte leap into action.

With cool precision she clipped on a safety line, crawling for'ard to undo the halyards and drop both sails. The horizon returned to normal and she jumped back into the cockpit, starting the diesel.

As the engine throbbed and the yacht pushed comfortably through the water despite the elements, she breathed a sigh of relief, smiling brightly at Harper. 'You okay?'

'I'd have gone pale if I could,' he joked.

'Our weather has a habit of springing nasty little surprises like that,' she said. 'Hasn't spoiled your lunch, I hope?'

'Not so far.'

It was raining heavily and they were both soaked to the skin. But the wind was warm.

Reducing throttle, Charlotte scanned the tiny island beside them: 'We'd better take shelter until this stuff blows over.'

Steering the yacht around to the leeward side of the island, she cut the engine completely and they drifted into a small cove with an old stone jetty.

'This place is called *L'Aconit*, the Monk's Hood. It used to have a monastery and leper colony, but nowadays it's deserted.'

In calm water, she let the yacht edge close to the jetty. Harper, feeling more useful now, hopped off and looped the mooring line around a bollard.

Partially dried off with a towel and fortified with a sip of rum, they waited till the rain stopped and went exploring among the ruins of the monastery, then climbed the central clump of cowl-shaped rock that gave the island its name. A few stunted palms clung to the slopes, and as the sun reappeared they sat down in a grassy crevice at the summit.

Charlotte lit one of her cigars. They were facing West, and they watched a huge American cruise liner, like a floating apartment block, slide by.

'Funny way to enjoy the Caribbean,' she mused. 'The elderly passengers hardly ever leave the ship. They step ashore, take a few pictures of each other, do a bit of shopping in so-called duty free rip-off malls, then toddle back aboard to eat in the restaurants and swim in the pool.'

'You never took a cruise?' Harper asked.

'God forbid! I can think of nothing worse! Anyhow, when you live in this paradise you seldom even think about a holiday.'

'How about living in Europe again?'

'Oh, I might do that, perhaps when Angeline is older,' Charlotte said. She spun her cigar butt over into the sea. 'Are you sure you want to go through with it tomorrow?' she asked.

Harper shrugged. 'Too late to pull out now. Why? You worried it could go wrong?'

She turned to him. 'Just don't try to be a hero on your own. Follow the briefing. That's the rule.'

'Can I break one right now?' he said softly.

Before she could reply, he put his arm around her and drew her close. She didn't resist. At first it was just a light kiss, but then he pulled her down on the grass. Their mouths became hungry. Tongues desperate. Their damp clothes took ages to get off, her T-shirt especially, taut against her nipples. Naked, they basked in the sunshine, pleasuring each other for a long time, before finally enjoying the greatest pleasure of all.

As they lay back, Harper could hear her snuffling. His fingers touched a shiny wet patch on her cheek. She pulled her body away from him abruptly.

'Damn, damn, damn!' she said.

'Is that how you feel?'

'This never happened, you understand?'

'No, it didn't happen,' said Harper.

And she turned on her tummy, and when she raised herself on her knees, he made love to her again.

Forty-eight

Shortly after it opened for business, Harper sat at a desk in the Caribbean National Bank, watching the Manager counting the money. Everything about him was discreet. He was discreetly attired in a dark suit, crisp white shirt and bank tie, discreetly incurious as he placed bundle after bundle of notes in the suitcase, and he even wore the discreet expression of someone who, though he regarded actual cash going out of the premises as a dubious transaction, wouldn't ever show it.

Occasionally he stopped to work his calculator, since one dollar too many, or even one less, would be a fiscal sin. If only, Harper thought, they'd had guys like this heading British banks that nearly went bust, while the bosses ran off with their huge bonuses.

'There we are, seven hundred thousand US dollars, as arranged.'

He closed the briefcase. The money had been issued on instructions from Head Office. All the customer had to do was to produce his passport. It said he was an English salesman. No questions to be asked, except a polite one of his own: 'That's quite a sum of money. Do you have an escort?'

'Waiting outside,' said Harper.

'Glad to be of service, and have a pleasant day, sir,' was all the Manager could think of saying, while maintaining discretion.

'Thanks,' said Harper, lifting the suitcase and walking out.

As he watched him leave, the discreet Manager said under his breath: 'Shit, who wouldn't have a fucking nice day with a suitcase like that!'

The sham taxicab was waiting at the kerb, Ben Thomson behind the wheel. The young cop eyed the suitcase as if it contained plutonium.

'You ever get the feeling you'd like to go to Las Vegas?' said Harper, getting into the back and holding the suitcase on his knees.

'All the goddam time!' said Ben, driving off. He spoke into a hands-free mobile phone: 'Just leaving the bank,' he announced.

Carmona's voice answered from one of the two unmarked police cars parked downhill from the cemetery. 'Right, we're waiting in position. Everyone keep their lines open. You got that, Sergeant Plennard?'

'I read you, Chief,' said Charlotte, who was nearer, her jeep hidden in a clump of trees, with a good view of the road by the graveyard gate. She'd seen Harper earlier when he came into the Bureau for the briefing. They'd barely exchanged a word, now back to being just two cops on a job. But privately she was more concerned about his safety than she was prepared to admit.

'Has Tabard shown up yet?' Carmona asked.

'No sign of him so far,' she reported.

'Looks like Harper's ahead of him. But Ben, if you're sitting outside and Tabard arrives, play the bored taxi driver up to the hilt. Go to sleep if you like.'

'No problem.'

'And all of you, just remember that Raphael Tabard is the man we badly need,' Carmona added.

The taxi drew up at the cemetery gate and Harper got out with the briefcase and went in, slowly mounting the steps through the silent gravestones. There was a rustling sound, and he expected Charlie's armed guards to pounce once again. But it was only a large razor-backed iguana, disturbed from its warm slumber. The monster-in-miniature flicked its tail and gave him a beady-eyed look before scuttling away.

Continuing his climb, Harper reached the top of the steps. He gave a slight cough to herald his approach. Still nobody materialised. And then, as he walked into the glade he saw why. The place was quite deserted. No Charlie, hammock, or office staff. Just a couple of empty beer cans left on one of the tombs.

Harper tensed, sensing in seconds that something had gone wrong. It had been agreed that for him to be armed would be dangerous, but now he felt completely vulnerable, and a moment later when he heard a twig snap underfoot, he hurled himself into cover, down the side of a grave. Just in the nick of time, as a hail of bullets smashed into the stonework.

The same two sentries he'd encountered on his previous visit, had moved out of hiding with their guns blazing.

Still clutching the suitcase, Harper scrambled back into some bushes as they closed in, bullets ricocheting everywhere. When they discovered he'd eluded them, they began a search. Harper crawled to yet another hiding place between two mausoleums, but he upset a vase of dead flowers and instantly they raked the spot with another fusillade.

As soon as he heard the gunfire from above, Ben Thomas, shouted the news into his phone.

'Get up there right now!' Carmona ordered. 'We're on our way.'

Ben hauled his .38 from the glove compartment and ran into the graveyard, leaping up the steps as fast as he could go.

Charlotte, who'd overheard, hurriedly started up her jeep and drove out of the trees, accelerating along the road towards the cemetery gate.

Uphill, Harper was desperately continuing hide-and-seek with his attackers. He knew it would only be moments before they flushed him out. All he had was the suitcase, and he decided to use it. One of the men was very near, looking the other way.

Harper waited for the right moment, stood up and heaved the case into some neighbouring bushes and ducked down again.

Instantly the man turned to the source of the noise and walked over, close to Harper, who waited till he'd just moved past, then stepped out and felled him with a trained blow from behind. In a flash, Harper grabbed his fallen gun and fired at his companion, who bobbed down in the undergrowth and returned fire.

Just then, to his alarm, Harper saw Ben coming to his rescue, running into the clearing.

'Ben, look out!' Harper shouted, but too late.

There was a single shot from the bushes and Ben took the bullet right in the middle of his forehead. He spun with the force of it, then pitched face down.

Grimly unheeding the risk, Harper broke cover with his gun to get the assailant. But when he pulled the trigger, there was a dull click. He was now a simple target, out in the middle of the clearing.

As he raised his arm to hurl the useless gun in a bid to thwart the other man's aim, there was a loud shot from one side, and blood spurted from the man's shoulder, his gun dropping from his hands. Charlotte moved swiftly up to him and savagely coshed him unconscious with the butt of her handgun.

Harper kneeled beside young Ben, knowing there was little hope. He shook his head sadly as Charlotte came over. 'He's dead.'

Numbly, the pair of them sat on a gravestone, Charlotte mouthing obscenities in French as Carmona and Joe Guarnac arrived in the clearing.

Harper said bitterly to Carmona: 'The fucking money's over there in the bushes.'

Forty-nine

Surprised to see him and even more shaken by the news of the shoot-out, Jimmie Buchanan led Harper upstairs to an untidy flat. His latest partner, a shapely Cuban dancer half his age, was lying in bed watching TV. Jimmie closed the bedroom door.

The old man was adamant. 'Harper, I swear on your sweet Mother's life, I never told a livin' soul about you!' he said. 'You gotta believe it, ol' calypso-mouth kept your secret to himself, just like you asked.'

'You're positive, Uncle?'

'Told me your life was at stake, didn't you? So far as I knew, you'd flown back home. You never even let me in on it, that you were still on the island!'

Harper sighed. 'Yeah, that's a fact.'

'Maybe now you can tell me more about what's going on, huh? We're family, after all,'

'I just made it three shambles in a row, and a good young cop is dead,' said Harper morosely.

'You were double-crossed, that's obvious. How about this American dude?'

'No, he's an undercover man, living dangerously.'

'Somebody at your hotel, then?

Harper said: 'Nobody at the Trade Winds could have known. I'm certain of that.'

'And you were carrying seven hundred thousand bucks, for Chrissake?'

'On loan.'

'What about the manager at the bank?'

Harper shrugged. 'Unlikely. He didn't know what the money was for.'

'So how about a Judas in this JIBOC outfit?' Jimmie ventured. 'The drug traffic corrupts a lot of folk. How do you know there isn't somebody who just don't dig the idea of a London cop coming out here, winnin' kudos?'

Harper shook his head. 'Today's scam was my idea. But they were all involved, Inspector Carmona and his team, including Sergeant Plennard, whom you met.'

'I know it sounds like some of them narrow-minded little Englanders, Harper, but we don't ever trust the white French. It's our history, goes back over two hundred years, all them wars. Even Nelson fought the frogs, remember. They'd have owned the whole of the Caribbean if they'd had their way.'

Jimmie stopped, looking a shade guilty for making what amounted to a racist attack. He was also surprised by Harper's nettled reaction.

'Listen, put any notion like that about Charlotte out of your head,' said Harper, rebuking him. 'I know her a whole lot better now. We're colleagues. She'd be the last person to shop me.'

Jimmie gave him a shrewd, even slightly lewd look. 'Don't tell me, you gone real sweet on that chick? You got somethin' goin' there?'

'A fine thing to ask me at a time like this!' Harper snapped. 'Anyhow, that's a private matter.'

'So's your own life, nephew,' Jimmie reminded him. 'With all this danger around, maybe you ought to go straight back home?'

'Not yet. I'm taking them on,' said Harper firmly. 'I've one advantage. They don't know I'm still alive, just like somebody else a long way from here is still very alive,' he said without explanation.

The atmosphere in the Bureau was decidedly gloomy. Yolande, red-eyed, brought in the usual lunchtime sandwiches and coffee, but nobody touched anything.

It didn't help that the secretary placed them on the dead cop's desk, alongside a few of his personal things, a stack of his favourite CDs and a tennis racquet he was hoping to sell to supplement his low wages. Ben was married with a mortgage problem.

Eddie Carmona came out of his office, having just talked with Ben's wife.

'Anyone want my fucking job?' he said bitterly.

Charlotte nodded in sympathy. 'How did Ben's wife take it?'

How would you expect?' said Carmona. 'For her it's back home to Jamaica with two kids and a shitty little pension.'

'What I can't figure out is why it misfired,' said Joe. 'Floyd set it up, he's very thorough. He's given us a dozen tip-offs. Yet Tabard never showed up with the goods, only a couple of Charlie's gunmen.'

'Maybe we'll wring something out of the bastards who survived. What's the hospital report on the injured one?'

'Fractured skull, still unconscious,' declared Joe.

'Sorry I hit him so hard,' Charlotte apologised. 'Couldn't help it with Ben lying there.'

'I'd have done the same,' Carmona replied. 'In fact I might have put a bullet in his fucking head,' he added, lifting a sandwich and putting it down again. 'Where's Harper gone?'

'He went to see his Uncle Jimmie, but he was convinced he wouldn't find the leak came from that direction,' Charlotte said.

The phone rang and Yolande took the call at her desk. As she listened, her face registered shock. 'Right, I'll inform him straight away.'

She put down the receiver. 'That was a call from the traffic police about Mister Kinthly.'

Carmona reacted. 'Floyd? What the hell's happened?'

'There's been an accident. They got the JIBOC number from a book in his pocket.'

Floyd Kinthly's car had been discovered in shallow sea water at the foot of a cliff. In the tangled chrome-and-maroon remains of his prized Pontiac, a motorcycle patrol cop found the Texan's body, with a single shot through the back of his head.

The car radio, amazingly, was still playing Country and Western when Carmona and Charlotte arrived.

Bleakly they surveyed the scene as the FBI man was cut out of the wreckage by firemen and examined on the beach by a doctor.

'That answers any doubts about Floyd giving Buchanan away,' said Carmona, grim-faced.

Charlotte picked up the dead man's stetson from the sand, dusting it off. 'Well, one thing's clear, they were rattled. Maybe Operation Hurricane's blowing too close to them for comfort.'

Harper and Jimmie drove over to the Green Hat. It was late afternoon, and they sat at a table as the sun dipped low over the ocean towards the horizon, a bottle of rum between them. There was nobody else about except for the owner, raking out the barbecue and piling in fresh charcoal ready for the evening's diners.

'So what can you do that your police pals can't?' Jimmie asked.

'I don't know. But I have some unfinished business here, and I aim to stay around for a while.'

'The trouble with you Harper is you're just like your father. When he was a boxer, Arthur wouldn't quit, even if he was taking a beating. He never got knocked out. Your brother Lennie's the same. Look at that goal he scored in extra time for Spurs last month.'

'Yeah, I know,' said Harper, pouring them both another stiff one.

The owner, wiping his hands on a rag, came over. 'You sure you gentlemen couldn't use a bite to eat? I can light the barbecue now, if you like. Got some real nice barracuda to grill.'

'Thanks, Benjie, but…'

'Barbecue!' Harper exclaimed, cutting him short, slamming his glass hard down on the table.

They both looked at him, baffled.

'That might just be it. Why didn't I think of it before!'

Jimmie frowned. 'You do want somethin' to eat, then?'

'No, I'm not talking about food, Uncle. I'm thinking of another barbecue ,' Harper said.

'Suppose you speak some sense, Nephew?'

'There's one person who could have listened to a phone conversation at lunchtime yesterday at the Chateau Mirabeaux… I was careless, talking near the barbecue. If the housekeeper understands any English, she could've overheard.'

'You mean that fading blonde, Claudine?'

'I should have guessed you'd know her,' said Harper wryly.

'We once played music for a party at the Chateau. Don't mind admittin' I fancied her, until she gave us rotten old fish pie – coley! – when the rest was eatin' lobster and caviar.' said Jimmie. 'By the way, Raphael Tabard was one of the guests.'

Harper shook his head: 'You see Uncle, you really are a Caribbean intelligence service all on your own.'

Jimmie suggested: 'Why don't you quiz your friend Charlotte about her?'

'No, I can't do that,' Harper said.

'Why not?'

'It might destroy Anglo-French relations,' Harper replied. 'Maybe I'll take a closer look at Claudine.'

'Well, there's something else you'd better know about her,' said Jimmie. 'She sleeps with Leon Plennard.'

Fifty

Harper spent the night in the spare room above the barber's shop. He went over to Martinique on the first flight, piloted again by the ruddy-faced Irishman.

They took off with minimum visibility in a ground mist, which he jovially described as 'a touch o' rising damp,' forecasting a blue sky just above. He was right.

There were just two other passengers, an Australian couple with backpacks as big as armchairs, who spent the entire journey munching Vegemite sandwiches for breakfast, and furiously working out what a few nights in the French island would cost them.

'Well now, Mister Buchanan, have you had a successful sales trip?' the Irishman asked.

'Things have been a bit quiet so far,' Harper replied impassively.

'And how is that lovely man, your Uncle Jimmie?'

'Oh, he's in great form. Still has the voice of a heavenly humming-bird,' said Harper, remembering Charlotte's graceful tribute.

'I expect I don't need to tell you, but Martinique's the best island to sell sports equipment,' said the pilot. 'The French are mad about physical exercise. Tennis, volleyball, cycling. For a nation who claim to have more sex than anybody else on earth, you sometimes wonder why they have to work up such a sweat playing games,' he said.

Harper was about to make some suitable observation, when a helicopter suddenly crossed their path only a few hundred feet below. There was no real danger, but the pilot swore loudly.

'Military choppers! Come buzzing out of nowhere, as if they bloody well own the airspace!'

Having made the trip by yacht, Harper was now familiar with the Martinique coastline, and five minutes later he watched with surprise as he saw the same army helicopter hovering over the blue necklace of the lagoon just below the Plennard plantation, then eventually settling down on the lawn of the Chateau Mirabeaux.

'Could you do me a favour?' Harper asked the pilot. He pointed down towards the chateau. 'Can you change course a bit and fly over that mansion?'

'Sure. What's your interest?'

'Oh, some friends of mine live there. I'd like to see what it looks like from the air.'

The pilot obliged, banking the Twin Otter and reducing height for a better view.

If it seemed odd that a military aircraft was visiting the place, something else had attracted Harper's attention. Ranged in front of the house were at least a dozen cars. A group of people, mere dots, could be seen clustered outside, watching the helicopter's descent.

For a moment, Harper wondered if there might be some kind of social gathering taking place, but then he remembered it was still only eight o'clock in the morning. A working breakfast for Leon Plennard, perhaps? But with whom?

Hiring a moped from a shop near the airport, Harper drove as close as he dared to the estate, before hiding the bike in some bushes. The gates were closed, so he climbed a fence and made his way uphill through thick undergrowth on the lower slopes of the plantation.

As he emerged from the trees skirting the formal grounds, he heard the sound of a car coming up the steep road nearby, and dodged out of sight.

A 2CV driven by Claudine headed up to the Chateau, parking alongside the row of cars he'd seen from the air. Some of them were chauffeured limousines, the drivers lounging about, smoking and chatting to each other. The housekeeper took a few shopping bags from the backseat and went inside. After a few moments, his hands deliberately in his pockets, Harper boldly strolled across the lawn on which sat the army helicopter. To the chauffeurs, he hoped he looked like an indolent estate worker.

Without being challenged, he made it to a corner of the Chateau and started to edge his way around towards the rear.

The windows of the library, one of the larger rooms Charlotte had shown him, were wide open, but flyscreens inside remained in place. From within he could hear the murmur of voices.

Harper crept softly to one of the windows, and heard:

'It seems slipshod to say the least. You don't know whether this British policeman was eliminated. You don't know the fate of the two men whose job it was to kill him. Such doubts are dangerous.'

Harper tensed as he listened. They were talking about him! And the voice sounded familiar. It belonged to someone he'd seen on television...

Moving closer, Harper managed to peer inside. As he'd guessed, Maitland Harbinson was the speaker. That explained the helicopter.

'In other words, gentlemen, our overall plans could be at risk as a result of an entirely unsatisfactory and uncertain resolution of this matter,' Harbinson added. Within a week of taking on the Acting Prime Minister's role, he'd already adopted a leader's lofty tone.

They were all seated in conference around a long Louis XIV refectory table, fifteen of them, including the host, Leon Plennard, his friend, Raphael Tabard, now familiar to Harper from JIBOC pictures, and Colonel Theodore Marcel, the Army commander and Minister of Defence, whom Harper had also seen on television supporting the coup.

Although Harper didn't recognise the others, they all had one thing in common: an air of power and wealth. Except for the man next to Harbinson, an albino European with an obsequious manner, who echoed his neighbour's words.

'Mister Harbinson is right,' he said, with a Dutch accent. 'It's a highly risky moment, and yet against such a background, we are asked to a meeting to go through a completely different agenda.'

'Van Molder has a point,' said one of the men, an imposing, white-bearded Indian in a turban. 'We wanted this conference to clear up our inter-island business alliance following the coup and the shift of power.'

Tabard defended himself. 'It's not my fault. Caubec was taken care of, and as soon as we discovered who Buchanan really was, we had to do something. Whatever happened after that is down to our man, Charlie Kalipha. The American agent, Kinthly, was dealt with, and so far as we know, Buchanan likewise.'

'So where are Charlie's men? And where is Charlie?' asked Harbinson.

'I expect he's gone to ground,' said Tabard. 'No doubt in one of his rainforest hideouts.'

'Very convenient,' Leon Plennard said scathingly.

Harbinson intervened. 'Alright, there's no sense in squabbling among ourselves! I can assure you that our partnership is safe so far as events in my island are concerned. We will be making changes, and the bureaucrats on the other side of the Atlantic, especially in Whitehall – who still think they can control things – will know that they no longer have any say.'

Harper decided to scout around. He came past a kitchen, glancing in to see Claudine preparing a tray of coffee and biscuits. Little did he think that it wasn't just her who blew the whistle on him, it was her boss, Leon!

Retreating to one of the nearby warehouses, Harper called the Bureau on his mobile, speaking under a vast, almost surreal roof of huge bunches of bananas hung on hooks.

After a moment Yolande answered. 'This is Sergeant Buchanan. Let me speak with the Inspector,' he whispered urgently.

When Carmona spoke he gave him a quick run-down, and suggested an immediate armed swoop on the Chateau by the Bureau's helicopter unit.

'But make it quick,' urged Harper.

Stunned to learn where the meeting was being held, Carmona was even more concerned with the fact that Charlotte Plennard, Leon's sister, was one of his JIBOC team.

'Where is she?' Harper asked.

'Because of what happened yesterday, I gave her some time off,' said Carmona.

'Good, then you can leave her out of this one,' said Harper, relieved.

'Not so fast, Harper,' Carmona cautioned. 'I have to alert the Martinique police. What the hell do we use as justification for busting in there? Those people at the Chateau aren't breaking any laws just by holding a meeting.'

'Oh, come on, we know who hired Caubec then killed him – and tried to kill me. I heard them with my own ears!'

'We need more hard evidence,' insisted Carmona.

'Listen, this is your big chance. Move in now and Paris will give you a medal. Do nothing, and Operation Hurricane will be a failure, because the cartel already knows you're breathing down their necks,' Harper argued.

Carmona was silent.

Harper continued: You can be a step ahead of the French cops,' he said. 'Spring the old trick, bring a stash of drugs. You know... "found in possession of..."'

It was a dishonest device often employed by police officers over-eager for an arrest, and one which Harper abhorred. But he didn't say so.

Carmona said: 'Even JIBOC can't touch Harbinson. Right now, he's an acting Head of State.'

'As soon as news of the raid gets out there'll be an instant public reaction. And it'll be followed by another big shock, I promise you. Harbinson and his UPP buddies won't survive for long.'

'What does "another big shock" mean?' asked Carmona.

Harper decided this was the moment to tell him the truth about Sir Walter Julien's condition. Not only had he survived the shooting, he wasn't in a coma, suspected of being brain dead.

'Jesus, Harper, you kept that from me?' Carmona shouted down the phone.

'Sorry, I had to. Orders,' said Harper.

'You weren't bloody well following orders when you flew out here!' Carmona said, his voice full of resentment.

Switching off, Harper decided there was nothing much for it but to sit tight where he was. He helped himself to a free banana, peeled it and took a bite. It was unripe, and he tossed the green skin into a metal wheelie bin, and thought about Charlotte's reaction to this latest development that would reveal her very own brother as a member of a crime syndicate.

It was was bound to be a shattering blow. Somehow he wished he hadn't been the one who'd uncovered it.

He still had her mobile number, and was tempted for a moment to ring her and try to prepare her for the news, but decided it would be a senseless move. How could he possibly explain by phone that Leon had almost caused Harper's death, and certainly that of a JIBOC colleague, young Ben?

He was staring up at the roof of bananas, and because of the whirring sound of the warehouse temperature control equipment, he didn't hear the footsteps. But he felt the cold touch of metal against his throat. An elderly Creole stood over him, holding a machete with a firm grip.

'Who are you? What are you doin' here, M'sieu? You better keep nice and still,' said Jean-Claude, the gardener.

Harper had laid his mobile down beside him on a workstool. The old man lifted the phone, and with his free hand plonked the house number.

In the library, Leon waited for his housekeeper to answer the phone. But the phone on a side dresser kept ringing insistently. Irritated, he left the conference table and went over to take the call.

As he listened to the gardener, he tried not to betray his alarm. Maitland Harbinson was in the middle of another speech to the assembly.

Leon said softly: 'Very well, Bappy, I'll be over straight away,' He hung up and decided to quit the room discreetly, without explanation.

Fifty-one

On his way to the warehouse, Leon collected a shotgun from his gun cupboard. He thrust two cartridges into the breach.

The old gardener still had the machete at Harper's throat as Leon arrived, reacting with surprise and not a little chagrin when he saw who the intruder was.

'Thank you, Bappy, you did well,' Leon said, dismissing him, menacingly covering Harper with both barrels.

'Sorry to gatecrash your summit,' Harper said. '*Un peu maladroit.*'

'Trespassing's the word, as any policeman should know.'

'I'd be a dead cop if you people had succeeded,' Harper reminded him.

'Yes, indeed, we had hoped you'd have been – how shall I put it, Sergeant Buchanan – marginalised' said Leon. 'Now, alas, I shall have to see to it myself.'

Harper, playing for time, needled him: 'Surely you aren't going to commit murder right here on your doorstep, on your own precious plantation? I thought French aristocrats, even pretend ones like you, had more style?'

Leon shrugged: 'They'll find your body washed up on a beach on the other side of the island.'

'You and your pals wanted Sir Walter out of the way to give you all a free hand?'

'He was becoming really tiresome,' said Leon. 'All that stuff about upholding what he called strict moral values, but what we call the "upright colonial hangover". You might say he was bad news to certain other parties in the Caribbean.'

'You mean he was cracking down too hard on organised crime?' Harper suggested.

'I'm a businessman, belonging to a group of like-minded entrepreneurs,' Leon claimed defensively.

'Like your friend Raphael Tabard, the fragrant drug dealer?'

Leon ignored the jibe. 'In my case I'm fighting to preserve this estate. I told you about the fall-off in the banana trade. It's getting worse. I was in debt to the bank. I needed to find some other way to make ends meet.'

'Oh, sure, keeping your hands clean while lining and soiling your palms?' scoffed Harper. 'Willing to go along with murder when your sister's a cop. Some kind of loving brother!'

'Charlotte won't ever know,' said Leon. 'Why should she?'

'She already does,' Harper lied. 'I just called her,' he said, indicating his mobile which the old gardener had replaced on the workstool.

Leon looked down at the phone, momentarily off-guard, and Harper lunged at him.

As they struggled, the loud clack of helicopters erupted above the Chateau.

In the same instant, the shotgun in Leon's hands went off with a roar. But the barrels were pointing away from them, exploding into a stack of bananas, in a flail of pulp.

Harper grabbed the shotgun and sent Leon crashing back, where he bounced off the big metal bin and staggered, trying to keep his feet.

'You've had it, you bastard,' said Harper, covering him.

'Not quite. The gun's empty, I pulled both triggers,' Leon said.'

Confidently, he moved in on Harper, who turned the shotgun around, holding the barrel, ready to use the stock as a club.

Dodging Leon's advance, he swung the weapon in cricket bat fashion, as if smashing a rising ball to the boundary, and the sheer force laid Leon clean out.

'Umpire's signalled a six,' said Harper wryly. 'You French have been in the West Indies for over two hundred years, and you never mastered the fucking game.'

Discussion in the chateau was interrupted by the noisy arrival of the two unmarked helicopters that JIBOC used for its secret operations. The meeting broke up and its members, mystified, went outside to find the machines landing on the lawn.

'What's going on? Where have they come from?' Harbinson demanded.

'No idea,' said Van Molder.

'Where's M'sieu Plennard?' he asked Claudine, who'd come out onto the terrace. She shook her head and shrugged.

Both choppers' doors burst open under their spinning blades, and Carmona and his colleagues jumped out. There were at least a dozen of them, in flak jackets with machine guns at the ready.

'Police! Get your hands up!' Carmona shouted. He and Joe Guarnac covered the assembly on the pool terrace. The other cops began to surround the house.

Colonel Marcel tried to shout an order to his own helicopter pilot, standing amidst the limousine drivers some distance away, but a snarling Carmona ordered: 'Keep those hands in the air, Colonel!'

Carmona, somewhat superfluously displayed his badge. 'Inspector Carmona, JIBOC.'

'We know perfectly well who you are, Inspector,' said Harbinson brusquely. 'And you know that I am currently acting as Prime Minister. Why have you landed here?'

'We have reason to believe that there is a large consignment of drugs on these premises, Narcotics is our job.'

'Utterly preposterous!' said Harbinson.

Carmona added: 'We're also investigating a gunfight in which one of my men was shot dead yesterday.'

Harper, interjecting, walked onto the terrace, machete in hand: 'Plus the cold-blooded murder of an American, Floyd Kinthly. *C'est vrai M'sieu Tabard?*' he said, deliberately over-accenting.

Harbinson stared at him: 'And just who the hell are you?'

'This is Detective Sergeant Harper Buchanan, from London,' Carmona explained. 'Who has a very big bone to pick with you.'

Tabard blustered: 'May I point out that you are on French soil. You have no authority for this intrusion.'

'Your infringement will be taken up at the highest level on both islands,' Van Molder threatened.

But even as the Dutchman spoke, two Martinique police cars, with sirens howling, came speeding up the drive towards the Chateau.

'I think our authority just arrived, with a local search warrant.' said Carmona calmly.

At that moment, over the sound of the police sirens, they heard the loud report of a shotgun going off.

'Shit!' Harper shouted, sprinting towards the warehouse, Carmona running behind him.

They found Leon Plennard sprawled among the bananas with half his head blown off. The shotgun was still incongruously in his grasp. Harper and Carmona gazed down at him.

'He tricked me. He must've had more ammo in his pocket,' said Harper bitterly.

Carmona shrugged and thought to himself: Harper did him a favour leaving the gun.

Fifty-two

Sir Walter Julien's convalescence from his bullet wound was nearly over, and with the news of his "resurrection" and the downfall of the coup leaders, he was moved back from the country to the hospital in London.

They were having a hard time handling the Press and TV reporters who wanted interviews. Professor Hardwicke, however, put a firm ban on them, insisting that his patient needed all his strength in readiness for the heart operation he still had to face. But the story of Sir Walter' secret survival had captured the headlines worldwide.

In the Juliens' hospital suite, decked with flowers and messages of congratulation, Jonathan Walmsley filled Sir Walter and Emilie in on the details sent to the Commonwealth Office.

Harbinson and the rest of the group had been arrested at the Chateau Mirabeaux on a drug charge, six kilos of cocaine having been 'found' in an exquisite Sevres soup-toureen in Claudine's kitchen.

In fact, as Carmona and his team later discovered, Tabard actually had a parcel of the stuff under the spare wheel in his Mercedes.

'What with this other French chap, Plennard, shooting himself, and the cocaine charge, the whole gang just fell to pieces,' said Walmsley. The important confession was Raphael Tabard's. He incriminated Maitland Harbinson, especially in hiring an assassin to kill you.'

'How about Sergeant Buchanan?' asked the Prime Minister.

We owe a great big debt to that man,' said Emilie. 'If you British don't give him a medal, my husband will have to bestow some kind of honour.'

Walmsley sighed. 'I'm afraid that as far as the Commissioner is concerned, he's still guilty of negligence over your safety, Sir Walter.'

'Surely that matter can now be overlooked?'

'Well, there is a possibility that Sergeant Buchanan may not be available to attend a disciplinary hearing,' Walmsley replied.

Sir Walter frowned: 'What do you mean "not available"?'

'I gather he's being made an offer of a new job on a year's attachment,' said Walmsley.

Harper sat in Eddie Carmona's office while the Inspector poured them both a hefty dark rum from his bottom drawer.

It seemed a lot longer than just a few days since Carmona had shouted at him, telling him to go back to London. Now here he was being invited, officially, to become a colleague.

'Are you serious?' Harper said, astonished.

'Of course I am. I was thinking about replacing young Ben, then I thought, why start looking elsewhere when I might interest you,' Carmona said. 'It's a solid offer.'

'Has the Met approved this?' Harper asked.

'Yes, they're all for it.' His eyes twinkled. 'Maybe they're all in favour of getting rid of you for a bit!'

'Have you told Sergeant Plennard about the idea?'

'Not yet. Charlotte's in a daze. Can you blame her? On top of everything she inherits the entire estate from her brother.'

'Will she give up being a cop, d'you think?'

Carmona shrugged. 'I just don't know. Anyhow, you'd be a useful addition to our team, Harper. I like your style, and you speak French, a big advantage in this part of the world. You want to think it over?'

Harper shook his head. 'I don't need time to think about it.' He raised his glass. 'It's a deal.'

Harper, who hadn't talked to Charlotte since they flew her over to Martinique to officially identify Leon's body, found her in the basement garage of JIBOC headquarters, servicing her ancient jeep.

Despite the ordeal of the last twenty-four hours she wasn't as numbed by events as Carmona had suggested; at least she didn't show it. She looked quite composed.

He greeted her rather tentatively, wondering if she might hold him responsible for her brother's suicide. After all, he'd inadvertently left the weapon to hand.

'You all right?'

'Busy, as you can see. The Inspector has stood me down, but I still have work to do,' she shrugged, a Gallic shrug, determined to tough it out.

'I'm really sorry about Leon,' was all Harper could muster.

'Thanks. But don't be. And let's not talk about it.'

'Okay. As you wish.'

He wanted to put an arm around her, but it didn't feel like the moment, especially as she was wearing oil-covered overalls.

'You'll be going back to London now, I suppose?'

'Not yet,' said Harper. 'At least not for a while.'

Charlotte frowned. 'What does that mean? You giving up your job?'

Harper shook his head. 'Not quite. Look, why don't you climb out of that boiler suit and let me buy you a Fish Outa Watta?'

Sir Walter Julien duly underwent heart surgery. It took seven hours, successfully performed by Mr Carl Hardwicke, not, as he had intended, at the London hospital in St John's Wood, but away from any media interest, at a discreet private hospital in Wiltshire, which nevertheless had a fully equipped theatre for cardiac operations.

With Emilie at his side, Sir Walter's recovery was swift. In a post-surgery recuperation annexe of the hospital, overlooking peaceful countryside near Stonehenge, he talked regularly by a specially-arranged TV satellite conference link to various members of the island's properly restored government.

And then, most important of all, to his family.

The kids at Government House were especially thrilled to have a Dad who was supposed to be dead, but, like Lazarus, he had come back to them, reportedly – for public consumption – 'coming out of his coma', even though the family had known the truth, that he had regained consciousness after the bullet had been removed.

Now there he was – large as life on the conference screen! Hattie, at three months, gave a delighted gurgle every time he appeared.

Meantime, the island's TV news and radio channels, as well as those all around the Caribbean, carried the story, which included, inevitably, interviews with Uncle Jimmie Buchanan. It was Jimmie's finest hour, and he was even invited to sing some of his old calypso hits on air, resulting in a planned brand new album to be entitled *Jimmie Buchanan Beats his Best!*

He kept his hairdresser's shop open, but quietly let it be known through an agent that he was ready for offers of new gigs.

Sir Walter and his wife were driven from Wiltshire in a Rolls (courtesy of the Royal Household) to Buckingham Palace, for an audience with the Queen.

Thinner, in a sober, dark grey suit, he looked otherwise in good shape. Emilie, all the stress of the last few weeks gone, wore a bright, hand-painted floral balloon dress. During the interview she reckoned the Queen had given it the odd admiring glance. Perhaps, Emilie thought, she's got one of these exuberantly-coloured Caribbean dresses in her wardrobe, a memento from a past visit to theirs or one of the other West Indian states.

They were accompanied, naturally, by a puffed-up Hon Jonathan Walmsley, on his first occasion at the Palace.

Sir Walter declined the offer of a drink from the Duke of Edinburgh, and after coffee and biscuits were served, Her Majesty, as Head of the Commonwealth, asked Sir Walter to give her an update on the current political climate in the Caribbean (she and the Duke said it was one of their favourite parts of the world). She asked, particularly, about the rising crime rate on some of the islands, so often related nowadays to drug-trafficking.

When Emilie – despite Walmsley's official line about the whole affair – mentioned the valuable role that a London police officer, Detective Sergeant Buchanan, had played in the downfall of the coup leaders, Walmsley skilfully managed to imply that Harper's pursuit of the hitman who'd tried to kill the Prime Minister, had had the full blessing of Whitehall mandarins.

Fifty-three

To begin with, Inspector Carmona thought it better to keep Harper and Charlotte on separate assignments, but pretty soon they had arranged a yachting weekend.

As he stepped onto the deck of *La Moqueuse* in the harbour, Harper, who'd brought a hamper of food and wine, headed for the galley from where he could hear, through a porthole, Charlotte rattling dishes, when a small voice cut in:

'Bonjour! Bienvenue à bord...'

Angeline, in nautical white jeans and T-shirt with the yacht's name emblazoned, grinned at him as she bobbed up into view over the boom.

For a split second Harper taken by surprise and – though he'd hate to admit it – feeling a slight tinge of disappointment at not spending the day sailing alone with her mother, grinned back at her. He reached up and fondly tugged at one of her pigtails.

'Angeline! Quelle surprise!'

Charlotte appeared from below. Like her daughter she was in jeans and the yacht T-shirt.

'I hope you don't mind? I decided to take her out of the convent for the day.'

'Of course I don't mind,' Harper assured her. 'Tip-top! as we say in English. Hoist the sails, Bo'sun!'

But just as she replied 'Aye aye, Cap'n,' giving him a jokey salute, there was the loud hooting of a workboat entering the harbour. At the same time a car screeched to a halt further along the quayside, sounding its horn in response to the boat.

Harper and Charlotte reacted as they saw Carmona and Joe Guarnac jump out. They watched as the workboat edged into a mooring space and tied up. A derrick was swung out from the forward section, holding aloft – suspended with ropes attached to its hook – a bright orange inflatable.

In the rubber boat, escorted by two uniformed cops, was the massive figure of Charlie, sitting dejected and Buddha-like in his voluminous kaftan.

The "cargo" was set down on the quayside, and Charlie, handcuffed, was hauled out. As he caught sight of Harper walking towards him with Charlotte, his whole body began to shake, but this time it wasn't with his usual rumbling laughter.

Carmona was savouring the moment. 'I believe you've met Sergeant Buchanan, Charlie.'

Charlie stayed silent, fearful of what Harper might do to him. Even with witnesses.

'I bet you never thought you'd run into me again, did you, you evil bastard,' Harper said vehemently. 'I ought to lecture you about the harm you and your drugs do in the world, but I'll leave you to ponder that in prison.'

'Fifteen years at least,' growled Carmona. 'On fucking bread and water if I had my way. Alright, squeeze him in the car,' he snapped.

'How did you find him?' asked Harper.

'Co-operation from the Pentagon,' said Carmona. 'They used one of their military spy satellites and pin-pointed another of his makeshift offices – on a small deserted island called Monk's Hood. The rest was easy.'

When they drove off, Harper exchanged a startled look with Charlotte.

'Monk's Hood – *L'Aconit* – isn't that where we...?'

255

Abruptly, she cut him short: 'I don't think anyone needs to know that. They mightn't appreciate the irony.'

As she started the boat's engine and it chugged out to sea, Harper wondered if she would decide to give up being a cop and take over the family estate. Or maybe they'd still be working together in a year's time? After that, maybe they'd... Hey, thought Harper, checking himself. You're jumping a bit ahead, aren't you?

And then maybe not.

2 201